Books by Sue Hardesty

The Truck Comes on Thursday
Book One of the Loni Wagner Mysteries

Bus Stop at the Last Chance Saloon
Book Two of the Loni Wagner Mysteries

Taking the Long Road Home
Book Three of the Loni Wagner Mysteries

Running Through Fire
Book Four of the Loni Wagner Mysteries
(forthcoming)

The Butch Cook Book
Co-editors: Nel Ward and Lee Lynch

Taking the Long Road Home

Book Three
The Loni Wagner Mysteries

Sue Hardesty

Launch Point Press
Portland, Oregon

ISBN: 978-1-63304-206-3

E-Book: 978-1-63304-237-7

FIRST EDITION
First Printing: 2019

Cover: Jove Belle

Published by:
Launch Point Press
Portland, Oregon
www.LaunchPointPress.com

Dedicated to the One I Love

Thank you for planning things that I never would. Like shopping, and dinners, and parties, and vacations. It's not that I don't want to do these things; it's that I'm mostly oblivious to even think of it.

Thank you for driving. I feel bad that I drive in the direction I look and scare the crap out of you, and you always take the wheel without complaint. Or survival. I'm not sure which!

Thank you for making me feel like the greatest fix-it person in the world. And the greatest spouse in the world. And the greatest friend in the world. And the greatest butch in the world. And the greatest . . .

Thank you for hugging me and making me laugh every single day. And for loving me. I really like that one.

Thank you for being forgiving, understanding, and patient with me. I know that when I am difficult and moody and grumpy, but you love me anyway. Or maybe you really do like my wrinkles and gray hair and fat nose and the irritating way I forget words.

But most of all, I'm telling you how grateful I am for finding you all those years ago and for letting me keep you. So thank you. Really, really . . . thank you!

And thank you, Coco, for your part in Loni's life in these novels, and to all our other special animals who have shared our space over these many years.

Many More Thanks!

I thank my readers who enjoy Loni's adventures and hope you like Loni Book Three as well.

I thank my best friend Lee Lynch who kept me writing when there were times I believed I didn't have another word in me. On paper that is. I always know how to talk.

I thank my partner, Dr. Nel Ward, who loves to tear my scenes apart with a heavy hand on the delete key and demands rewrites in her edits of the first round of my many mistakes.

I thank those very good friends who were my beta readers: Taylor West, my writer friend and tech editor; retired Judge Nancy Campbell Mead, who answered my questions on procedural legal scenes; friend Chrystal Bell, the head of quality control at the Oregon State Police forensics labs who answered my questions on crime scenes; and Dr. Carol Federiuk whose many years in emergency and sports medicine gave me the plot line for the children in the hospital and who corrected my many erroneous medical errors.

And I thank my editor Lori L. Lake who can make any writer look good.

Sue Hardesty
March 2019

Taking the Long Road Home

by

Sue Hardesty

Chapter One

"What the . . . ?" Lieutenant Loni Wagner almost dropped her coffee cup. She reached for the door frame, fighting the feeling of a huge wave rolling over and knocking her down as she clung on to the wood. Shock ricocheted through her as she watched a woman with long, curly, honey-gold hair stand at the front desk in handcuffs. The woman stared, unseeing, past Loni.

Although she didn't seem to recognize her, Loni remembered those eyes and full lips from her freshman year at Lewis and Clark College. Loni had been sitting at a lunch table, lonely and homesick, when she looked up to see the friendly face.

"I'm Jenna. Do you mind if I join you? I saw your dimples when you smiled at the proctor." The soft, lilting voice matched the warmth of the girl's eyes. Without responding, Loni watched her move her dishes from the tray to the table. "You don't mind, do you? People keep telling me how amazing my dimples are. I never really see mine so I thought I'd check yours out to see what the fuss is about."

Jenna's green eyes sparkled, and Loni fell in love for the first time. They spent two amazing years together before everything fell apart.

Now, all these years later, sea green eyes flashing with fire slid through Loni's memory as a rotund male detective grabbed the woman's arm and steered her toward the interrogation room. Loni stepped back into the dark of the police chief's open office door, taking in the blood-soaked knees of Jenna's off-white dress slacks. More blood was smeared on her pale green button shirt, partly untucked from her slacks. Jenna stared straight ahead. Detective Piggy Washington nodded to Loni as he pulled Jenna into the interrogation room.

Loni hurried into the observation room behind the one-way glass window of the interrogation room and turned on the sound. Piggy pulled out a metal chair from the table and motioned for the woman to sit down facing the one-way mirror. Waves of hostility poured off her as she rested her handcuffed hands on the table, laced her fingers together, and leaned toward Piggy, demanding, "What possible evidence do you have to arrest me? I didn't do anything wrong!"

Oh, God! The voice. Even twelve years later, it resonated with Loni. Jenna must be thirty-two now, Loni thought as she remembered she was five months older than Jenna. "Smile, dammit." Loni whispered to herself, "Let me see those dimples." Their age was all they'd had in common when they met. Loni's dark olive skin and black eyes of her Southwest Indian heritage was the opposite of Jenna's Scandinavian pale skin and green eyes. That was back when Loni's black hair fell down her back in a long French braid, and Jenna's honey-blonde curls fell in rippling waves across her shoulders.

Loni soon learned that there were other differences between them. She had always been poor, but even Jenna's casual demeanor screamed money. As they got to know each other, they laughed about how they were like the toy black and white Scottie dogs with the magnetic attract and repel.

Piggy slammed his short, fat hand onto the gray metal table, and Loni was jolted back into the present. Jenna jumped. "Tell me why you murdered Carlotta Carboni," Piggy yelled.

Jenna straightened her spine, and her angry voice exploded in the speaker over Loni's head. "I didn't hurt her!" Shaking her head side to side, she said, "Why would I hurt her?"

Piggy slammed the table again and once again jarred Jenna. "Kinda obvious considering you were there, Doctor. What happened? You catch your lover in bed with someone else?"

Doctor? Loni and Jenna had both studied pre-law during their two years together at Lewis and Clark. Jenna swore she never wanted to have anything to do with medicine because her family had built the Harborville Hospital from their lumber money. Even though a large corporation had purchased the hospital from her family, Jenna's grandmother had been allowed a seat on the board and took her job seriously as she pushed all her grandchildren to stay home and work at the hospital. Jenna refused and decided law would upset her grandmother the most. Obviously, Loni realized, Jenna didn't continue studying law. She wondered what kind of doctor she'd become.

No matter her profession, the beautiful teen Loni had once loved became a gorgeous woman.

Jenna held her head higher, and her voice tightened. "I will repeat this one more time so listen closely. Then I want a lawyer. The house was hers, not mine. I found the door partly open. Carlotta was behind it. I think she had probably been dead for at least an hour which, I'm sure, a coroner will tell you. I didn't leave work until a few minutes past eight. I stopped once for a bottle of white wine. There's a receipt in my purse if you don't believe me. They will remember me because I often buy wine there. I repeat. When I got to Carlotta's house, she was dead. Now. I want to call my lawyer." Staring in defiance at Piggy, Jenna sat back and folded her arms as much as the handcuffs would allow. In frustration, she sat forward and shoved the cuffs in Piggy's face.

Loni backed away from the window, leaving them to argue about the cuffs. She rushed into the hall. Ever since they'd separated, Loni had searched for this woman in every honey blonde she saw. Loni didn't know why Jenna had disappeared from her life, but she knew she wanted to find out, and she wanted to work this investigation.

Stopping by the booking desk, Loni asked for a copy of the arrest information Piggy turned in. Loni rushed up two flights of stairs and burst into the squad room, ignoring the looks she got from the detectives sitting around. Everything that she and the police chief had talked about that morning at their Monday morning briefing vanished from her mind. She could only focus on finding out what charges were levied against Jenna.

Loni rapidly navigated around the desks in the long room, ignoring greetings from her dispatcher and the five detectives sitting at various desks. She banged her office door shut and flipped on the computer. Waiting for it to boot up, she stared back at the detectives' surprised expressions through an office glass window. What were they looking at? None of their business.

She returned to the computer and the report.

Jenna Ann Giovanni was on the report in front of her. Loni didn't recognize the last name. Piggy accused her of murdering her woman lover and she's *married?* Loni typed *Giovanni, Jenna* into the computer and stared at the information scrolling down her screen. She'd graduated from the Georgetown School of Medicine, specializing in emergency. She was married to Barelli Giovanni, owner of research labs in New York and Portland and had one daughter, four years old. Eight months ago, Jenna had taken a job in the emergency department at the Harborville Hospital. Loni sat back in wonder. Jenna had come home.

A knock on the door dragged Loni out of her thoughts. She closed out the contents on her computer screen and motioned for Piggy to come in.

He sat across from her, shaking his head. "She lawyered up, o' course. I don't get it, Lieut. How could such a good-looking woman be so evil? You wouldn't believe all the blood ever'where. I'd swear she took an axe to the vic."

Loni ran fingers in frustration through her spiky short hair. "About that, Piggy. I didn't send you to the scene. In fact, I haven't gotten a call on the crime at all. What's up with that?"

"The DA called me in, o' course. I told you afore we're fishing buddies and when somethin's serous, he calls for me."

Loni studied Piggy a minute. "That's not how it works, Piggy. I'm your boss, and I say what cases you work. But I'll get back to that later. Your report here says you arrested her for interfering with a police officer, and you wrote the reason for the arrest was that you found her at the scene of a murder. And in interrogation, you accused her of murder. Would you explain that?"

"You see the blood all over her?

"So?"

"Obviously she was up close and personal with the vic. Proves she was the killer."

"If she's the killer, why didn't you list murder on your citation?"

Piggy ignored Loni's question. "She argued with me about ever'thing and pissed me off, so interfering's what I thought of at the time when I wrote it. Stupid woman don't know nothing."

"I don't think arguing with you will be a prosecutable offence. Did she threaten you?"

"No."

"You find the weapon?"

"Not yet."

Loni sat back and stared at Piggy. "Where is Doctor Giovanni now?"

"I called Jansom to take her to the cells."

"You can't do that on the citation you wrote."

"Sure I can, Lieut. The DA's adding murder on the arraignment as we speak."

"You put her into a single cell, right? By herself?"

Piggy harrumphed. "Of course not!"

Loni flipped open her phone, fast dialed a number and pressed speaker. "Jansom. This is Lieutenant Loni Wagner. Detective Washington brought the prisoner, Doctor Giovanni, down to you. Please make sure that she is immediately placed in a single cell by herself."

"Why?" The tinny speaker squeaked. "Is she dangerous? Don't look dangerous to me. Mostly she sits and stares. Aside from a few funny comments about rich bitches from her cellmates, nobody's bothering her."

"Jansom!" Loni's voice turned brittle. "If she has to spend the night those few 'comments' can turn fast. Play nice and do what I'm ordering!"

"Okay, okay, Lieutenant. Consider it done."

"Sorry," Loni said, taming her tone. "She's a VIP. Handle with care. Understand?"

"Sure. I got it. Another care package for the city jail. We love them all."

Loni hung up and turned back to Piggy. "Is the body still at the house?"

"Last I know. Somebody said the coroner got hung up elsewhere."

"I need to see the scene."

"Now?"

"Yes, now!"

"Why?"

"It's my job, Piggy. I want to see the body before it's taken away. And I want to see the scene."

"What the hell, Lieut? It's a slam dunk. She did it! It's always the wife or girlfriend. One time a train runs over this pickup pulling a horse trailer. Somebody said he must've been drunk, the parts of him left stank so bad of rotgut."

"Piggy—"

"Don't interrupt, Lieut. This is important!"

"If this is another one of your tall tales . . ."

"No, no, no." Piggy's voice immediately over-rode her. She'd learned the hard way that not even Chief could shut him up until he finished his long-winded, fabricated stories.

"So. Sheriff said it was an accident until the coroner pulled a bullet out of the feller's head." Piggy cackled like an old red Cornish hen scratching in the dirt. "The wife did it, sure as hell."

"What do you mean, sure as hell. Didn't you prove it?"

"Nope. Never could. He was a mean sonofabitch and would beat her fearsome. Everybody hated him and protected her. She took the insurance and married a farmer raising hogs up on the ridge. Now ain't that how it always works?"

"You done now?"

"Don't you get it? She can't be allowed to get away with it."

"Piggy. It's not her husband who's dead."

"Same as, only but worse. It's perverted. Them's the worst."

Loni tried to keep from looking disgusted and wondered how long she could put up with him before she exploded. She feigned a patient expression and pushed out of her chair. In the squad room, she said, "Listen up, guys. I'm headed for Piggy's crime scene. Anyone need anything before I go?"

Four people at their desks stared up at her.

"Bobbi?" Loni looked at her clerk dispatcher who was fiddling with her displays and monitors. "Anything I should know or do before I go?"

Bobbi Wittier's short brown frizzy hair shimmered as she swung her stool around to face Loni. "No, Lieutenant. *Barney* is quiet right now. Most of the dispatch calls are being handled by patrols."

"Ginger? Cleatus?"

Ginger answered in her familiar Texas twang. "Checking up on Piggy, Lieutenant? I'm sure he needs it. As usual." Her partner, Cleatus, grinned at Ginger's sarcasm. Sometimes lack of patience matched the fire-engine red hair she wore short and kinky. Loni noted that the rawboned, muscle-bound butch wore a pale blue shirt with a cobalt blue suit and floppy tie, matching her bright blue eyes.

"Nahhh, Ginger." Cleatus corrected her in a deep Southern drawl. "Piggy's a lost cause. When he was just a li'l baby, his mama left him in a parking lot." Loni grinned at his dialect, so thick that sometimes Ginger had to translate for the rest of them. His courteous manner and beatific smile made some people think that they could beat down the short, slender man, but any aggressive opponent had to face his black belt skill, which also helped him keep his feisty partner out of trouble. "We good, Baws," Cleatus assured Loni.

Ginger echoed her partner. "Yeah, boss. Should've left him in that parking lot."

"She did, Ginger." Harry Truman responded with ridicule written across his craggy face. "He was raised by bears. Don't you notice how much he hibernates?"

Loni worked to control her chuckle as she turned to her last team, Don Thurston and Harry Truman. Both were good-natured and good at their jobs. Harry was the younger one in his early forties, taller and more attractive. Don was almost to retirement age, and he showed it with thick gray hair and a paunch.

Don smirked. "Go on and cover Piggy's ass, Lieutenant. We're good here."

"If any of you do need me I'll be at—what's the address, Piggy?"

"Ninety five thirty eight West Coast Street. Wait! It's nearly lunch time."

Loni resisted the desire to tell him to stop whining and complaining. She checked her watch and grinned at him. "Damn. Would you look at that. So it is." She headed for the stairs down to the basement garage.

Piggy reluctantly followed. "Jesus, Lieut! Why can't we take the elevator? Better yet, wait 'til after lunch?"

"Suck it up, Piggy. Exercise is good for us."

"You a coward, Lieut." Piggy cackled behind her as they hit the bottom of the stairs into the garage. "You scared of that fine elevator."

"Just get in the goddamn car, Piggy!"

"I'm driving."

"Like hell you are." Ignoring Piggy's outstretched hand, Loni took the set of keys from the garage attendant.

"You get the black Audi R8 in space eleven, Lieutenant." The young man dressed in grease-laden bib overalls said, "Don't let Piggy drive."

"Why not?" Piggy looked outraged.

The young man scoffed. "The last time you took one of these cars, you flew out of here into the street in front of a cement truck and burned rubber for half a block before you almost skidded into a blue Prius."

"So? Missed him, didn't I?"

Loni opened the passenger door. "Get in, Piggy, before I fire your ass."

"Ha! You can't. Chief hired me, makes him only one who can fire me."

"Unfortunately," Loni muttered to herself, waiting for Piggy to climb into the passenger seat and buckle up. She carefully pulled out into the traffic and drove on the busy highway through town. They passed workers exchanging Thanksgiving turkey flags for Christmas decorations.

Dark rolling clouds hung low above the heavy gray haze, and rain began to spit on the windshield. Even the Christmas colors reflecting on the glistening streets didn't lighten the darkness. They drove past the blocks of square business buildings. As they came to the edge of town, the buildings turned into residential houses.

"I'm worried, Lieut. You takin' me off this case?"

"Hmmpf," Loni muttered. Piggy had decided to talk to her. "Why?" she asked, glancing over at the hesitant-sounding man.

"I want this case, Lieut. Can't stand to see another woman get away with murder."

Loni shook her head and didn't answer.

"Stop!" Piggy shouted.

Loni slammed on the brake. Both of them flew forward until the seatbelts jerked them back into their seats. "What?" she shouted back.

"You see that, Lieut?" Piggy jumped out of the car and left the door standing open to the rain and wind. Before she could shove the car into park and climb out, Piggy grabbed a young girl with chestnut hair. No more than twelve years old, the girl had tears rolling down her cheeks from her huge brown eyes, and her mouth formed an "O" shape. She shook violently in his hands.

"Let her go, Piggy!" Loni ordered.

"She's jaywalking. She needs to learn her lesson."

The girl looked ready to faint. "Piggy. She's just a kid. It's pouring down rain, and there aren't any crosswalks on this street."

"That's right, Lieut. That makes it jaywalking."

"Piggy! Let her go and get back into the car. Now!"

"Wait, Lieut. Looks like some illegal to me." Piggy flapped an arm at Loni as he pulled on the girl. "Don't she look Mexican to you? Jaywalking's a good reason to deport her."

"Piggy. Let. Her. Go. Now."

Piggy finally grunted in disgust and released the girl. She almost fell to the pavement before she scurried down a sidewalk into a house and slammed the door behind her. Loni saw her peeking out from behind a curtain. The girl gave them the finger as Loni put the car in gear.

Pulling back onto the street, Loni kept her eyes on the road and her mouth shut while her anger simmered. Her interactions with Piggy were becoming increasingly hostile, and she wondered if her unfamiliarity with both her new home and job mixed with her loneliness caused her negative reactions.

Or was she extra sensitive because of Jenna? No doubt, seeing her ex-lover at the booking desk was creating a plethora of unwanted emotions.

The reason for her stress and hostility didn't matter. She knew she had to do something about changing her attitude because even in the short time she'd been at the job, she'd quickly come to realize that there was no changing Piggy.

A wind gust rattled the car, and the black clouds opened up with nearly impenetrable sideways rain. Loni turned onto a narrow road that led to the ocean cliff. Below them, angry black waves lifted high in the air, foamed and crashed in rooster-tails on the rocks.

"See that, Lieut? See those rooster-tails on those waves? East wind's what causes that. Reason it's so cold." Piggy fake shivered. "Glad I'm not out there today."

Hurtling dark clouds smeared the sky in front of them reminding Loni of the darkness boiling inside from her own losses. Jolting away from her thoughts, Loni said, "Somebody's got to knock on some doors. If you want the case, I guess it's going to be you." Loni decided to list Piggy's hostile mutter as the first feel-good part of her day.

A rain squall pounded on the car as Loni drove by old cobbled houses that had survived years of assault by heavy winds and salty spray from the wild surf. Most had managed to hang on while the town grew up around them, but some of them sat too close to the edge of a cliff steadily eaten away. Each year houses collapsed or had to be demolished as the Oregon coast inched its way eastward.

The weather didn't let up as Loni turned down a street so narrow that two cars couldn't pass or park. Shattered oyster shells mixed with sand reflected a mica white glow on the road. Skinny tall houses sided with grayed cedar shingles perched on quarter lots fronted by cracked asphalt stained with plush green fungus. The weight of the water had made roofs sway-backed, and the same green fungus covered the old wood shingles. Gnarled shore pines with gangly moss-covered limbs surrounded the houses and leaned eastward, permanently bent by the buffeting southwest winds.

Spotting a number of emergency vehicles ahead, Loni rolled to a stop behind an ambulance. She turned off the motor. As they waited for the rain squall to pass, Loni stared around her.

"Jeez, Lieut. You drive like an old woman. This car was built for speed."

"Piggy, I drive the speed limit."

"I don't care. Ever'body needs to just get outta the way."

"Hell, Piggy, talking to you is like talking to one of those pine trees."

"Shit, Lieut," Piggy grumbled, "that's cuz you women have no business making decisions no-how."

Loni sputtered a few swear words under her breath before she changed the subject. "Our vic." Loni nodded at the cabin. "You know what she did for a living?"

"She's a nurse, I think. She works at the hospital."

"Worked, Piggy."

Piggy ignored Loni's correction and launched into one of his rants against the government, about excessive spending on Medicaid, Medicare, Social Security, and government costs. Loni tuned him out and studied the one-bedroom house partly sheltered by the spindly shore pines. She admired the trees' determination to hang on and survive in the sand that piled against walls and filled cracks of the brittle shingles.

The squall let up, and Loni opened her car door and stepped into the misty aftermath that some people called Oregon dry rain. Watching the long, dark bands of heavy moisture flying over her, Loni was grateful for the brief break in the storm. She sniffed the salt and the pine scent hanging in the cool damp air. The smell of smoke told her that somebody had a fire nearby. The sun briefly broke through a hole in the low flying clouds, and she tilted her head back and closed her eyes to enjoy the warmth on her face. Storms changed by the minute on the coast—just like her life lately.

Nine months earlier Loni had left dry, hot days of her Arizona home, left her family in the ground, left the girlfriend who had dumped her. Looking around, she smiled at the irony.

The sandy yard supporting a few sprigs of pale green sea grass led to a porch barely big enough for the platform rocking chair sporting a faded, cracked plastic seat. The garish red door and a four-by-ten-foot deck on the second floor completed the front of the house. A purple BMW i3 coupe sat in the rock-laden driveway.

"A beaut, ain't it, Lieut." Piggy brushed his hand across the hood. "Bet it cost way over a hundred thou." Piggy kicked a tire. "Didn't know nurses made that kind of money, did you, Lieut?"

"Is it in the vic's name?"

"Yup. I asked Bobbi to check on it."

"What about the house?"

"Yup. I had Bobbi check on that, too. Said it belonged to the vic."

Loni climbed up onto the porch. "What's really interesting, Piggy, is a hundred thousand-plus car at a hundred thousand-minus house."

"On the beach like this you gotta add another two hundred thou for the view. You pay for the view around here." Piggy pointed to the back of the house. "You gotta see it."

Loni opened the red door, and a young cop, a new trainee she didn't know well, handed her shoe covers and purple latex gloves. "Thanks, Reynolds." She somberly pulled the covers on her feet and slipped on the gloves.

On the floor behind the door lay the body, close up and personal, on top of a paisley rug. The violence inflicted on the body sickened her before she regained enough control of her emotions to study the scene.

"See what I said," Piggy gloated. "Took an axe to her for sure."

Loni silently corrected Piggy. Not an axe. The woman's face was finely slit in strips. One of her ears was missing. Her long, auburn hair was cut out in hunks, and her tiger-patterned jump suit was shredded and covered in blood. It looked as if a raging killer had flung and scattered the pieces. Something very sharp like a straight-edge razor or a fisherman's boning knife had been used for the cutting. Or maybe a doctor's scalpel. Somebody really hated this woman.

Loni nodded hello to both Jumbo Hart, who was taking photos of the scene, and Adanna Steller, the primary criminologist carefully picking up debris around the body.

Adanna said, "Looks like she opened the door to someone she knew."

"Why do you say that, Adanna?"

"She didn't try to run. All the cast-off blood spatter looks consistent with a full-on frontal assault."

Studying the blood pattern on the back of the closed door, Loni had to agree. Murmuring to herself, Loni said, "Yet who would have thought the old man to have had so much blood in him?"

Jumbo snapped another photo before he looked up. "Quoting Shakespeare, Lieutenant?"

"Lady Macbeth."

"Uh huh," he said.

The older man's emaciated, almost anorexic, body belied his name. Loni had asked Jumbo once why he was so thin. He laughed before he answered, "You think I'm skinny? You should see my ma. If you could find her."

"Coroner not here yet?" Loni asked him.

"No. He's coming, but he's been busy with a death at the Old Pioneer's Home."

"Yeah?" Piggy said. "Anybody I know?"

"I couldn't tell you, Piggy. Natural causes, though. Somebody's mother, I'd guess. How's your ma, Piggy?"

"Good, Jumbo. Had her gall bladder removed. I got the bill. Ought to be ashamed charging that kind of money."

"Isn't she on Medicare?"

"Yeah, thank God. Still have to pay some on her pills. What's up with that?"

Loni interrupted Piggy before he got onto another diatribe. "You said something about a beautiful woman, Piggy. How can you tell?"

"Upstairs. Her photo's ever'where." Piggy snickered. "I'll just wait for you upstairs. Boy, is it something!"

Two sets of tracks surrounded the body, one set smeared in the blood and the other on top of the blood. The first set looked like a dress shoe with a slick leather bottom from either a man's or a very large woman's foot. "Looks like someone walked through the blood and kneeled here at her head. Maybe a woman's dress shoe." Loni turned to Adanna. "Can you call the evidence room and have someone bring me the suspect's shoes and clothes. I'd like to see how they match."

"You do know you need a release from a judge to get them here. On top of possibility contaminating your evidence."

"You got a judge on speed dial? I could do a telephonic."

Jumbo said, "Be easier to use a Photoshop overlay, Lieutenant."

"I will if this goes to court. But I've got a problem with what I'm seeing, and I really need to know now before I go forward with a murder indictment."

Loni listened to Adanna's phone conversation as she explained the issue to the judge. To clarify matters, Loni took the phone. "Your Honor, I need to either clear or confirm a murder, and I need the suspect's clothes and shoes and would much appreciate your help."

After some further conversation, Loni handed the phone back to Adanna and said, "Thanks. It's a go."

Loni moved around Jumbo while Adanna called her office to get the clothes and shoes delivered. "Make sure you get a good photo of every footprint and measure for size, please," Loni told the photographer as she carefully circled the body.

"Always, Lieutenant."

"Sorry. Of course, you will." Embarrassed for questioning him, Loni watched Jumbo carefully lay a ruler down beside a print, his long hand and fingers extending out of his too short sleeves. As he squatted, his joints popped. "Lordy, I'm getting too old for this." Jumbo groaned. "Give me a few, Lieutenant, and I'll be done here."

"What's takin' so long?" Piggy whined as he stepped in front of Loni. "Whatcha think about this love nest, Jumbo? Wouldja want one?"

"Get out of my way, Piggy." Jumbo gestured for Piggy to get back and squatted down. "You're in my shot."

"Whatcha say, Jumbo?" Piggy took a half-step back. "This fine layout. Sickos have all the fun."

Jumbo looked up at Piggy and shook his head. "Don't look like she's having fun now. What are you doing here anyway? Thought you went upstairs?"

Circling a sputtering Piggy, Loni continued into the large, open room, nodding to Molly, a cute tech so small she looked like a child playing house. Her fragile waiflike essence was highlighted by her porcelain pale skin, and her light blond hair tied back in a ponytail made her look like a teenager. She had to roll up the pants and sleeves on the tan jumpsuit that she wore to prevent contamination. Her hair bounced with every movement as she intently dusted for prints on cabinet handles.

"Hey Molly, anything interesting?" Loni waited for an answer as she looked around at the compact and open kitchen-breakfast bar and the living room, all painted a pale yellow. The large Jackson Pollock and Andy Warhol prints hanging on each side of the front door on the flat living room wall broke up the pale wall color. A bulky rug atop the polished hardwood floor added more color to the room along with the surrounding short red couch, glass-top coffee tables, and two red upholstered chairs.

"Two sets of prints, Loni. No others so far."

"Two will do, Molly, especially if one's the murderer."

"If we could be so lucky," Molly sighed, returning to her task.

Loni's eyes moved back to the body before she scanned the room again. Between the kitchen and living room a black metal spiral staircase wound up to the second floor. A compact desk and chair were tucked in behind the staircase. "Anybody know? Is this the victim's primary address?"

"Yes," answered Molly as she pointed at the desk. "At least her mail has this address."

"Thanks Molly."

"You're welcome, Lieutenant." Molly grinned and winked at Loni.

Staring down at the desktop between the kitchen and the living room, Loni noticed a blank space among the papers and a newspaper with articles partially cut as though someone had not finished. She wondered where the scissors were. She rejected them as the murder weapon, and her interest moved on. "Hey, Molly? Where's her computer?"

"None here, Lieutenant. And no cell phone. No land line either."

"Really? What about her purse?"

"No purse either."

"Did you find the weapon?"

"Not yet."

Half listening to Piggy and Jumbo, Loni flipped through the mail on the desk, stopping to open and study some of the mail. Credit card bills showed big charges, especially at places in Portland that sold clothes and jewelry.

"Hey, Jumbo," Piggy said. "Bet she's one of them bleeding heart liberals."

"Was, Piggy. Was." Jumbo looked around the room. "Where do you get a bleeding heart from, Piggy?"

"Didn't you see that bedroom upstairs? Them kind have no morals. They're—"

"Oh, for God's sake." Adanna Steller interrupted Piggy's diatribe. "I swear I've been transported back to the bowels of Georgia." Adanna stuck her fists on her hips and leaned into Piggy's face. "And what do you know about morals, Piggy? You so white bread you even bleed Maalox. Do you know what that means, honey?"

"I'm not your honey, Adanna—"

"Stop, Piggy," Loni demanded with a hard look. Piggy stopped in mid-sentence and squirmed. Loni turned away from him. "Find anything I should look at, Adanna?"

"I did. Follow me." Adanna headed for the stairs.

Molly stopped her rummaging through a kitchen cabinet. "Wait until you see that bedroom, Lieutenant."

Curious, Loni trailed up the steep staircase after Adanna's long legs. Tall and beautiful, Adanna looked like an African queen. She was in her early forties, but her prematurely white hair, close cropped, accented her dark eyes and skin. She was also the smartest criminologist Loni had ever worked with.

As she neared the top of the stairs, Loni understood the stunned expression on Adanna's face. "Wow!" Loni said. "Now I understand why Piggy asked the suspect about the bed."

Adanna said, "I know. It's a good thing you can't see me blush."

"Unfortunately, my Apache Indian heritage isn't dark enough to help me. Oh, my!" Loni stood at the end of the round bed and stared in amazement at the velvet red bedspread on a heart-shaped bed piled everywhere with pillows. She got uncomfortable imagining Jenna on it. "Find anything on the sheets?"

"No. The bed's been changed today. Sheets and bedspread were clean."

"How about in the wash?"

"Nope. Everything's washed, vacuumed, and cleaned up. I think our deceased is a little OCD."

"So," Loni paused, "whoever killed her probably hadn't been sleeping with her last night."

"No way to know. We haven't found any evidence of that yet."

Loni continued to stare around the room. Except for two slanted walls, the room itself was almost the same size as the downstairs. The flat part of the ceiling was covered with mirrored tiles, and one of the walls was painted black behind erotic posters adding to the titillating effect of the décor. The other wall had a sled-roof pop-out with a three-by-three-foot table and two chairs. Loni gazed out the wide window revealing an ocean view of heavy waves crashing on rocks and blasting in the air in amazing shapes. Even though the tide was in, she could see a staircase winding down to where the low tides would uncover the sandy beach and tide pools around the rocks.

"See what I told you about this whore's den?" Piggy's whiny voice disturbed Loni's focus on the amazing show below. Turning away from the window, she ignored Piggy and refocused on Adanna.

Piggy snickered. "Sure know where this broad spent her time." He winked at Adanna.

"That why people call you Piggy?" Adanna snapped. "You so good at rutting in the dirt."

Piggy snorted. "Nah, I always wanted to be a cop since I was a little sucker and always been chubby. Mostly they made fun of my pug nose, so my brothers started calling me Piggy and it stuck."

"Don't you hate it?"

"Nah. It's what I am."

"Okay, I guess it would be like an Italian calling himself a dago, or a Chicano calling himself a wetback."

"Or black people calling hisself—"

"No. No. No." Adanna interrupted, her voice rising. "Do not go there! That's the one word I cannot stand."

"It's just calling a spade a spade."

Adanna sputtered, "You're an insensitive jerk."

"How come you're not tougher, Adanna. You can't be a good cop if you go all bleeding heart all the time."

"I'm not a cop, Piggy."

"Then what the hell are you?"

"A scientist!"

The loud fight between Adanna and Piggy dragged Loni out of her reverie. She had been remembering the apartment she and Jenna shared their second year. Their dinky, shabby place was homey, but certainly nothing like this. "Hate to spoil this happy reunion, but did you find any items of interest?" Loni asked.

Adanna pointed to a box. "This is what I've packed. The dildos include strap-ons and doubles implying female lovers as do other toys in the bedside drawers. You might also be interested in some of the men's clothing that I found in one of the drawers. A little of everything. Shorts, tees, socks, all expensive. Shirts and ties in her closet."

Piggy snorted. "Maybe she was a cross-dresser."

"One could think that Piggy, if they were in her size." Adanna moved toward the bathroom. "Check this out."

Loni followed her into the bathroom with white walls and a white-tiled floor. At the end was a two-person Jacuzzi beside a glassed-in shower with shower heads from a number of angles.

"Wow!"

Adanna laughed at Loni's reaction. "My sentiments exactly. Maybe a little much?"

"It's so clean it looks unused. Where's the toothbrushes, makeup, and other usual bathroom crap?"

"In here." Adanna opened a double-mirrored cabinet that went from floor to ceiling. Pullout shelves were filled with rows of makeup, perfumes, soaps, lotions, designer drugs, and items that Loni couldn't identify. "Some of these perfumes are very expensive, Lieutenant." She picked up a one-ounce amber-colored bottle with a crown-shaped lid and waved it in front of Loni's nose. "Clive Christian Number One. Maybe eight hundred dollars."

Piggy crowded into the bathroom. "A bottle?"

Adanna rolled her eyes at him. "Yes, Piggy. A bottle." She opened another drawer. "Look at these soaps!" Adanna shook her head in wonder. "My first memory of soap was my grandmother's grey lye soap, so hard on our skin that my mother used Lava soap bars when Granny wasn't around. If we were lucky, we got Lifebuoy soap bars for our hair." Her face softened. "I remember how Lava soap smelled, sort of acidy with sugar cane spice. Always tickled my nose. And I remember my brother always used orange Lifebuoy soap."

"What is this?" Piggy whined. "Old memory time?"

Adanna glared at Piggy until he turned away, muttering about women. She said, "This room hasn't been fingerprinted yet, so don't touch." She opened a drawer that held a shaving cream, razor, and toothbrush. "Looks like she had a frequent male visitor. I shouldn't have any trouble getting DNA from these. And I'll look for fingerprints, but they've probably been wiped clean like everything else."

"Interesting," Loni noted as she looked at the evidence of a male inhabitant. "Bisexual?"

"That'd be my guess." Adanna led Loni back out into the room to a long black modernistic-styled dresser with round set-in handles. "This is a Brownstone, Lieutenant. Very high end." She carefully avoided the fingerprint powder when she opened the second drawer. Picking up a bra from the stacks of lingerie, Adanna said, "This is a Jean Yu. It runs over three hundred dollars." She dropped it back in the drawer.

Loni's eyes widened in amazement. "Damn, Adanna! How do you know all this?"

Adanna laughed at Loni as she pulled her phone out of her pocket and tapped the face. "Hey! You can find out anything on these."

Loni spun on her heel, appraising the opulence. "We must be in the wrong business. I had no idea nurses made this kind of money."

"I'm pretty sure they don't. I also found a Carine Gilson robe in the closet."

"Let me guess. Eight hundred?"

"Maybe closer to two thousand."

"Two thousand what?" Piggy asked.

"Dollars, Piggy. Dollars." Adanna answered.

Piggy's eyes popped as his nearly non-existent eyebrows climbed to the top of his short forehead. "For a housecoat? How many sugar daddies did she have?"

"Piggy!" Loni shook her head. "You're assuming again."

"Kind of hard not to, Lieut. I know doctors are rich. We know a man visits a lot. From his clothes, he's rich, too."

"Or maybe she inherited it, Piggy. Ever think of that?"

"I might if this didn't look like a whore house." Piggy flapped his arms. "Look at it!"

Adanna admitted, "Piggy, you do have a point."

Loni nodded. "Could be enough motive for a jealous lover to kill. When you tag and dust these, Adanna, put a priority to the lab for DNA testing."

"You in a hurry on this case?"

Loni looked Adanna in the eye. Speaking low to avoid other ears, Loni said, "I am. This one's personal."

Adanna nodded her understanding. "Maybe we could have a sit-down sometime soon."

With an acknowledging glance, Loni left the bathroom and walked over to the fireplace and picked up a photo of Carlotta, carefully studying the professionally staged half-nude body and the "come fuck me" smile. "I know this woman."

Piggy looked over her shoulder. "Told you she was good-looking. And sexy as hell. Don't say you jumped her, too."

"*Was* sexy as hell, Piggy. Was."

"Not so beautiful now though," Adanna reminded Piggy. She lifted a questioning eyebrow at Loni. "Just how well did you know her, Lieutenant?"

Flushing red again, Loni nudged Adanna with her hip. "Not *that* well." Loni looked at the photo again and lost her shy grin. "I met her right after I moved here. I got a call to Freddy's on a shoplifter. She was still raging when I arrived and got in my face screaming 'setup.'" Loni put the picture back, thinking about Carboni's violent temper. "She never shut up the entire time I walked her out, put her in the car, drove to the station, led her to the interrogation room, and questioned her. And she was still screaming when her lawyer showed up and bailed her out."

"Did she get out of it?"

"She paid the store for the merchandise, promised to never go into the store again if they didn't press charges, and walked." Loni had warned Carboni she had better pay because it was her only chance. Still swearing, Carboni wrote a check and stomped out of the prosecutor's office in righteous indignation. Loni remembered thinking what an amazing actress she would have been. And how much she reminded Loni of Lola, her last girlfriend. Beautiful, volatile, verbal, bisexual, rejecting. Still smarting from Lola's last words about how she wanted a man, Loni had walked.

Loni shook herself back into the present by asking, "Can you tell yet how many different people have been in here?"

"Looks like three so far, maybe four," Adanna said. "Hard to tell. Somebody did a good job cleaning this morning."

"Sure," Piggy added. "Killers cleaning up after."

"Don't think so," Adanna said. "Looks to me she had a germ phobia. Probably the nurse in her."

"Thanks, Adanna." Loni scrambled downstairs to the kitchen. She walked through the kitchen looking for anything that didn't seem right. The dishwasher was empty and dry. The immaculate refrigerator had an open bottle of white wine, a few squares of cheese, some cut-up vegetables, a melon, several containers of fruit yogurt, and two dozen eggs. Closing the door, Loni surveyed the pea-green cement counters. A fry pan big enough for a couple of eggs sat on the glass-top range, and the oven was so clean that it looked unused. The half-full pot of coffee on the coffee maker was slightly warm, but the counter held nothing else. No sugar bowl. No spices. No canisters. Loni turned to find Adanna and Molly coming through the doorway. "Where's the coffee cup?"

"Didn't see any dirty dishes," Molly answered. "Maybe they got washed and put back." She stretched up and opened one of the glass-door cabinets. "Check this out. This is some really spendy dishware."

"Fiesta ware?"

"Eight servings. The real deal, too. Vintage all the way. Feel how heavy." Molly handed a plate to Loni. "The red is richer, too. They don't use lead to make it any more. One place setting probably costs almost a thousand dollars."

"Damn, Molly! Take it back before I drop it."

Laughing, Molly accepted the plate and picked up a bowl. "This one alone is two hundred."

Loni silently counted the coffee cups. "Looks like one of the cups is missing." Loni looked around. "Strange. Maybe somebody was drinking coffee with her and took the cup."

"Could be. I haven't found any fingerprints to tell me anything."

"Let me know if you find the missing cup. Oh, and bag it. Make sure Jumbo gets photos of all this." Loni began opening drawers.

Molly pulled open the drawer next to the sink and took out a boning knife and tested the edge on a page out of her notebook. "Only possible weapon I found. Not even sharp. I used the precipitin test on it as well as others. No human blood residue. The weapon's not here."

Piggy pushed into Molly's space and took the knife, twirling it around. "Looks like a murder weapon to me." Tossing the knife back into the drawer, he continued with dripping sarcasm, "Never assume, Molly. Didn't you get the lieut's lesson?"

"Guess I missed that day, Piggy."

Loni starred Piggy down for interrupting. "So did he, Molly," she said, turning her back on Piggy to continue looking around. "So did he."

Unlike the bedroom, the first floor contained no personal items, as if nobody spent any time there. Loni got back to Carboni's body at the same time that a young female cop came into the entry and handed Adanna the sealed plastic bags with Jenna's shoes, blouse, sweater, and slacks that she brought from the police station evidence room. Adanna cut the bags open and pulled out the shoes, matching them to the footprints on top of the blood. "Looks like a match for the top shoe prints." The slacks also matched the knee impressions at Carboni's head.

"Indicates she was already dead when the good doctor walked in her blood." Adanna completed Loni's sentence.

Holding up the shirt, Loni said, "I don't see any blood spatter on this." She passed the shirt to Adanna who resealed the evidence bags and returned it to the cop. "Thanks. You can return them to the evidence room. Please."

Loni and Piggy watched the coroner, a heavy-set short man, remove Carboni's body. Adanna and Jumbo left with the coroner.

"Ever seen a body sliced and diced as good as that one before, Lieut?" Piggy asked. "A woman could've done that, easy-peasy."

Loni was disgusted by Piggy's gross description, but she worked to be civil. "I agree, Piggy, but I think you jumped the gun here. There's no conclusive evidence against Doctor Giovanni to take to trial. Now we've got a suspect in jail who's no longer a suspect and who's already lawyered up."

"The other shoes could be a partner."

Loni gritted her teeth before answering. "Maybe so, but you've got no proof of that either. Obviously, she's not the killer, and until we find who is, we can't prove anything."

"You think she didn't do it."

Loni was close to losing control. "What you're not hearing is that you have no proof," she said in a harsh tone.

"I know, I know. I got it!"

"Got what, Piggy?"

Piggy threw up his arms. "Never assume. Don't try to force the facts to fit a theory."

Loni eased up. "Very good, you're learning." At the same time, she was thinking, I hate wiping horsepucky all over your sorry face even if I do think you deserve this one.

Loni looked around one last time. "I'm going to go get her released since we don't have any criminal charges."

The black clouds had rolled on, opening another hole of blue sky that followed Loni and Piggy as they returned to the station. Loni drove down into the secure underground parking. Piggy complained every stair step of the three floors that the elevator worked fine, but Loni laughed at his grunts and gasps. "Suck it up," Piggy she said as he fell farther and farther behind her.

"But I missed lunch and I'm shrinking."

"Losing weight is a good thing, too."

Several phone calls later, Loni couldn't find anyone who knew where Jenna's booking or first appearance file was. The DA's office finally called Loni back saying the DA wasn't in and didn't know when he would be back.

"How about the assistant DA? Isn't there anyone else who can help me?"

"No, the DA insists on reviewing everything first."

At least, that's what the sweet voice on the phone said. Disappointed, hating to see anyone innocent behind bars, even someone who once hurt her, Loni left for the day. There was nothing else she could do.

Chapter Two

Loni was bombarded by the memories from long ago as she drove home. After all these years, she was still angry with Jenna for leaving her, and yet the good memories of Jenna had brought her north to the Oregon coast, to the place where she'd spent two of the happiest years of her life. At the crest of the last hill to her home, Loni stopped and idled a few minutes. She stared out at the old homestead she'd bought two miles out of town. Her new home was surrounded by forty acres in the middle of a pine forest on a hill overlooking a trickling stream that anyone could jump across. She especially loved the path beaten through the woods that made easy access to the beach and ocean.

Loni's thoughts of Jenna led her to wonder what Jenna would think of her having only two bedrooms and one bath, much different from Jenna's home on the lake. The squat salt house with shingled siding blackened from the relentless southwest rains was in front of a slightly listing barn that held a stack of hay, two stalls with horses, and enough parking for three cars. Or maybe two cars and a tractor. After years of battering sun, rain, and hail, the barn's red paint was almost gone, leaving a few rusty streaks over the dark gray. Loni hoped to put on a new roof as soon as the rain let up, but that wouldn't be until summer. A five-acre rolling pasture of timothy grass stretched tall and green out behind the barn. The incessant rain wouldn't let her mow the weeds encroaching on the house.

Driving down the hill, Loni was relieved to get home. She parked in the barn next to a Ford F-150 pickup truck, her one luxury item from selling the ranch in Arizona. Sharp barks greeted her as she approached the house. She opened the door and was nearly knocked down by a large ball of brown wool that circled her before the standard poodle dashed off to the back of the barn. Loni hated to lock Coco in the house all day, but too many animals were brave enough to go through her dog door into the house for her food and water. An occasional squirrel was okay, but raccoons were mean and didn't want to leave. And the skunk that once got in made Loni grab Coco and head for the barn until it finished eating the poodle's food and left. Didn't seem to help, though. The acid skunk smell stayed around the dog door for weeks.

Back at the barn, Loni reached out to Roani, a reddish quarter horse who nickered in greeting, and she rubbed his velvet nose. Roani had been with her since she was a kid. His saddle and battle scars left white patches spotting his body, and the creases and wrinkles around his eyes told his twenty odd years. Other people thought the over-sized head on his short neck, along with knees too big from all the falls chasing cattle across the Arizona desert, made him ugly. They laughed at the awkward tilt from his powerful hind-quarters until they saw his speed in action. And Roani just wouldn't quit.

"Hey, guy." Loni clucked as she lifted his head and checked his teeth for any needed floating. She didn't have to grind them down very often so that he could chew better, but checking was a habit. As was checking each of his hoofs and legs for hot spots and swelling.

Loni filled the gunny sack feeders with oats to hang on both horses leaning out of their stalls. She hung the gunny sack on Roani and moved on to Gladys, repeating the same checks. "Hey girl. You have a quiet day? Any visits from vermin you want to talk about?" Gladys was a common brown American Standard horse with a white star the size of a child's open hand in her forehead. She was tall with good conformation. A plodder, she could sustain a running walk for hours. She was a sweet girl with no expectation or drive who loved Roani and refused to be parted from him. Loni didn't want to take two horses when she left Arizona, but she couldn't separate them. Smiling, she sat on a bale of hay across from them and watched them chew, their eyes half closed and their ears wiggling in ecstasy.

Coco sniffed around the yard doing what Loni called reading her evening newspaper while Loni pulled the feed bags from the horses' heads. She dropped a flake of hay in their troughs and filled their water pails with a hose. Finished with the horses, she called Coco and headed for the house.

The dog curled up in her favorite place where she could watch all the doors while Loni fixed dinner in what she considered her kitchen, a tiny stove, fridge, and sink at the end of the main room. Loni had covered the four-foot long counter with a swirly purple Formica that made her smile. Cast iron pots and skillets brought from Arizona hung from nails pounded into a board hanging over an island where Loni cut up meat and vegetables. She didn't use anything for cooking except for a seven-inch ceramic fry pan that didn't burn her food, but her grandmother's cast iron pots and pans were memories, and she kept them oiled to prevent rusting.

The long room contained several pieces of antique furniture that came with her from the Arizona ranch. Her great-grandmother had brought the sideboard and dining room table surrounded by eight chairs to Arizona from the East in the eighteen-eighties. They were massive and left little room for her worn La-Z-Boy recliner in front of the wide screen television.

Loni put two frozen green corn tamales into the microwave oven and fed Coco while they heated. Without her friend Yammy and his tamales, she'd probably starve. She threw together a salad, gobbled her dinner and dragged herself into the undersized bedroom which contained a full-sized, ornate antique Murphy bed, so old it would no longer fold up. The original mattress had to be replaced after it broke in half. As tired as she was, she sat on the bed and made herself open her computer. She had an email from Sandi, the sister of her late partner, Maria. Seeing Sandi's name brought it all back as the night Maria was shot flickered through her mind and she watched the scene again for the millionth time, Maria running ahead of her, the young rooky cop, mistaking her for the perp, stepping out and shooting her in the back. Holding her, begging her not to die. Loni shook the painful images away and focused on Sandi's email.

> TO: Loni Wagner
> FROM: Sandi Havir
> Date: December 12
> Subject: Where are you?
>
> Momma and I have not heard from you in too long and
> we are getting worried. Please write me!
> Sandi

Sighing, Loni settled in to answer the email.

> TO: Sandi@gmailyahoo.com
> FROM: Loni Wagner
> DATE: December 12
> SUBJECT: Sorry!
>
> Sorry it's so long since I last wrote. Tell Momma Sanchez
> I miss her and that I'm good. There's so much to tell you. So
> much change. So much loss. I couldn't write about it for a
> long time after I lost my grandparents. One morning Bahb
> couldn't wake up Shiichoo. At her funeral, Bahb said he

stayed to take care of her and now he was done. He went to bed and twelve days later died in his sleep. I am so lucky to have been raised by such loving people. I told you about losing Willie when I visited you last spring. His funeral following Maria's was hard enough. With the family gone I didn't want to stay on so I sold the ranch and moved back to Oregon where I spent two wonderful years during my college days. I got a job as a lieutenant heading up the crimes investigation division in a medium-sized town called Harborville.

I'm pretty settled now although I can't say whether my horses and dog are happy with me or the place. They're used to the hot, sunny Arizona desert, and now we live on the windy, cold, very rainy Oregon coast. I did find an old farmhouse with a field full of grass and a barn for Roani and Gladys.

Coco doesn't go to work with me much anymore unless we're working a drug case because I have to spend most of my time in my office on paper work. It's a lot easier for her to do her drug sniffing up here because the scent hangs on longer in the damp air. Unless it rains. Which has been most of the time.

I hung Maria's jacket in my closet, the one she was wearing when she was shot in the back. It's shoved far enough inside so I don't see it every time I open it, but I know a part of her is there and it eases me. It also reminds me to watch my back no matter where I am. I do wish our sister-in-law had left me something of hers when she stripped our apartment while I was at Maria's funeral. I'm still having trouble forgiving her for that.

On a better note, I love it here, especially the green and cool weather. I've even made a few friends and found a sort of relative of a relative. And I ran into someone I knew back when I lived here before. But that's another story for another time so I'll sign off for now.
Take care,
Loni

Loni spent a restless night chasing her past lovers in a dance with Maria, Lola, and Jenna fading in and out. Sleep finally came when a sliver of light appeared in the east.

Chapter Three

Looking forward to her second cup of morning coffee, Loni hit the last step into the squad room and heard her name. Police Chief Alden was beckoning to her from the doorway of Loni's office. The big bear of a man possessed gentle brown eyes that always made her feel more at ease. Gray spurts of hair sprouting around his ears and his mostly shiny bald head revealed his sixty-some years. He had a squishy essence, contradicting the hard-muscled body from years of championship weight-lifting.

"What are you doing coming all the way up here, Chief? Don't you know you'll get altitude sickness? Some of you VIPs have even been known to get nose bleeds."

Chief laughed. "More out of hostility than altitude, I'm thinking." He followed Loni into her office and closed the door.

"Did I forget something from yesterday's meeting?"

"No." Chief stood at the office window for a few minutes looking out at her squad and shook his head. "Can't believe your detectives. You got black-as-the-ace-of-spades Cleatus with Rambo redhead." Chief glanced over at Loni before he turned back to watching her detectives. "Cleatus is smarter than all the rest of your detectives put together. Did you know that? His IQ tested in the one-sixties. Harry looks just like his great-uncle Harry Truman. Talks like him, too. That sign on his desk? 'The Buck Stops Here.' Really? Sometimes I think he channels his uncle to speak for him."

Chief turned back to Loni who was sitting on the edge of her desk. He said, "I know you lost a good detective to narcotics when you took over, and I understand why you assigned Harry and Don as a team, but why Ginger and Cleatus? I thought Ginger and Piggy were a good team."

"Not according to Ginger. She asked for the switch." Loni slipped off the desktop and went to stand beside the chief at the window. "It also helps Ginger's from Texas. Her dialect comes the closest to Cleatus's, so she's his translator."

"That's right. He's from Mississippi. Who's *her* translator?"

"Most of us can work it out now we've toned down her dialect. We're working to get her to use her R's." Loni grinned. "They seem to really like each other. More to the point, I can't get anyone to work with Piggy. Ginger calls him a demented drugstore cowboy. Harry calls him a sociopathic hotshot. Don says he invented depraved indifference."

Chief laughed. "Harry psychoanalyzes almost everything, and Don legalizes the rest. What does Cleatus say?"

"When he's not calling Piggy a turkey turd, he dubs him Ignert or Machiavellian depending, he claims, on his benevolence at the time."

"Machiavellian, huh? I bet not even Ginger can translate that one." He rubbed his head a minute. "I do know what a trial Piggy, is but when it comes to hunting down low life, especially along the coastal hills, no one is better."

"Are you saying he's a political hire?"

"Aren't we all?" Chief snorted and changed the subject. "So. Then there's you."

Loni laughed. "Then there's me. I got to tell you, I give Piggy the easy ones, hoping he gets it right. I do worry about leaving him out there alone too much. I try to work with Piggy when I get the time."

Chief turned away from the window. He sighed and stepped over to sit in the visitor's chair at her desk. "Can't say I blame you. At least you got Don. He's not got the intellect Cleatus does, but he's the best damn detective I ever saw. Too bad he's set to retire in a few months." Chief sighed again, rubbing his nose. "Thinking about joining him." Chief moved his hand from his nose to rub his eyes a few seconds and sighed for the third time. "This job's not fun anymore."

Loni had never heard the chief sound so forlorn. She wasn't even sure she'd ever heard him sigh so much and it worried her. "I think Piggy would agree with you." Loni moved around her desk and sat across from him. "Consider how he feels being bossed by a lesbian half-breed Apache Indian."

Chief laughed. "Tell me the truth. Being Apache ever scare anyone?"

"Being a lesbian scared them more, but yeah. Back when I was young and stupid I had this homeless guy always getting himself busted every Friday to get his weekly bath and a few meals. So, I put a few stripes on my face and feathers on my head before I did a war dance outside his unlocked cell. Never saw him again. Heard he sobered up and got a job. Was afraid of having more alcoholic hallucinations."

Chief laughed. "Don't think that would work here."

"Probably not." Loni asked the question she had been wondering about since she was hired. "Considering my age, why did you give me the lieutenant's job? There's good people out there to choose from."

"Nobody else wanted it."

"You're kidding?"

"What's the pay like in southern Arizona?"

"Why? You gonna move there and become a snowbird? Work part-time?"

Chief's grin didn't show his teeth. "Might, one of these days. You have a good chief there?"

"The last one, yeah. He was a good friend. Older than me, but I grew up with him living at the ranch next to us. We often worked our cattle together. When his dad died, he leased out his ranch and became a cop." Loni remembered Carl's kindness over the years she knew him. "The one before that, not so much."

"Really? What was wrong with him?"

"Aside from the fact that he was a pedophile, a psychopath, a misanthrope, and hated most especially me, not much else."

Chief barked a laugh. "That all, huh? Could've been worse."

"I don't know how. Not when I ended up arresting a girl I was dating for nailing Chief on the wall like Christ and gutting him like a deer. With her father's help." Loni felt the sadness roll over her. "During his previous job as a cop in California, they were neighbors, and he had molested her for years. When he got caught, he accused her father and had him thrown in prison. Her mother believed her husband did it and committed suicide, and her brother got lost in drugs." Loni wiped her face attempting to clear away the memories. "She was an amazing artist and teacher. A beautiful woman. I still have one of her paintings." Loni nodded at a painting on the wall with a pastoral scene where fall leaves exploded with wild colors among brilliant greens.

Chief stared at the painting. "Cheery."

"I keep it in sight to keep me vigilant."

Chief nodded. "Things are never what they seem."

Loni nodded in agreement. "Wander into the lounge sometime." Loni nodded toward the conference room beside the elevator. "Bobbi painted it in the colors of a grand old lady. Says it's to bring calm into our stressful lives."

"Grand old lady?"

Loni delighted in the expression on the Chief's face. "That's what she calls it. Like an old Victorian house."

"I could use that in my office. Does it work?"

"Don't know but it does look really good."

Chief studied Loni a minute. "You doing okay? You been here, what? Six, seven months now? Rain not getting you down yet?"

"More like nine, but God no. I love it. I got so tired of the hot sun every predictable day after day that it can never rain enough for me." Loni took a closer look at the chief. "Can't say the same about you, Alden. You still look like you don't feel good. You losing weight?"

"Asking for my job?"

"God, no! No, no. No campaigning for me. Ever. Just worried about you."

"I'm good. Still getting over a bout of really nasty flu."

"I heard it was going around. You should go home and eat some chicken soup." Loni leaned back and sighed. "Wish my grandma was here. She made the best."

"You were raised by your grandparents, that right?"

"Yes. My mom died when I was born. My dad disappeared. They say he was too heartbroken to stay. After I was grown, heard he died in a salt mine."

"And your grandparents were Native Americans?"

"On my mother's side. My grandma was Apache and my granddad was Navajo, mostly." Loni grinned. "Claims he was part of a horse trade, though, and mostly raised Pima."

"You miss them."

"They left me too soon. After I buried them, I didn't want to keep the ranch anymore."

"Why here?"

"Back in my Lewis and Clark school days I knew someone from here. Visited a few times and loved the town. Saw an ad online for someone to head up your detective department, so here I am."

Chief nodded. "Glad to have you.

Loni was touched at his sincerity. He seemed to genuinely mean his words.

"Rather impressive credentials. Two years of pre-law, graduating the police academy, street patrol in L.A. where you also trained in profiling and negotiating. Highway patrol and town detective in Arizona, now here. You could be chief!" He grinned at her. "You would think after all that you would know how to answer your phone."

"Sorry. I just got back from a crime scene." Loni checked her phone, but she didn't see a call. "Must have called me when I was in one of those dead zones we have out of town." Loni dropped her phone back into her pocket. "Come to think of it, there was no land line at the crime scene. And no cell phone. No computer either." She jotted down a quick note before focusing her full attention back on the chief. "What can I do for you?"

"About this Carlotta Carboni case. I really think you have enough to do. Let Piggy run with it and see what happens. Looks like a 'love did me wrong' case to me. Piggy thinks it's a slam dunk."

Loni raised an eyebrow. "When did you talk to Piggy about the Carboni case?"

"I didn't. He called the DA yesterday when he was bringing in the killer. DA called me." Chief gingerly pushed himself out of the rickety armless chair in front of her desk. "He said to tell you to stop investigating, that Piggy had arrested the killer. Said to tell you he would be filing a murder charge when he gets back."

"No, no, no. Piggy only thought he did. But it wasn't her. We found enough evidence at the scene to prove her innocent so we have to let her go."

Chief's gray bushy eyebrows shot up. "I don't understand. What happened?"

"Piggy arrested her without checking out the evidence at the scene."

"How was it wrong?"

Loni leaned back in her chair. "Well." She rubbed her dark eyes in thought. "The woman he brought in, Doctor Jenna Giovanni, was still at work when the murder occurred. Also, her footprints at the scene were on top of dried blood, and there was no blood spatter on her clothes. No murder weapon found. She wasn't the killer."

With a disappointed sigh, Chief Alden trudged to the door. He reached out for the knob and turned back to Loni. "You know who we're dealing with here, right?

"Not really, Chief. I've only been here a few months, remember?"

"True." Chief stared at Loni and spoke quietly. "Jenna Giovanni's grandmother, Maud Davenport, not only owned the hospital, she has a hand in supporting a lot of businesses in this town. Old lumber money. I want to be kept informed on this case. Don't drown me in surprises."

"Got it, Chief. I'll do my best." She wondered about the mixed signals she was getting from him.

Chief opened the door and stood in the doorway another moment watching Loni's detectives. "You'll be down next Monday at your usual time for a report on your cases, right?" He waited until Loni nodded in agreement. "Maybe you should hold off on working this case for now. Let me get an okay from the DA."

"Sure."

"Good." Chief finally walked out of her office.

"Hey, Chief?" Loni followed him. "Would you help me get a release for Doctor Giovanni since it's not a murder charge?"

Chief Alden stopped but didn't turn around. "See a judge for that. Anyway, I have a meeting with the mayor over the other side of town, and I'm late." Without a backward look, he walked through the squad room to the elevator and banged on the button.

Don looked up and smirked. "Won't get that elevator up any faster."

"Probably not, but it makes me feel better." Chief gave a weak grin.

Loni stood in her doorway and watched the chief as the elevator squawked its way up to the third floor. Chief stepped in and grabbed on tight to the hand rail. When he finally turned and faced the front of the elevator, Loni noticed that he looked paler than before.

"Come back soon," Loni called to him.

The elevator jerked, and Chief's eyes widened. "Not in this lifetime."

Loni laughed as the ancient door slowly closed. Back at her desk, Loni dialed the courthouse. "The DA in?"

The high sweet voice from yesterday said, "Sorry. He had to leave on a family medical emergency for a few days."

"I thought he didn't have any family."

"I can't tell you what I don't know."

"Okay. I'm still looking for Doctor Jenna Giovanni's booking or first appearance file. Anybody there who can help me get a release for an innocent prisoner?"

"No?"

"Is that a 'no' or 'no I'm not sure'?"

After a long silence, the timid voice squeaked, "No?"

Loni hung up and walked over to Piggy's desk. "Piggy, you know anything about the DA's family?"

"Don't have one, Lieutenant. They got washed away in the big Boxing Day tsunami some place in the ocean. I think it was called Bad Ache?"

"Banda Aceh," Cleatus corrected Piggy.

"Right." Harry added. "Anyway, Lange was somewhere in California at law school. He never went back home. He's not married."

"God, Harry," Bobbi's voice quivered. "All of them?"

"Yeah, Bobbi. Every blessed one of them."

"That must have really been heartbreaking," Don mused. "Remember the flooding during the great Hanukkah Eve storm here in 2006?"

"Lordy, Lordy." Cleatus looked up from his reading. "Three of them storms piled together was devastating. Lost eighteen good souls."

Don shook his head. "House parts, logs, dead animals floated out of all the rivers and streams up onto the beaches. Took months to clean it up. Storms getting worse every year."

Harry scoffed at Don. "The Columbus Storm of 1962 was worse than that. Forty-six lives lost then."

"Really?" Don said. "Forty-six? That all? How do you compare that to the three hundred thousand wiped out in the Boxing Day tsunami?"

"That was an earthquake, ignorant one, not a storm." Harry poked at Don.

"How about the Great Nor'easter of 1992?"

"How many died in that one?"

"Have no idea."

"Cleatus would know." Ginger reached over and lightly knocked on the top of Cleatus's black head to take his attention away from the file he was back to reading. "How many people died in the Great Nor'easter of 1992?"

Cleatus sat back in thought. "Twenty speaks to me."

Don said, "I was with my mom and dad on Fenwick Island and got caught in the Ash Wednesday Storm of 1962. Nearly lost our lives. I was just a kid but I still remember the water piled up everywhere and no way out. Gotta tell you, I've never been so scared."

Loni raised her voice above the discussion rolling around her. "People! Could we focus here?"

"So," Ginger wondered out loud, "whose family has the medical emergency?"

Piggy snorted. "That's what Jimmy says when he wants a few down days. He just takes off."

"Where to?"

"I can't say."

"Can't or won't?" Ginger tossed at Piggy.

"Who's Jimmy?" Don asked.

Piggy snorted again. "The DA, dummy. That's his name. Jimmy Lange."

"Hmmm," Cleatus said, " 'Curiouser and curiouser, cried Alice after she fell down the rabbit hole.' "

"Huh?" Piggy gave Cleatus a strange look. "As usual, you don't make no good sense. What'd he say, Ginger?"

"He said your name ought to be Alice you're so good at rabbiting."

Loni groaned in exasperation. "I got it. None of you knows anything about the DA's whereabouts either. Would you get your asses back to work!" She shook her head at the giggles caused by the conversation churning around the room. One by one, Loni stared the group into silence and heads down.

Back in her office, Loni made another call, this one to the Port Bar, a bar and grill across the street from the police station. "Doreen? I hoped you'd answer. Do you have time for a few questions?"

"Will I get a date out of it?"

"Do you want to get paid?"

"Considering what you pay your snitches, I'd rather get laid."

"Doreen!"

Doreen giggled. "Can't knock me for trying. So, what do you want to ask your favorite snitch."

"Two things, actually. Is the mayor there?" Loni paused a few seconds. "Well, maybe three. Is Chief there? And do you know anything about where the DA goes when he slips out of town and why?"

"Yes, to number one. You know he's always here for lunch. No to number two. And I can't say on three. I'll ask around. You coming over now?"

"On my way. Doreen? Ask around on the QT."

"Always. Good thing the bar is just across the street from you. Don't know how anybody can get lost as fast as you."

Loni wanted to smack her. Would she never let it go? "Once, Doreen. I got lost once. You ever going to drop it?"

Doreen giggled. "Why should I?"

"Because you gave me the wrong address. Should've told me First Place, not First Court, and you know it."

"Everybody knows where the Rochester Motel is."

"I was new in town, remember?"

"Sure. You assumed with such a fancy name it would be in the best part of town. I don't think the owner of the Manchester Motel will ever forgive you for your Rambo tactics."

"Goodbye, Doreen." Loni hung up. "Okay," she mumbled to herself. "It really is getting curiouser and curiouser." Where the hell was the chief really going? And where did the DA take off to? Loni grabbed her long black leather coat and her rainproof western hat and hurried out of her office, stopping long enough at Bobbi's to give her a set of directions. "I need this ASAP. Okay?"

"Let me get this straight. You want me to call the hospital and ask security to find anyone who can verify that Doctor Giovanni left work at eight-fourteen yesterday?"

"Yup. That should do it." Loni was headed for the stairs hollering over her shoulder, "Thanks, Bobbi." She hurried down to the second floor to the forensics lab and knocked on Adanna's office door.

"Come!"

Loni stuck her head in the door laughing. "You have any idea of the image that conjures up?"

"Hey, Loni. I was just thinking about you."

"That's even scarier." Loni fished a plastic baggie out of her pocket and handed it to Adanna. "I could use a rush on the DNA with this. I found gray hair under the body when it was removed. Could be nothing."

Adanna took the baggie and stared at it. "Damn! How did I miss it?" She looked up at Loni with a chagrined expression. "Want a job?"

Loni grinned. "No. But I would like to see Doctor Jenna Giovanni's purse. She told Piggy she had a recipe in it proving she wasn't there at the time of the murder."

Adanna picked up the phone and asked that it be brought to her office. Hanging up the phone, she said, "And in the meantime, I've got something for you." She handed Loni a file. "Found some of Carlotta Carboni's prints. The second set of prints belongs to Carboni's housekeeper. She showed up here when she heard about the death and let us fingerprint her. Said Carboni's neighbor called her. Said she cleaned the day before Carboni's murder. She did verify that Carboni was a germaphobe. Her prints matched so we eliminated her."

Loni opened the file and stared at a middle-aged Hispanic woman with tired brown eyes. "Whoever our murderer is, he or she knew how to clean up after."

A young woman walked in to Adanna's office and handed her the purse. Fishing around, Adanna pulled out a receipt. "Yup. Time is stamped at eight-thirty a.m. Have you verified when she left work?"

"She said she talked to the doctor on the next shift about several patients. When she got in her car, the car clock said eight-fourteen a.m. Her shift ended at eight a.m. Bobbi's verifying that now."

"Have you verified she bought the wine?"

"Not yet, but I will."

Adanna nodded. "Coroner says the victim had been dead for approximately an hour. Looks like your girl's in the clear. Wanna talk about it?"

"Not my girl, Adanna."

"But there is a story there."

"Maybe another time. I've got to find the mayor to help me get her released." She continued, "He knows how to sweet-talk the judge." Loni left the station and quickly walked across the street.

The narrow Port Bar stood out like the splint on a broken ring finger, rising above the two buildings squatted on either side. The front was painted in *trompe l'oeil* style, made to look like the back of a battleship with the rusty-stained door hidden in a huge rusty-stained propeller that gave the illusion of spinning. The rest of the windowless building was painted battleship gray, and a realistic turret and gun on top pointed across the street into Loni's third floor office window. Looking down the gun barrel every morning gave Loni the willies.

Inside, Loni paused to get used to the darkness. After her eyes adjusted, she searched for the mayor. Vaguely familiar faces of men and women in blue watched her cross the room, and Loni nodded to them. To her left she saw Doreen serving a table filled with cops, and Charlie Orville sat at the bar on her right. Perching on the stool beside Charlie, she sucked in the dank hop smell of the old beer bar, amazed that her twice-broken nose could still smell.

Across from her a mirror was fronted by glass shelves loaded with sparkling wine glasses and liquor bottles. She looked at her reflection and thought about the first time she had broken her nose. Her cousin James had shoved her into her locker at school, and the bump never went away. She started to think about the second time when she caught Charlie's piercing blue eyes looking over at her. Loni was amused, wondering if Charlie had tossed a few more beers than usual. "Need a perp released. She didn't do it."

Charlie was a tall, stringy man in his late fifties wearing his usual pin-striped blue suit and tie. The red tie stood out against the light blue shirt. His straight black hair made it hard for Loni to guess his age. Though usually respectful in the office, Loni knew him to be a real Lothario once he got a few drinks in. He grinned back at her. "Saw you eyeing Doreen. She is cute. I do love a full-bodied woman with such luscious brown hair. Especially long like that."

Loni frowned at Charlie. Clearly he was already good and soused. "She's got pretty brown eyes, too. But I still need a release."

"Geez, Loni. You sound more like Piggy every day. You related to Ira Hayes? Heard he was also a man of few words."

"Can't believe you just said that. All Indians look alike?"

Charlie smirked. "They do to me."

"You ass." Loni slugged his arm. "No, I'm not related to Ira Hayes. I'm from the O'odham Nation in Southern Arizona. He was a Pima from the town of Sacaton on the Gila River Reservation."

"Never heard of it."

"On the way to Tucson, around Casa Grande."

"Who's Ira Hayes?" Doreen asked as she brought Charlie another beer.

Loni said, "He helped push the American flag up on Iwo Jima. There's a statue of it in Washington, DC."

"What's Eewoh-what?" Doreen asked.

"Iwo Jima. It's an island in the Pacific Ocean," Charlie said. "World War Two."

"Oh, ancient history. That's way before I was born."

"So true, Doreen," Charlie said as he turned to Loni. "So what happened to Ira Hayes?"

"Died in a ditch in front of his house. Got beat up and fell. Then froze. They said he was probably drunk."

"Isn't there some famous photo of him lifting the flag?" Charlie asked.

"Rosenthal," Loni said.

"What?"

"Leo Rosenthal. That's the photographer who took that famous picture on Iwo Jima."

Doreen leaned on the counter. "How do you know so much, Loni? You ever meet Ira?"

Loni stared at Doreen in amazement. "Jeez, Doreen. He died sometime in the Fifties. How old do you think I am?"

Charlie laughed, a loud, raucous sound that caused heads to bob up and stare at them. She poked Charlie in the ribs in embarrassment. With a grunt, he took a protective stance and held Loni's hands against another assault. "Never understood you desert lizards. All you do is jump from one stick to another trying to keep your ass outta the fire. Didn't you ever learn genteel behavior?"

"About as well as you never learned how to be mayor."

Charlie threw his head back and laughed again. He let Loni go. "Touché!" He nodded his head a few times. "Good one. Still. Didn't anyone teach you manners where you were raised, Lieutenant Wagner? How about a hello, how the hell are you, before you go pounding on me?"

Doreen shoved a beer glass filled with diet Coke and ice in front of Loni. "Anything else?"

Loni saluted Doreen with the glass. "Thanks, but no, Doreen."

"You not eating?"

"Don't really have the time. I'm working over the mayor here to get an innocent friend released from jail." Tongue-in-cheek, Loni pretended to apologize to the mayor. "Hello, Mister Mayor. How the hell are you? I need Doctor Jenna Giovanni released. Now. Please."

Doreen reached over and bumped Loni on the chin to get her attention. "How close a friend?" she demanded to know.

"Not really a friend. It's been years since I last saw her."

"Oh." Doreen seemed to lose interest. She waved at a cop banging on the bar with his beer mug.

"That cop drinking on the job?" Charlie asked Doreen.

"Stop it!" Doreen laughed. "He just got off shift, and he's on his way home."

"Yoo hoo, Doreen. Down here!" The cop banged again before Doreen finally sauntered over to him.

"Hey," Charlie pulled Loni's attention back. "You're wasting your time talking to me. Not my purview."

"I know it's not your purview. Which reminds me. Chief had a meeting he said couldn't get out of. Something about meeting the mayor? Know anything about that?"

"Not that I remember." Charlie took out his phone and checked his calendar. "Nope. No meeting until the city council meets at seven tonight. I hope to be good and anesthetized by then."

"You staying here all afternoon?"

"However long it takes."

"Why? You expecting problems tonight? Should I be there?"

"Nah. Just got decisions to make about the wave action electricity. The fishermen are upset and I don't blame them. Getting a net hung up on those bobbers gets spendy fast. Heard you got a call from dispatch. Some guy complaining he got attacked by water-wave debris and was injured. He wants someone arrested? What did that mean, attacked?"

Loni laughed. "Seems the big waves from our last storm busted a bobber off its cable and beached it. Some scavenger rolled it over on his foot and broke a toe."

"Big toe or little toe?"

"I didn't ask, Charlie. Told Piggy to collect the bobber off the beach, find the owner and return it."

"What'd Piggy say?"

"First he complained that it was probably too big. Then he wanted to borrow the chief's sand buggy. After that round of 'no you can't,' I told him to get the information off the bobber and contact the owners to come get it."

"And then?"

"Don't know. Piggy hasn't handed in his final report. Speaking of wave energy, I read about that new invention. Lays flat like an air mattress with billows that inflate with waves passing through and it disturbs nothing. Sounds good for the fishermen. You looking at that one?"

"Don't ask me. I'm not the scientist on this project. Sounds like it would still get caught up in their shrimp nets. Can you see a fisherman hauling that in?"

Loni elbowed the mayor. "About that release?"

"Can't you see? I'm preparing for my meeting tonight."

Loni grinned. "So, any problem at all tonight, you'll call?"

"You know I will. Speaking of waves, I heard Piggy got wiped out by a sneaker?"

"Yup. That was when he was down checking on the bobber. That storm last night wasn't quite done. He came in a mess, sand in his ears. Up his nose. And, according to him, every other orifice in his body. Says he's going to quit the cops and sell 'Golden Tickets to Heaven.'"

"Golden Tickets?"

"I asked him about it. Said he'd heard about a couple down in Florida who made so much money selling Golden Tickets they decided to sell franchises and he was getting one."

Charlie threw back his head in raucous laughter again. "Seriously?"

"Yup. Want a ticket?"

"Not right now. How much?"

"Didn't ask him. Want me to find out?"

"I want to know if the couple got arrested."

"Don't think so. They said it's what Jesus told them to do."

Charlie shook his head in disbelief. "I get so sick of assholes getting away with hiding behind the cross or the flag as they foist dangerous ideas on the desperate and vulnerable."

"That a no? You want me to tell Piggy you don't want one of his tickets?"

Charlie groaned. "Oh, Lord, *Deliverance* is back. Does Piggy have a cousin in North Carolina who plays the banjo? Reminds me of a story I read about this town called Woodland whose city council voted to close all their solar farms because they took all the sunlight and all their plants were dying."

"Did I ever tell you about the rancher on the Arizona desert that dismantled three of his windmills because someone told him he had too many and they interfered with wind getting to the others?"

"You're kidding?"

"No. True story. Of course, he was slow. Met him once when he was very old and I was really young. He was nice to me. He inherited this ranch along with two cowboys who were paid out of the estate to take care of him but he outlived both of them. My uncle Herm kept an eye on him when he could." Loni smiled, remembering. "I never believed it either until one time some asshole vandalized one of our windmills. It just so happened one of the windmills the old rancher piled up was the same brand and had the broken part we needed, so my uncle and I dug through the pile until we found it." Loni patted Charlie on the shoulder. "So, you see? Piggys are everywhere."

Charlie shook his head. "Yeah, yeah. We're turning into Trumpland. Got an election coming up and Piggy votes." Charlie lifted his glass and drank until it was empty. Belching, he plopped it down with a sardonic laugh. "Winston Churchill once said he believed in democracy until he spent five minutes talking to a voter. After this last election, I have to agree. I still can't believe that Trump won."

"Gosh golly, Mister Mayor. They keep electing you. What does that say?" Loni laughed, watching Doreen beckon her with a slight tilt to her dark brown head as she sauntered toward the bathroom, swaying to an old perky "my achy breaky heart" Western song blaring from the jukebox. Patting Charlie on the shoulder, she stepped off her stool to follow Doreen. "I'll be right back so don't go away." Then she whispered, "Good luck with your election.

"Hey," Charlie hollered to Loni's back, "your next boss could just fire your ass. Thought of that?"

"I vote, too. Thought of that?" Loni retorted as she ducked inside and the bathroom door slammed behind her. "Hey, girl. Whazzup?"

"Whazzup?" Doreen shook her head in mock dismay. "Charlie's right. You have been hanging around Piggy too long."

"Hell, woman. One day is too long."

"Try one minute when he's hitting on you."

"He giving you any trouble?"

"Nah. He's harmless."

"Doesn't he know you bat for the other team?"

"Yeah, but he's one of those Trump wannabes who thinks he can cure me."

Loni nodded in understanding. "You find anything out about the DA for me?"

"Not yet. Nobody seems to have any idea where he disappears to."

"Damn."

"Why do you care, Loni? Maybe he's got a girlfriend."

"I don't know. Something my gut is telling me."

Loni followed Doreen out of the bathroom and returned to her stool where she watched Doreen fill a pitcher of beer for two cops who'd just got off rotation.

Charlie called out, "When you're finished there, Doreen, a beer for Loni."

"Thanks, Charlie, but you know I don't drink. Another Coke please, Doreen?"

"She's a hottie. You doing her in there?"

Loni groaned in frustration. "Jesus, Charlie. *No, I am not 'doing' her*, especially in the bathroom!"

"It looked that way to me."

"You know what, Charlie. I should let this go, but if I do, you'll have this gossip scattering across this town like a cockroach chopped up in pieces put back together as a stink bug." Loni leaned close to Charlie's ear. "She's my snitch."

"She is pixy cute, but she's too young for you."

"I know. That's what worries me. She's so young she won't be careful. Look around you, Charlie. Look at all the secrets she hears. Every law person in here has talked to her at one time or another. Not counting what she overhears." Loni groaned. "Even if I did go out with her, it would put her life in danger. So, how about helping me get Doctor Giovanni out of jail?"

"Tell me again why you aren't asking Jimmy?"

"Told you. The DA's gone. Said it was a family emergency."

"Really?" Charlie stared at Loni in disbelief. "Jimmy doesn't have any family. Who told you that?"

"Some court clerk. I don't know. Harry told me that he didn't have any family, too."

"I know for a fact he lost all his family in that Indonesian tsunami years back. He became a citizen to get away from his loss." Head down, Charlie sighed before he looked back at Loni. "Whatever Jimmy's up to, I hope it doesn't come back and bite me in the ass. Again."

Loni giggled. "Sounds like a story here. Share!"

"Oh, go away. What do you want anyway?"

"I just told you. I need a charge dropped."

"What charge?"

"I just told you! She didn't do it!" Loni threw her hands in the air in frustration. "Dammit! Help me get to the judge."

Charlie shook his head. "Told you. Not my purview. You have to talk to the judge yourself."

"You know I can't. It's against the law for the judge to discuss a case."

"There you are. I don't know how you think I can help you."

Loni shook her head in exasperation. "I realize you're having me on, but I'll explain it to you anyway. Seeing as what good friends you are to the judge, maybe you could tell her I just need a little friendly advice?"

"You mean now?"

"Yup."

"You saying you got proof she didn't do it?"

"Yup."

"Irrefutable?"

"Yup."

"You know more words than yup?"

"Yup."

"Try two."

"Bite me."

"The short answer is No. The long answer is Hell No."

"Does that mean no, hell no? Or is that a judgment you just pulled out of your ass?"

"Enough! Before I interrupt the judge at her meditation and get myself shot, or, even worse, run out of my lovely office, give me your reasons again."

Loni sighed. "I tracked Doctor Giovanni's movements. I can prove she wasn't there when the murder went down."

Charlie groaned and downed his beer. "Why are you such a pain in the ass? Can't you ever let anyone be plain old guilty and avoid all this paperwork?"

Loni's frustration level began to climb in her need to get Jenna released. "You just don't want to get Judge Wentworth off her meditation rug."

"Glad you see reason, my child. You know she doesn't really meditate. It's their 'Helen and Marlene' time during her lunch hour."

"Come on, Charlie. She's a pussy cat."

"It's not her that I'm scared of. It's her wife."

"Who? Helen?

"Yeah."

"What did you do?"

"I pranked her during their private time. That was years ago, and she still won't forgive me."

"You going to tell me what you did?"

"Not until you're older, my child."

Loni laughed. "Payback's hell, as my grandpa used to say. I still need a release."

"I don't care if you beat or shoot me. I'm not facing that woman one more time today."

"Guess that's why you're sitting here getting drunk off your ass. Should I be worried?"

Charlie stared at Loni with a haughty expression. "Not in your lifetime. Which may be short if you don't drop it."

"If I told you Doctor Giovanni is Missus Walter Davenport's granddaughter, would you talk to the judge then?"

"You do know how to hurt a man." Charlie feigned disappointment. "But you are so right. That old lady owns half this town. Having her come at me is definitely worse than facing Helen. But it still doesn't matter. Like I said. Once she's been arrested on a murder charge, the judge can't release her without arraignment and a bail hearing. If bail's possible."

"What if no one's around to arraign her? Can the judge get her released then?"

"Ask the assistant DA to schedule an arraignment."

Loni shook her head. "Can't. DA told his department that nothing happens until he sees the arrest file first."

"Sounds to me like your friend hasn't even been arraigned. The judge couldn't help you anyway."

"I have to try. Maybe she can help me find another way."

Charlie scoffed. "Wouldn't count on it."

Disappointed, Loni slid off the stool. "I still want to hear that story!"

Chapter Four

Loni had to spend an hour getting case updates from her detectives before she could break away. She rushed down to the basement floor of the court house where prisoners were housed. The building was one of the oldest in town, and the bricks had been brought in by a railroad track that was long gone except for the occasional rotting trestle along the river's edge and across a ravine. She grabbed the yellow-painted metal handrail leading down to the jail entrance and waited in front of an eye-level window for the clerk to recognize her and open the thick glass sliding door.

A sad-looking woman with beige hair and large light brown beagle eyes answered Loni's knock. "Haven't seen you for a while."

"Miss me?" Loni grinned, taking in the too-tight blouse with a missing button.

Judy shook her head. "Is there anyone you don't flirt with?"

"Not when they look as good as you."

"You should know that my husband loves his guns more than he loves me."

"And you let him live?"

"For now. He looks really good staked out in my back yard."

Grinning, Loni hurried past Judy and down another flight of stairs. The damp air retained the smell of old sweat, vomit, and cigarette smoke no matter how many times the floor and windowless walls were scrubbed or painted. She breathed through her nose and thought about the majority of prisoners who were either hard-partying loggers escaping the dangers of sharp saw blades or falling logs or tough fishermen celebrating one more survival at sea. If these old walls could talk. Even with several coats of white paint, the walls and ceilings of the cells were dank and cold with greenish splotches leaching from the bricks' mortar. The heat from overhead vents never warmed the cold floor and walls.

Janson, a heavy-set powerful female guard with short salt and pepper hair, turned to the electronic key box behind her and unlocked the door to Jenna's cell. "You got maybe a half an hour."

Loni nodded her thanks. "I'll be gone."

Janson returned the gesture. "You know your way out."

Hurrying by Janson, Loni fast walked down the hall to the cells and found herself slowing down to a shuffle. Oh, my God, she thought. I can't do this. She finally reached the cell and grabbed a bar to keep herself from turning around and running. Frozen in place, Loni's old need to protect Jenna flooded her senses. She wiped her sweaty hands on her black trousers before running them through her short black hair. Straightening her spine, she took a deep breath and opened the metal door. She still wasn't prepared for the emotional barrage that hit her as she walked into the cell. Twelve long years. The curled fetal shape of Jenna's body blocked out her world. Jenna always did this when she was stressed, especially when she had to face her domineering grandmother. The jail's bright orange jump suit reflected an unhealthy orange tinge on her pale face, and her closed eyes. Her sleep hair tangled around her head in strange shapes.

"Hello, Jenna," Loni said softly.

Hearing her voice, Jenna pushed herself up into a sitting position on the single bed. When she looked up, her deep green eyes darkened.

"I'd ask how you are but . . ." Loni stood just inside the door and waited, watching Jenna's eyes widen in recognition.

"Loni?" Jenna sounded startled.

Loni smiled. "It's been a long time."

Jenna slowly stood and walked over to Loni, reaching out to her face.

Loni grabbed her fingers and stepped back, circling around Jenna into the room. "Please, Jenna. Sit. We need to talk."

Jenna slumped back down onto the cot beside Loni and stifled a sob. She pulled her legs up, wrapped her arms around herself, and stared in amazement at Loni before she burst into full-throated sobs. "Can't you get someone to get me out of here? I didn't do this terrible thing."

Loni patted Jenna's arm. "I know. I'm working on getting you out."

"Seriously?" Jenna wanted to believe her.

"Of course."

"Thank God and thank you! But that's not what I meant. What do you mean you're getting me out of here?"

"I'm in charge of your case."

"How?"

"I'm a lieutenant here in the crime squad."

Jenna still didn't seem to take in what Loni was trying to tell her. "What? How long?"

"Nine months now."

"No. I mean how long before I get out of here?"

Loni grinned, remembering how Jenna's conversations would leap from one topic to another, sometimes in the middle of a sentence. "I forgot about your multitasking."

"Time-sharing," Jenna reminded Loni as she slightly unwound her body. Loni knew that Jenna was moving away from her fear of not knowing what would happen.

"Right," Loni agreed with her. "I forgot. Multitasking isn't possible."

"So?" Jenna swung a hand in a circular motion.

"I'm working on it. Could you answer some questions while we wait?"

"I don't understand. Should I be talking to you?"

"What did your lawyer say?"

"He's in Portland and can't come until tomorrow. When I told him it was a murder charge, he said I have to stay here until the arraignment and probably longer." Fear crossed Jenna's face and marred her beauty as tears formed in her eyes.

"I promise you there won't be any charges. I checked into it, and I can prove you're innocent. Just tell me what happened."

Jenna closed up again. She snuffled and wiped at the tears rolling down her pale cheeks. "Can you really get me out of here? Are you sure we should be talking? My lawyer told me to keep my mouth shut."

"This isn't an interrogation, Jenna. You're not guilty of murder. I just need you to help me find who is guilty."

Hope settled on Jenna's face as she regained some color. She focused on Loni's eyes. "I work the night shift in emergency so I can be with my daughter during the day. Night before last, Carlotta called me up to the pediatric floor on an emergency. We lost the child. That morning I watched the autopsy. After that I returned to the pediatric floor to check for puncture wounds on the other children." Jenna paused and wiped a tear. "I had another doctor with me verifying the wounds as he took photos." Jenna's voice faded into a sob. "All I wanted to do yesterday was go home and see my baby, but I had a breakfast date with Carlotta. I knew she'd be really pissed if I canceled, but, even more, I needed to talk to her about the boy that died."

"I don't understand. Why her?"

"She's the night charge nurse for the pediatric floor."

"Go on."

"When I got to her house, the front door was open. I looked in and saw her and blood everywhere." Jenna rubbed her face. "Oh, God, so much blood! Poor Carlotta. I called 911 and tried to help her, but she'd been dead for a while."

"You got her blood all over you. That's why they thought you did it."

Jenna took a long hard look at Loni. "Where have you been all these years?"

"I've got questions for you, too. But before we go there, tell me the rest."

Jenna paused and gave in. "I tried to save her, Loni. Even though I knew it was too late." Jenna sat up straight and defiantly stared at Loni. "I tried to show your detective I couldn't have done this terrible thing. I wasn't even there."

"I know."

"I have an alibi. I have a time-stamped receipt from the grocery store, but he wouldn't even look at it."

"I know that, too. Although I did wonder about buying wine in the morning."

Jenna explained, "Carlotta likes white wine with her breakfast. She loves making omelets. It's really her dinner because she works all night."

"Right. You said she had probably been dead around an hour by the time you arrived. How could you tell when she was killed?"

"I know when someone is dead. There was no pulse and way and too much blood for anyone to survive. Some of the blood around the edges was dry. The pooled blood that was thicker and hadn't dried got on my clothes. I also know it was less than two hours because the cornea in her eyes had not clouded yet."

"Did the detective tell you why he arrested you?"

Jenna scoffed in disbelief. "He said arguing with him proved I had no respect for the dead so I must have been the killer. Can you believe that crazy logic?"

"You told him you could prove you weren't at the scene, right?"

"I tried but he poo-pooed everything I said. He said the doctor I talked to when I left wouldn't know what time I left because doctors are notoriously late to everything. He said I could have picked the wine receipt up off the floor. It didn't prove anything. I told him the wine-buyer would remember me because we always talked about good wines."

"You said a young boy died and you wanted to ask Carboni what she knew about it. Do you think her death might be connected to the child's death?"

"I have no idea."

"Tell me about the boy."

"Tell me how you ended up here."

"Jenna!"

"Okay. But we still need to talk."

"And we will. But right now getting you out is more important."

Capitulating to Loni's request, Jenna continued. "After the autopsy, I called Carlotta to see if she noticed the puncture wound when she was changing or bathing the child. Clearly she was still alive then. She said we could talk about it the next morning when I got to her place for our breakfast/dinner date." Jenna used air quotes around the words breakfast/dinner. "That's when I grabbed another doctor to check out the other children on the floor. This morning I left the hospital at a few minutes after eight, stopped by for a bottle of wine, and drove to Carlotta's house."

"Do you know what time you got there?"

"Not exactly. I could guess. The time stamp on my receipt would tell you when I stopped for the wine. Like I said before, the clerk will remember me. I'm a regular customer." Jenna's voice trembled and got so low that Loni leaned over to hear her. Her long fingers tucked her golden blond hair behind her ear. "I kept the receipt because he told me about a new Oregon wine, and I wrote the name of it on the back. It's about a fifteen-minute drive to Carlotta's house from the store."

"What bothered you about the puncture wounds on the children?"

Jenna wiped a tear off her face. "I checked but nothing was charted on any of them."

"Did you know Carboni well?"

"I knew her. Sometimes when we had the same time off I would visit her. And yes, including the bedroom and bathroom, But I didn't go inside the house this time. I called 911 and waited in my car. Your detective drove up and arrested me."

"What was Carlotta Carboni to you? Was she your lover?"

Jenna closed her eyes again and sighed. "No. Well, sort of, but only as a friend. Nothing serious."

"Sort of. What's that? Sort of like friends with benefits?"

Opening her eyes, Jenna glared at Loni. "No!" Then she slumped against the hard wall. She tapped the back of her head against it a few times in frustration and took a deep breath. "Yes." she repeated quietly. "We weren't even that good of friends." Jenna paused. "Truth be told I really didn't trust her or even like her that much. She had a bad habit of reporting her conquests to anyone who would listen. She even told people lies about who she went to bed with."

"And you were on that list."

"Yes."

"She was beautiful."

Jenna almost smiled. "Yes."

"You're wearing a wedding ring."

"I leave it on to avoid unwanted interest."

"No husband? Or wife?"

Jenna smiled for the first time, her dimples showing. "No wife. Just an ex-husband."

"So, you're bi now?"

"No. I still prefer women."

"Yet you married."

"Yes." Jenna sat up and faced Loni. "I wanted children. You weren't there so don't judge me."

"Sorry." Loni changed the subject. "You said home?"

"For the time being, until I finalize my divorce, I'm living back home with my sister's family and my grandmother whenever she's not flitting around the world. She's in New York right now visiting my brother. My ex-husband also lives in New York."

"What's his name?"

"Barelli Giovanni."

"Is your husband a violent man?"

"My ex-husband, and no, he's not a violent man. Stupid, careless, a liar and a cheat, but not violent. Why do you ask?"

"Just wondering if he could be jealous enough to kill."

Jenna inhaled a half-laugh. "Not a chance. He's Italian aristocracy. Or thinks he is. Actually, he's way out on the periphery. Claims to be a baron, but he's not. He's a distant part of the Baroncelli family from the Tuscany valley. He claims to own a villa in Baroncello, but he doesn't."

"That's why you married him? Impressed by barons?"

Jenna flared. "No. That's why my grandmother married me off to him. She was impressed."

"You had a choice!" Loni exclaimed in disbelief.

Jenna's ragged laugh echoed in the cell, but she didn't answer Loni.

"Would your ex-husband murder someone?"

"No, I told you he isn't violent. He might hire someone, but he wouldn't do it himself."

"Were you intimate with anyone else who might be jealous enough to kill her?"

Jenna vigorously shook her head. "I've only been in Harborville a few months. I've been too busy getting myself out of a nasty divorce so there's no way in hell I'd jump back into another serious relationship so soon."

"Where did you live before that?"

"New York for the past few years. That's where my ex's lab is."

"What kind of lab?"

"Pathology lab. It performs tests to analyze DNA, tissue, and other substances for clinics and hospitals."

"Tissues such as bone marrow?"

"He never said he handled bone marrow tissue, but I don't know why he couldn't. He certainly has lab people that can."

Loni changed the subject. "Earlier you said you needed to get home to your baby?"

Jenna gave Loni a hard look before she answered, "Yes. She's four years old."

"What's her name?"

"Why do you want to know?"

Loni shrugged. "Just curious."

Jenna looked Loni in the eyes. "Her name is Loni Lyn."

Loni's eyes widened in surprise. "Really?"

"Really. She's with my sister now. You remember Louise? She's married now with three kids. She says one more won't make a difference. She lives on the floor below me."

"So you're all living at the Lake House."

Jenna glanced at Loni with a warm smile. "Yes, where you and I swam in the lake and—"

"I'm not going there, Jenna. Tell me. Do you have any idea who would do this? Or what's going on?"

A single tear rolled down Jenna's cheek. "Oh, God, Loni. I have no idea. Can you get me out of here? Please? I really need to get home."

Loni stood and looked down at Jenna. "I'm working on it."

"Are you leaving me?"

"Just until I talk to the judge."

Jenna seemed so defeated that Loni leaned over and threw an arm around her shoulder for a brief hug. "Hang in there, Jenna. It's going to be alright."

Jenna clutched Loni to her and buried her face in Loni's chest. Prying Jenna's arms from around her waist, Loni grabbed her hands as she backed away. They quietly stared at each other a minute before Jenna nodded her head, releasing Loni.

Turning to leave, Loni reminded her. "Get some rest. I'll be back as soon as I can."

Loni let herself out of the cell. "Keep her safe," she said to Janson. She waved over her shoulder and ran back up the steps, hurrying to the court house to see the judge.

Loni waited impatiently outside the judge's chambers. It felt like years before the silver-streaked, black-haired women in her early sixties came out waving a piece of paper at Loni, demanding, "I can't talk to you about an impending court case. Why are you dragging me out for this?"

"Because she's innocent of murder and I'm trying to get her out of jail?"

"There's nothing about murder on this."

"What! Piggy said that's what he turned in."

"This says she's in jail for interfering with a police officer. What's that about?"

"That's Piggy. Said she argued with him that she was innocent and it was the first thing he thought of to charge her with."

"You're saying she didn't interfere?"

"Not illegally."

The judge stepped into Loni's space. "You can't just manufacture facts out of thin air."

Backing up, Loni held her hands up as though protecting herself from assault.

"Looks to me like no one arrested anybody but you didn't hear that from me. Got it! Don't make me slap you silly."

"Good thing we're sort of related or I'd arrest you for threatening an officer of the law."

"You and what army, big bad brave."

"The release, Judge?" Loni held her hand out.

"What'd I just say?"

"I wish I knew."

"Last time I looked, weren't you a cop?"

"So?"

"I thought you studied Oregon law."

"That was years ago and it was prelaw. Besides that, I've only been back here a few months. Haven't gotten to the charging part in that twenty-one-book set of ORS you so kindly sent me."

The judge laughed. "Bet they look impressive on your shelves."

Loni whirled her hand in the air, motioning for the judge to get to the point.

"She could have walked anytime. In fact, she shouldn't have been in jail in the first place."

Loni tried unsuccessfully not to groan as the judge laughed at her. Loni sputtered, "Shit. You're saying she didn't have to spend the night?"

"She'll have to get the charge dropped at a preliminary hearing, but she didn't have to be in jail. Her lawyer should have known that. Didn't he even check at the desk? Didn't you?"

"I did, but Piggy said he told the DA to add murder to the charge."

"Does it say anything about murder on this?" The judge waved the form in Loni's face. "What's your next move?"

"We never had this conversation?"

"Good."

Before the judge demanded her first born for Loni's carelessness, Loni changed the subject in embarrassment as she started to back away. "Have you checked your Facebook page lately?"

"No. Why?"

"Remember that kid last Friday accused of robbing his girlfriend's family and who got his mother to alibi him out?"

"So?"

"So, he's saying if anybody needs a stupid judge who buys any story you tell her, make sure you go before Judge Wentworth. Easy-peasy, dumb broad."

"God! Who says easy-peasy anymore?"

"Piggy says it all the time."

"Figures."

"Want me to bring him back in?"

"Nah. Print a copy and put it in his file. He'll be back." She grinned. "That's when it gets fun. Night, Loni."

"Night, Judge. Thank Helen for me."

"Oh, yeah. I'm supposed to invite you to dinner this Sunday. Bring your girl if you want."

"Don't have one."

"Then bring a friend."

"Don't have one."

"Okay." The judge threw her arms in the air in surrender. "Maybe Helen's got a friend for you."

"I'm not looking for a fixer upper either. I can find my own girlfriend."

Jenna's bloody clothes had to stay in the evidence lockup so Loni grabbed the change of clothes she always carried in her car for Jenna to wear home. Black clouds overhead absorbed what little light remained as Loni hurried down the stairs to hand the clothes to Janson. Loni waited for Jenna at the jail entrance and took her hand, walking her up the stairs.

"You need to know you didn't have to be in jail at all. Who was your lawyer, anyway?"

"You're kidding me. I spent the night in jail for nothing?" Jenna's voice reached a near scream in her anger. With a sigh, she immediately calmed. "Serves me right for getting one of the hospital's lawyers. Obviously, they know nothing about criminal law."

Reaching the top of the stairs, Loni led Jenna over to her car.

Staring at the car, Jenna shook her head in amazement. "My God. You still have Lulu."

Loni grinned. "Yup. The same. My 1955 T-Bird two-seater."

"Still that awful baby blue, I see. How many times have you repainted it by now?"

Loni grinned, remembering the argument they had about what color to repaint it when Jenna carved a large dent down one side while trying to dodge a wall. Her one excuse was "if it had just been moving…" They were still arguing about it when Jenna disappeared from Loni's life. "Yeah, well. What I remember you complaining about most was the lack of a back seat."

Jenna grinned. "The trunk lid wasn't bad. It had a great view of the stars."

Loni snorted a laugh. "Or the hood on a cold night."

"Baby powder blue." Jenna climbed in while Loni held her door. "I really wouldn't want it any other way."

On the ride home Jenna withdrew and folded within herself again. Loni could feel the wall that Jenna could so easily put up between them. All she could do was wait. Jenna finally sighed and looked at her. "Did it rain today?"

Loni's brief burst of laughter was a snort as she reacted. "Of all the things we could talk about, you want to talk about the weather?"

"That's what people talk about when they don't know each other, Loni." Jenna reminded her. "We're different people now."

"I don't think so, Jenna. Twelve years doesn't change us that much."

Jenna glanced over at Loni with a partly-suppressed smile. "Your twelve years or my twelve years?"

Loni turned off the paved, two-lane highway onto a graveled lane toward Jenna's home. It had been twelve years since Loni had been on this road. She avoided it after she moved back. "Don't let me get lost."

Jenna smiled. "I remember that last time we drove from school for a weekend to have some alone time." Jenna dropped into silence once more leaving her thought unfinished.

Loni stopped in the driveway and admired the three-story Victorian house. The stately looping home was just as she remembered it, but she had never seen it all lit up. "I don't remember all those lights down to the dock. It's really welcoming," she mused. Long white reflective streaks danced on the water in the gusting breeze.

"We put the lights down to the lake earlier this year. My sister's afraid of the dark."

"Do you want to get out here?"

"No. Take me around to the back."

Loni circled the building into a large garage area and parked under a light that shone on a gate and reflected onto Jenna's face. She turned to Jenna and quietly asked. "Just tell me. Where did you disappear to?"

Jenna pushed her hair out of her eyes and sat very still for a few minutes. "That last time we came down here," Jenna nodded toward the lake, "we were celebrating the end of the semester. We went swimming." Jenna took a deep breath. "We got caught, but you never knew that. David saw us and told my grandmother. I knew my grandmother had meetings in Portland for a few days and no one was home, but, apparently David and she got into a fight and David came home early. Before I even knew what was happening, she pulled me out of class, informed me how ashamed she was of me, threatened to kick me to the curb without any family support, destroy you, and shipped me east to Georgetown College. I admit she got to me. I was so demoralized and scared I went willingly. I tried to explain in the message I left you."

Loni snorted. "I got the message you left on our machine. Other than 'I'm sorry,' you were crying so much I couldn't understand a word you said. Not that I could call back and talk to you. The phone was disconnected. So were all the utilities. And while I was at school taking my last exam, someone took all your stuff. Then the landlord locked me out with a nasty note from your grandmother warning me to leave you alone. He finally let me pack my clothes."

Remembering those horrible days, Loni stopped talking and swallowed hard. Putting herself together again, she continued. "I had nowhere to go and no reason to be anywhere. I couldn't go back home to the ranch with my tail between my legs so I drove south. I stayed on the coast until I was too tired to drive and then stopped somewhere south of San Francisco. The next day I called around to find somewhere to go to school. When I checked with the LA police academy, the man on the phone was so friendly and upbeat that I thought what the hell. So I enrolled."

Jenna ducked her head. Her voice sounded regretful when she explained. "I thought you'd go home so I wanted to call there but I couldn't find a number. I called the police department, and your cousin James said you weren't home and they didn't expect you. He said he'd give you a message to call me."

"Oh, God. Leave it to James to fuck everything up."

"You didn't get the message."

"No, I never got your message."

"David said you found a new lover."

"Your brother always was a lying sack of shit."

"So, what happened to you? Thought we were going to be lawyers and open up an office together?"

Loni shrugged. "When you left, all I wanted to do was to get away from anything that reminded me of our time together. So I set about changing everything I could."

"Did it help?"

"Not really."

"Did you ever try to find me?"

Loni's voice was somber. "I did. The summer before I graduated, I drove up and I tried to talk to your grandmother and sister." Loni nodded toward Jenna's ring finger. "When I confronted your grandmother, she told me you got married. She said if she ever saw me again she'd have me arrested for stalking. I got so drunk that night and so angry I totaled this car." Loni patted the steering wheel. "I shipped her home in parts. When I decided to move back up here, my cousin Daniel helped me rebuild it."

"You got drunk? You never drink!"

A chagrined expression crossed Loni's face. "I did that night." She shivered in the memory. "I was a mess."

"Were you hurt?"

"Not physically."

"But you put this car back together."

"That's what you do, Jenna. You climb back up and put things back together again. And no. After that I didn't try to find you again."

"You became a cop."

"I did. I hooked up with a girl my last year at the police academy and after we graduated, we found an apartment. She wasn't you, but she loved me. We both got jobs as cops in L.A."

"Is she here with you?"

"No." Loni hesitated a minute before she continued. "She was killed on the job."

"Oh, God. I'm so sorry. How?"

Loni sat back, her voice dropping to a near whisper as she painfully recalled. "We were chasing a junkie leaping out of an apartment window of a home invasion. Maria came off a fire escape in front of me, and when she hit the pavement, she was shot in the back by another cop who thought she was the perp."

"How awful!" Jenna studied Loni a few seconds. "You loved her."

"It was different from the way I loved you but yes, I loved her."

Covering her ring with her other hand, Jenna frowned. "We were going to live in your hometown to help your grandparents. Did you ever go home to live?"

"After I lost Maria, I did go home for a few years. Then I lost my best friend Willie and my grandparents. And my girlfriend Lola dumped me. She had a big, homophobic Catholic family who tried to beat the crap out of me all the time, and they finally convinced her she was going to hell and they would disown her."

"What aren't you telling me?"

Loni grinned. "You're still doing that to me."

Jenna smirked just a little. "You're still easy to read. Tell me more."

"Maybe there was a little more to it. Along with siccing the priest on me to tell me how I was corrupting their sweet sister, she also had a homophobic ex-husband who joined her very Catholic homophobic older brothers who, except for one, were hell bent to hurt me. Bad!"

"The priest?" Jenna started laughing.

"You think that's funny?"

"What I think is funny is getting sex tips from an old celibate fart in a skirt."

Loni grinned. "Now that's funny."

"So, the one who didn't want to hurt you?"

"Got him off a murder charge."

"Nice of him to appreciate it. What happened next?"

"I sold the ranch, quit my job, and moved back to the Northwest."

"Green and blue were your favorite colors anyway. I always did wonder why you wanted to live on that prickly dead desert."

"The desert was home. I know it's hard to understand how the desert gets in your blood. The open vastness. The sense of freedom, of expansion."

Jenna laughed. "We've got an ocean for that." Jenna leaned over and rested her head on Loni's shoulder. "I think for me home is a person. That's why I was willing to move to Arizona with you. But then, I always was needier than you. How did you end up in this town?"

"I liked remembering our times together at school and at your house. Also, I have a sort of relative here. Judge Wentworth. She's my aunt by marriage. When I sent my application out to coastal cities, the police chief remembered she was from the same town and asked her about me. She knew me when I was a kid. So, here I am."

"You said you'd been here a few months?"

Loni nodded her head. "Looks like I moved here about the time you did."

Jenna shook her head. "This is scary. Does it feel to you like we've been traveling in a parallel universe?"

Loni laughed. "Seems like we did take the long road home."

Jenna sighed and looked up at the house. "Too long. I'm not even sure what that means although I did learn one thing. Family obligations always were our biggest dream killers." Jenna sat a few seconds longer before she reached over and squeezed Loni's hand. "But, in the end, family is all we have."

"If we're lucky."

"I am so sorry we lost each other the way we did." Jenna grinned. "I have to say, however, my daughter is not the only one making my trip back home worthwhile." She climbed out of Loni's T-Bird and quietly closed the door. Leaning back in the window, Jenna continued, "It does feel good to get some closure." With a tap to the top of the car, Jenna walked to a gate in the back patio wall where she punched in a set of numbers on the security box. The gate swung open and, with a quick backward look, Jenna walked through, shutting herself away from Loni again.

Loni watched until the light on the top floor blinked out. Realizing her anger was gone, Loni smiled as she drove away, understanding what Jenna meant about closure. So many things were finally resolved. Except how she felt about Jenna. Some things never change.

Chapter Five

A sleep-deprived Loni dragged herself into work. She'd been determined to bury painful memories of Jenna that kept popping up and disturbing her sleep, but she'd failed. The noisy squad room covered Loni's subdued "Good morning," as she passed through to her office, hoping to sit quietly and hold her aching head. She listlessly hung her heavy leather coat on the rack and slowly sat, trying to ignore the buzzing from her detectives.

"You guys tired of the rain? Just wait. A big one's due next week. Big. Big." Harry warned them.

"Cleatus? You hear about it?" Ginger asked him.

"Sho' did. Heard one of those strong Pacific cyclones were a comin' with a huge pressure gradient and strong winds to tha south. It's scary. Along with its low barometric pressure, there's a strong atmospheric river of subtropical moisture streamin' right at us. Harry's right. A big one's comin'."

"Ginger!" Piggy complained. "What did Cleatus say?"

"A big storm's coming."

"Why didn't you just say that, Cleatus?"

"I did."

Loni forced herself back on her feet back to her office door and wearily leaned against the door sill. Everybody had gotten hyper from the ever-changing barometric pressure. "All of you! Please! Settle!" She figured that yelling at them was the only way to get them quiet so that she could check their progress and assign jobs. Piggy always got the slam-dunk cases, and Loni hoped that he wouldn't mess them up too bad. "Settle! *Now!*"

Bobbi turned away from her console toward Loni.

"Bobbi? Any new calls?" She admired Bobbi's deep brown dress with a pencil skirt and drifting neckline that matched her hair and eyes. Bobbi winked. "Another one from Percyville. It's not an emergency so I put it on your desk."

"Don't give it to us." Ginger took a chocolate-frosted doughnut from the box on the communal table and waved it in the air before the red-haired butch handed it to her partner, Cleatus.

"Oh, my." Cleatus chewed. "'Tis good enough to make me want to beat ma' mama."

Ginger laughed. "Haven't heard that since I left home."

"You lookin' good, Ginga'," Cleatus commented.

"I agree," Loni echoed. "You look really sharp. I like it."

Ginger was dressed up much more than usual. Her light blue button-down men's shirt and dark blue vest were set off with a rainbow-colored bow tie, and the boot cut on the dark blue pants showed off her fancy stitched black boots. "Thanks, but that don't change anything. Don't try and butter me up, Lieutenant. Means you want something."

"Don't you and Cleatus have to go to Percyville this morning?"

"Yeah. We're hitting doors and interviewing about those murders. I thought to clean up because it's such a guy's town."

Don looked her over. "Aren't you a little butch looking for Percyville?"

"Shock value, Don. They'll be so busy trying to figure out what to do with me, they'll forget to be careful answering my questions."

"Oh, sure. And after they're done being shocked, then they'll beat you to death."

"Come on, Ginger." Loni cajoled. "You'll already be there."

"No! No! No! I don't care," Ginger said. We already got the ATV interviewing and the highway shooting interviews to do."

Ignoring Ginger, Loni said, "Bobbi? Tell Ginger about the call."

"A parolee jumped his court appearance on a minor charge. Everybody knows where he is, and he never appears for anything. Someone just needs to pick him up. He's harmless."

Vigorously shaking her head, Ginger defiantly crossed her arms across her ample chest.

Loni looked over to Ginger's partner. "Cleatus? What do you think?"

"It don't make no nevermind to me."

"There you are, Ginger. Cleatus will pick him up."

Ginger turned toward him. "Damn it, Cleatus! Do you always have to be so accommodating?" She shook a finger in his grinning face as she caved. "You gotta do the hunting."

"Yes, ma'am."

Harry and Don were still fighting over who got the French twist doughnut as Loni questioned them. She made a silent bet that Harry would win the flip. Maybe he had a two-headed coin. Harry won. The two settled in their chairs, Don glaring at Harry. "Let me see that quarter."

"You two have court this morning. You ready?"

"Got canceled, Lieutenant. DA's still out." Harry grinned at her.

One by one they quieted and twisted around to stare at Piggy who was still hollering into his phone. He got more and more agitated until he shouted, "Asshole!" The sound of his slamming down the phone reverberated throughout the room, and Piggy furiously stared around the room as if daring anyone to say anything to him. One by one, each detective turned away from Piggy. Loni shook her head. She could not get anyone to team with Piggy. Harry used the term "drugstore cowboy" when he told Loni why he wouldn't go out on cases with Piggy. "He's just too dangerous to work with, Lieutenant. All bluster, no brain. It's not safe."

"How so?" she'd asked him.

"Before you came to work here, we got a call about a homeless man blocking traffic on the highway. When we got there, the man was hopping up and down, swearing and threatening with a bat anyone who came near. We pulled up, and Piggy jumped out, pulled his gun and emptied it into the guy. Seven shots rapid fire. One of the shots almost hit me as I ran around the car to stop him. Another bounced off a bumper of a car waiting to pass." Don rubbed his face. "Jesus! That old man would have worn out soon. Piggy didn't have to shoot him!"

"Did the old guy survive?"

"He did, thank God. He was off his meds because he couldn't afford them. Ain't that the way?" Don exhaled a half-laugh. "Damn good thing Piggy's such a piss poor shot. He only nicked him on the leg and ass, which knocked him down." A short smile crossed his face as he recalled the incident. "You should have seen those motorists backing up, squealing tires and scattering like attacked ants, out of the way of those bullets. They bounced all over the place."

Loni turned back to her detectives. "Okay, everybody. Let's try this again. Good morning."

"Oh, yeah?" Piggy replied. "What the fuck's good about it?"

The group laughed.

"Yo, Piggy." Ginger hollered through the laughter. "Your case not going very well?"

Cleatus joined in with his thick dialog. "That because Piggy thinks his government job means he doesn't have to do squat."

Waiting for the laughter to die down, Piggy demanded that Ginger translate. "What'd Cleatus say?"

"He said you-all's a lazy shit living off the government teat."

"I ain't got no government job. I'm a cop."

Don groaned. "That's a government job, Piggy."

Piggy vigorously shook his head in denial opening his mouth for a rebuttal when Loni cut him off. "Piggy! In here!"

Loni waited for Piggy to settle in the chair by her desk before she closed the door and sat behind her desk, facing him. "I told you to talk to the DA about dropping your charges against Doctor Giovanni for interfering with a police officer. Why haven't you done that?"

Piggy waved a hand in the air at nothing. "Ain't seen Jimmy about."

"Since you're such great friends with our DA, I want you to track him down. you need to talk to him now."

Piggy sputtered in protest. "I ain't runnin' around all over town. He'll show up when he's ready."

"Now, Piggy!"

"Hey, boss." Bobbi interrupted. "You got a call on line two."

"Thanks Bobbi." Dismissing Piggy, Loni watched him leave her office before she picked up her phone and pressed the speaker button. Settling back in her chair. Loni answered, "Lieutenant Wagner speaking."

A soft laugh was followed by "Doctor Giovanni here."

Loni stuttered at the unexpected voice. "Ah…What can…I do for you."

"So formal. Is this your work voice?"

"It is today."

Jenna laughed again. "Maybe I should call you back tomorrow."

"Let me do this again. What can I do for you?"

"Have lunch?"

"Is there an agenda?"

"Just to thank you for getting me out of jail. I still can't believe my lawyer."

"Lunch would work. Maybe you could tell me something more about Carboni?"

"I'm afraid I told you all I know."

"How about meeting me at that little restaurant down the block from the hospital. It's on the corner of 101 and Pine?"

"The Feed Store?"

"The very one. See you at eleven-thirty?" The phone was dead before Loni could say goodbye.

The elevator door squawked open and Chief Alden dragged himself out like an old man carrying a heavy weight. Hurrying out to greet him, Loni wondered if his drawn face meant he was seriously ill. Behind the big man was Molly wearing a police jacket. Molly was so tiny that people sometimes underestimated her ability in the police forensic lab. When Loni had lunch with Molly, she found out that she worked there to keep busy while her husband was stationed in the Middle East as a troubleshooter. Molly had been the first person to welcome Loni with a lunch invitation.

"Hey, Molly." Loni walked over and hugged her. "You in trouble again?"

"Nope." Molly beamed. "But if you're intimating I found it, I brought my own protection."

"Hey, Chief. Not particular who you keep company with?"

Chief grinned at Loni. "Compared to what? Keeping company with you?"

"Funny, Chief. You're a very funny guy."

"You might change your mind soon."

"What's up?"

"Molly here has a proposition for you." Loni raised an eyebrow at Molly who winked back. "She needs help for a gun buyback program. I'm volunteering your crew."

Molly handed flyers around the room, ending up with Piggy who crumpled the flyer and threw it at Loni. "Hell, Lieut! You can't support this! It just ain't right!"

Loni caught the flyer and threw it back at Piggy, catching him in the mouth. Ginger broke out in a loud laugh. "Good one, Lieutenant. Hope it shuts him up."

"Hey," Cleatus said. "How about we turn Piggy into a Trappist monk."

"Whaaat?" Piggy wailed. "I ain't never gonna be no traipsing monk."

"Trappist, Piggy. They's never speak one word they whole lives."

"Not one word?" Don asked.

Cleatus nodded in agreement. "Total silence."

"Holy shit," Ginger said. "Now wouldn't that be nice."

Piggy gasped in exasperation. "You'd like that, Ginger. Just like you'd like to take my gun away from me. You and your bleeding heart."

"What the hell, Piggy? Don't be your usual jerk. You know most guns only have one purpose and that's to kill. Including you and me. Why not get rid of what people don't want."

Piggy smoothed out the flyer on his chest and waved it in the chief's face. "This ain't in my job description! You can't make us do this!"

Chief sat on the edge of Piggy's desk and stared at him. "Somebody make you chief now?" With a dangerous smile on his face, Chief calmly waited for the answer.

"Ask me and I will." Piggy declared. "Make a hell of a lot better decision than this!" Piggy dropped the flyer on his desk and pounded on it. He picked it up again and shook it in Molly's face. "You don't understand, you wannabe cop. Why aren't you busy working a crime scene anyway? Ain't that your job?"

"Jeez Piggy. You know most instances of self-defense violence were just petty arguments that escalated into violence."

"Tell me when a gun hurt more than helped."

"I can list thousands. A kid forgot his key and pounded on the door to get into the house. His father shot him through the door. Another kid got shot to death because he knocked on the wrong door for a party. Some guy shot his wife getting a drink of water in the kitchen because he thought somebody was breaking into the house. And there are tons more stories like that. And more people commit suicide with guns than anything else."

"You're saying self-defense is a myth. That's just bull crap. You're not even a real cop. You're just a crime scene investigator. You shouldn't be in a business you know nothing about. And who cares anyway if people kill themselves."

"You know nothing about what I know."

"You can't take guns from good folk. It's their constitutional right." Piggy whirled around. "Tell em, Cleatus. You know ever'thing."

"Piggy happenstance be right as the Supreme Court ruled gun owners don't have to belong to a militia."

"But Piggy!" Molly tried again. "We're not taking their guns. It's volunteer only. I think a hundred-and-thirty-dollar food gift certificate in trade is fair. Especially with no questions asked about where the gun came from."

"Why waste our time? You look at the shootings! This!" In agitation, Piggy's arms jerked in stops and starts as he kept waving the flyer. "Will not stop one shooting. Not one." The decibels of his voice ratcheted up again. "Why you pushin' for a thing that makes no difference?"

Loni held up her hand. "Piggy. How about it isn't right for you, okay? Nobody wants your guns."

"That's what I said."

"No. You said it isn't right for others. You're assuming again. We've talked about that over and over. You don't know what's right for them. Or me. Only for you."

"You're still violating my second amendment rights?"

"The flyer says we only want unwanted guns people don't want to have around anymore."

"Ain't no such thing as unwanted guns."

Chief turned to Molly. "You want to take that one?"

"Last year when we had our buyback, I asked people why they were turning them in. One said he'd had it for twenty years and never used it. He brought in ammo, too."

"Yeah. When somebody pulls a gun on him tomorrow, bet he'll be sorry."

Molly continued. "Another said he used to hunt but now preferred to spend time with his grandkids and didn't want a gun around where they were. Another said he didn't want a gun in the house with his kids."

Piggy scoffed. "Tell the kids leave it alone."

"How about this one? He said he needed groceries worse than a gun."

"Tell him to get a fucking job." Piggy belligerently crossed his arms.

Chief looked down at his large hands. "A woman whose husband killed himself with the gun said she never wanted to see it again. She thanked us for taking it. What would you tell her, Piggy?"

"Ask her what she did to drive him to it."

"Piggy!" Ginger nearly screamed. "Have you no shame?"

Loni intervened. "We'll be there, Molly." All the detectives except Piggy nodded in agreement. Leaning back in his chair with an insolent expression, Piggy declared, "Good thing it's a week from Saturday. I'm busy that day."

Shaking his head at Piggy, Chief pushed his bulky body up from the corner of Piggy's desk and slowly headed toward the elevator. Molly waved goodbye to the group and followed him. Turning around in the elevator, Chief looked back and pointed his finger at Piggy. With a big shit-eating grin, he cocked his thumb simulating a gun being fired. "Be there."

Loni collected her thoughts to finish the morning's rollout as the elevator's squeaking faded away.

"Hey, Loni." Don said. "Does Chief look right to you?"

"Yeah," Ginger added. "It's not the summer crud, either. Something's wrong with him."

Loni shrugged. The clock showed nearly nine o'clock and time to move on. "Ginger. Cleatus. You're on your way to Percyville for interviews. Pick up the jumper on your way back. Don, Harry, I want you to collect some interviews on the Littlelot case." Loni handed them a file. "Piggy, you got a DA to find."

Ginger grabbed her coat. "You ready to go, partner?"

"Does a hound dog hunt?"

"Oh, Cleatus," Ginger cooed, "you say the funniest things."

"That cuz I'm your favorite crocodile pet to make you smile."

"Nope. Crocs not funny, Cleatus."

"Yo, girl. I asked Piggy on it, and he said crocs are bad asses like me."

"Now that's funny, asking Piggy anything." Ginger's sarcastic laugh sounded like a raucous honk. "Why don't you just wag that bad ass of yours and let's get."

"Peace! You buyin' lunch?"

Cleatus and Ginger started for the stairs, and Loni reminded them once more, "Don't forget to pick the jumper up on your way back!" She got a third-finger salute from Ginger as the two of them charged down the stairs, bickering on who was driving until their voices finally faded. Don and Harry weren't far behind them as Piggy headed for the elevator.

Loni worked on her files until it was time to meet Jenna. She walked into the restaurant and found Jenna sitting in a back booth. "I ordered you a Monte Christo on marble rye bread," she told Loni. "Is it still your favorite?"

"Wow! You remembered that after all this time?"

"I remember everything."

"Really? Everything?"

Jenna's smirk had Loni blushing and Jenna grinning at her. Loni changed the subject. "What did you order?"

"Guess."

"Veggie Quiche."

A tall, thin waitress with a grim smile that never showed her teeth and dark brown hair in a ponytail appeared at their table and placed a glass of wine in front of Jenna and a Mexican coke bottle in front of Loni. She left as silently as she had arrived.

"About Carboni's case . . ." Loni got down to business. "Can you tell me anything about her history?"

"What kind of history?"

The waitress was back with the quiche and the sandwich. "Anything else?"

Both Jenna and Loni shook their heads "no." Jenna took a bite as she waited for Loni's answer.

Loni asked. "Do you know any of Carboni's other lovers? Did she talk about anyone? Did she mention any one who might hurt her? Anyone you know hate her? You know anything about her family? Education?"

Jenna chewed before she answered. "No, no, no, no, no, no. Any other questions?"

"Really? Nothing? Do you even know what food she likes?"

Jenna was becoming defensive. "I knew what wine she liked."

"That's it?" Loni pushed.

Jenna dropped her fork in exasperation. "Dearest." Jenna reached over and pinched Loni's cheek and held on, pulling Loni's face toward her. "Listen to me. All I did was stay long enough to enjoy the feel of a woman again. I never planned on marrying her."

When Loni returned from lunch, she approached Bobbi "I need you to help me research Carlotta Carboni, where she worked before, training, friends and lovers, finances. You know the drill."

The afternoon seemed to stretch on forever as Loni and Bobbi sifted through useless information to find the one thing of interest in Caboni's training and work history was Carboni's additional income in large deposits from a Chicago bank and excessive spending in Portland boutiques.

Chapter Six

Loni walked into the precinct after another restless night of obsessing about Jenna. By the time Loni had left Jenna off from lunch the day before, her anger at Piggy's treatment of her was spiking. She wanted to call Jenna and talk to her, but she was still uncomfortable with Jenna suddenly reappearing in her life. She knew she was living in the past and that she cared too much to be objective. Looking around, she asked, "Anybody seen Piggy yet this morning?"

"Nope," Don answered.

"How'd your case go?"

"Slam dunk, Lieutenant. We got them set for arraignment as soon as the DA shows up. The girl pled guilty to everything. Loaning her boyfriend her car to rob the convenience store, getting an out-town-friend to put them up for a while. She broke down and cried, really sorry she hurt her friend. Her friend told the same story, but it was too late for both of them."

"And the boyfriend?"

"Gone with the midnight storm. Took the money, car, and disappeared."

"Who disappeared?" Piggy demanded as he came out of the elevator and wound his way to his desk.

"The perp we went after. Gone."

"Ain't that the way of it?"

"Piggy, you found the DA yet?"

"Nope."

"Try again. Get on your phone and find somebody that knows something. A DA can't just up and disappear."

Piggy snorted. "Jimmy can."

"Piggy!"

Waiting until Piggy settled and appeared to be looking in his rolodex for phone numbers, Loni turned to Ginger and Cleatus. "How'd your interviews go?"

"Sad, Lieutenant. There ought to be a law that guns be locked up when kids are around."

"Don't make me mad, Ginger!" Piggy sputtered, looking up from his Rolodex. "Saturday is going to be bad enough watching those yahoos turn in guns. You can't tell people what to do in their own home."

Ginger snapped, "A ten-year-old boy turned killer, Piggy. Ten years old! His brother wouldn't let him ride his ATV. So what'd the kid do? He goes into the house, grabs a loaded rifle from behind a door, comes out and shoots his thirteen-year-old brother. Shoots him, Piggy! At ten!" Spittle flew out of Ginger's mouth as she closed in on Piggy, shaking her finger in his face. "Ten, Piggy. And then the kid gets on the ATV and rides until he's tired while his brother dies." Ginger's face streamed with tears as her voice quivered. "It didn't need to happen!" Ginger wiped tears off her face with the back of her hand. "You know the worst of it Piggy? The father lost two sons. And you know what he said? 'Guess I don't have to worry about locking up my guns now.'"

Loni gave Ginger a minute before she turned to Cleatus. "How'd the interviews go with the street shooting?"

" 'Bout like the ATV," Cleatus drawled. "This A-hole got mad at his girlfriend's brother for drinking his last beer. He got his assault rifle out and ran him, barefoot, half naked, into the street shooting until he went down."

Ginger sighed. "Like I said before, it's a guy's town."

"Did you get all the interviews you needed to turn the cases over to the DA for the Grand Jury?"

"We did," Cleatus answered. "Both confessed and we got plenty conclusives we's just finishing up."

"And the jumper?"

"Jumped him right in ta jail."

"Good work." Loni decided to ignore Piggy fidgeting at his desk and walked over to Don's desk. She perched on the edge and asked him and Harry, "So, guys. How are your cases coming along?" They always wore the same color suits, this time gray. Just the shirts and ties were different. Don's shirt was pale green with a dark green tie, and Harry had picked a gray tie to match his suit for his white shirt. Loni wondered if they called each other in the morning to make sure that their suits matched.

Don nodded toward Harry who said, "Got one case already wrapped up and ready for you to look over. We agree it's ready for the DA's office. It's the one where the two teens got caught robbing that service station over on Western Street. Said they searched the internet on how to rob it."

Don and Harry looked at each other, and Don giggled. Harry continued, "Guess the internet forgot to tell them not to hang around so long filling up with gas after they robbed the place."

"While they were paying the attendant for the gas with the money they stole from him, a patrol car drove up and arrested their sorry asses." They both broke out in laughter. "Get it, Lieutenant?"

"Got it. Good work, everybody."

Later, after lunch, the detectives had settled in when the phone erupted at Don's desk. He grabbed it, and Loni watched his anger grow exponentially as he listened. When he hung up, he raised a fist in the air. "You know that stalking assignment we caught last week where we got a restraining order? He ignored the order, and it's turned into an assault now. The bastard decided to visit her. He raped and beat her so bad he left her for dead. She'll survive, but she's scared to testify against him."

"You know where he is?"

"At his house if we're lucky."

Loni sat quietly for a moment. "Were they able to get a rape kit?"

"Yeah. But it was touch and go."

"See if you can find him."

"Oh, we will." Don stood and grabbed his bright yellow rain coat off the coat tree. "He's got a record of stalking women. Even did jail time for it. I am so looking forward to dragging his sorry ass in."

"I've never seen you so pissed before, Don."

"Shit, Lieutenant! I'll never understand how anyone can feel good about beating and raping someone who can't fight back. We know it isn't about power. They already got that! What makes them need to hurt the vulnerable to feel good? Where does that come from? For Christ' sake! Can't these sickos find another way to get their feel-good moments?"

Cleatus scoffed at them. "I tol' you a'for, you can't fix a predator. All you can do is take him off the street."

Don shrugged in defeat as he followed Harry's orange rain coat to the stairs.

Loni waited for the clatter to disappear and turned to Piggy. "Did you find the DA?"

"Working on it."

"Really? Playing games on your phone can find him?"

Piggy huffed and kept on playing. "Waiting for a phone call."

"Piggy!"

"Why can't Bobbi do that?" Piggy whined.

"I told you before," Loni snapped. "Bobbi only helps out when we don't have time to do it ourselves. You had plenty of time this morning."

"I was busy."

Loni gave up in disgust and turned back to Bobbi. "Would you check out Carboni's social sites and Facebook. Bring me any information you can find, please?"

Piggy objected. "What you doing that for, Lieut? Don't need to be done!"

Loni continued to ignore Piggy. "Bobbi?"

"Got it."

"Wait!" Piggy demanded. "Wait a minute! It's my case!"

"Not anymore. It's my case now. All I need is for you to get out of here and find the DA before I get even angrier."

"I keep saying. He ain't around. What do you need him for anyway?"

"Besides getting your charges against Doctor Giovanni dropped? I've got cases backed up needing indictments. Just get your ass back out there and find out where the hell he went. Somebody's got to know."

Piggy slowly took his jacket off the back of his chair and dragged it behind him as he meandered toward the elevator. He pushed the button, and Loni watched him wait. And wait. When the squeaking and squawking stopped, the door opened. Piggy wandered in, glared at Loni for a few minutes, and pushed the button to close the door

Two hours later Piggy dragged back in. He sat back at his desk, grunting nonsensical words before he lifted his head and hollered, "DA's still gone, Lieut. I even went by his house and banged on his door. His car's gone, too. No one's seen him or heard from him."

Loni closed Carboni's file on her desk. Carboni's social sites were a bust, and Loni had sat there too long. She stood and stretched her five foot nine-inch body, releasing the stiffness in her bones while she looked out at the rain, so heavy she couldn't see across the street. Cringing about going out into the storm, she took her long black leather jacket from its hook. "Isn't anyone worried about the DA?"

Bobbi smiled in sympathy for Loni as Piggy snorted, "What for? He's a grown man."

Shaking her head, Loni told Bobbi, "Wish us luck. Piggy and I are going hunting."

Piggy jerked in surprise as he continued playing a game on his phone. "Hunting? Hell no, Lieut. You looked out the window lately? The sky just opened up when I got back. I ain't no fucking duck. Take Bobbi. She ain't doin' nothing."

Loni grinned, watching Bobbi shake her head. "Just your work."

"Don't need doing anyway."

"Bobbi, I need to check on some things with Piggy. You okay here?"

"I got this, Lieutenant. Anything important, I'll give you a call."

"Good." Loni turned back to Piggy. "Where's your trench coat, Piggy?"

"Lord, Lieut. Wouldn't be seen dead in one of those."

"You won't stay dry in that jacket."

"Why not? It's got wool mixed in. I just shake it and the water falls off."

"It does have a really rough texture," Loni reached over and touched it. "Almost looks like butted steel chainmail armor. Why don't you spray on some waterproofing?" The knobby gray of the jacket was crisscrossed with red and black threads in the weave. Loni hoped it didn't look even more ghastly when it got wet. Or smell like wet sheep.

"Costs money."

"Okay, then. Let's go."

"I just said. It's raining out there."

"Piggy! If we waited for the rain to stop, we'd grow old and die in here. Get up off your butt and let's go."

"What we hunting, Lieut? Ain't got my deer tag yet."

"A killer, Piggy."

"You're right, Lieut." Piggy grinned. "Don't need no tag for that."

On the way to Carboni's house, Loni tried to explain to Piggy what she needed to know about Carboni's visitors. "Do they know any of them? What did they look like? When were they there? And, if possible, for how long? What did they drive? You know the drill."

Piggy groaned. "Not again? The doc did it, Lieut. There's no doubt."

"Don't you ever listen to me? She didn't do it."

"Like I said, she had a partner."

"You get a confession?"

"Get a life, Lieut. Don't need no confession." Piggy waved his arm in a circle, almost hitting Loni in the face. "Look at that rain. It's coming sideways, and I ain't got no leather like you! Where'd you get that thing, anyway?"

"One of the few things I kept from my past, Piggy. Good to have on a cold winter desert morning in Arizona on the back of a horse. Also good for dust storms. Sometimes when it even actually rained."

"Yeah, I heard you once were a cowgirl. What was that all about?"

"Just the way I was raised."

"Wouldn't loan it to me?"

"Not even if it fit you. Which it won't."

Dragging a baseball cap with POLICE stamped on it out of his pocket, Piggy tugged it onto his head. Groaning, he stared out through the thick raindrops splattering and running down the windshield. "I hate skinny people."

"Tough, Piggy. Run for the porches, and maybe you won't get too wet."

"What am I suppos' to be askin' anyway?"

"Who visited Carboni? How often? When? Is that so hard?" Loni pulled in front of Carboni's house and set the emergency brake. The quiet after she turned off the engine made the pounding rain smash even louder as murky sheets of water ran down the windshield. She sighed. "Just to satisfy you, Piggy. Give me supportable evidence for an indictment, and I'll take the case to the DA."

Piggy stared outside the car as the windows fogged up. His round face scrunched up in thought, he gave her a sideways glance. "A dead body?"

Loni's skinny stare got Piggy reaching for the car door handle. "You head up the street to the end of the block and come back down on the other side. I'll do the same in the other direction and meet you back here."

Piggy crawled out into the rain and hurried to the porch of the first house.

Loni unzipped the upper pocket on her jacket and clipped on her badge so that it hung in plain sight. As she shoved on her Western waterproof hat, she grimly clung to the handle to keep the door from slamming back against the car, bending the hinges. Holding onto her hat, Loni forced her way out of the car. Fighting the circling gusts, she finally heaved the door closed and ran for the first house on her list.

An hour later Loni met up with a very pissed-off, soaked, and bedraggled Piggy. He scrambled into the car, shivering from the wet. "Goddamn, Lieut. I hate this! You know this close to the beach, there ain't no place a block ends."

Tossing Piggy a towel she had used to wipe off her leather coat, she said, "Just tell me what you got."

"Give me a minute, for Christ sake." Piggy whined, swiping at his jacket. "Can't you see I'm busy here!"

Biting her tongue to keep from laughing, Loni gave him a few minutes, listening to his aggravated grunting. Piggy squirmed out of his soppy jacket and used it for a towel, unsuccessfully rubbing the water from the few sad hairs on his balding head. Loni patiently watched as he slowly tugged at his notebook in the inside pocket of his wet jacket. He flipped it open and separated the damp sheets. After groaning, he reported, "The old woman in the first house over there recognized Jenna Giovanni but only saw her a few times. Usually a Sunday morning about the time when Fox and Friends Weekend are on and stays awhile. Never when anyone else was around."

Piggy turned the wet page and pointed to the next house. "The guy across the street said the same thing. He never saw her car stay more than a few hours." Piggy smirked. "He wondered what they were doing an' I told him. He wondered if they would do a threesome." Not getting a reaction from Loni, Piggy pointed to the next house and struggled to read the smeared ink. "That one saw some young guy lots during weekdays except Mondays. Never at night, and never on the weekends." Piggy grinned. "Said it was probably because he were married to a very pregnant wife. He knew him. He said Ronnie Pierce was his name. He's a plumber and worked for him once. Said he had to dig up the sewer line and found a five-foot-long two-by-four board blocking ever'thing." Piggy looked up and shook his head. "What you think, Lieut. How could a two-by-four get in a sewer line?"

"Piggy! What does a two-by-four have to do with this investigation?"

Piggy grunted. "Nothing. Just found it interesting. Don't you find that interesting?"

"Fascinating, Piggy. Move on."

"Next neighbor saw a natty dresser. His words, not mine. Anyway, he would come Friday and visited Saturday a bunch of times." Piggy looked at Loni. "You know she worked nights during the week."

"Got it, Piggy. Go on."

"Next neighbor said the same thing. And so did the next one. Saw them kiss on the doorstep as he left and she went out to get her morning newspaper. Main reason he remembered was the car. Spendy looking red sports car with white racing stripes down the hood and trunk. Guess that makes her bisexual, huh, Lieut?" A strange gleam reflected in Piggy's eyes. "Must be nice to have all those choices."

"Piggy!"

"Oh, yeah. The neighbor third door down walks her dog and heard loud fighting. Wasn't sure about what sex but a red sports car was parked there. Also, Carboni screamed at her for letting her dog crap on her yard. Carboni had a temper, she said." Piggy flipped another page. "There's an asshole at that house," Piggy pointed across the street. "And he spit at me. I'm going back and arrest him."

"Did he actually hit you in the face?"

"No, but he hit my shoe."

"Sorry, Piggy. Spitting in the face is assault. Don't think shoes count."

"Come on, Lieut."

"We'll talk about it later, Piggy. Let's finish up with this."

Piggy closed his notebook and looked over at Carboni's house. "That's it for me. You hear anything to go ape-shit over, Lieut?"

"I got the volatile temper from her neighbors too, but no different visitors. Let's get back to the station to see what Bobbi found."

Piggy was still arguing at Loni's back when they walked into the squad room. The detectives looked up, watching Piggy scurry around in front of Loni to block her. "Listen! Maybe it ain't against the law to spit on my shoes, but it ain't right either. I could have arrested him for parking his truck on the street. We have a law against that do you know. Please, please let me go back and arrest him!"

"Is Piggy really begging?" Ginger said in mock wonder.

Loni refused to go around him. "It was a pickup truck, Piggy. Not one of those huge tractor trucks."

"Potatoes, potahtoes, Lieut. Truck, tractor. No difference. Anyways. His neighbor bitched to me, and I quote, 'Why don't you do something to get rid of my neighbor's goddamn ugly truck parked in front of my house all the time?' When I got next door I axed about it."

"And?" Loni queried, impatiently waiting for Piggy to finish.

Piggy grinned. "He said and I quote again, 'I'm not parking that ugly piece of shit in front of my house.'"

"Funny but not illegal, Piggy. It's still only a pickup truck."

"Then what do you call them monster trucks?"

"Land whales?" Ginger joined in.

Cleatus grinned. "Nah. Land whale's a rolling house. Tractors pull trailers."

"Right. It's a tractor," Don said.

"Can't arrest it." Loni shook her head. "A pickup truck is not a tractor."

Bobbi added, "She's right, Piggy. The law is referring to the big honkers that are hard to get around on a narrow street."

Piggy continued to argue. "So let's find another law to hang on him."

"Like what?"

"Like it's illegal to eat ice cream on Sunday."

Ginger laughed. "Where'd you find that law? You going on a stakeout every Sunday until you catch him eating ice cream?"

"Guess not. But we could untie his shoe laces. That's illegal."

"What's illegal?" Harry asked. "Say again."

"It's illegal to walk around with shoe laces untied."

Ginger shook her head in amazement. "We can't do that, Piggy. It's called harassing."

"Then how 'bout tossing a snake in his yard. It's illegal to own a reptile."

"That's called false accusation. Jesus, Piggy. Where do you come up with these things?"

"It's laws on the books, guys. Don't you use some stupid law to get the perp? Sometimes you have to get creative to arrest these assholes."

"I think they came up with crazy laws just for you, Piggy."

"You want to talk about crazy laws. I've got some doozies from my home state," Ginger tossed in.

Don looked up. "Now you got me interested in this stupid conversation. Like what?"

"Okay. It's illegal to shoot a buffalo from a hotel's second story."

Harry laughed. "I've got a better one from my state. You can't ride a mule to hunt ducks."

"You're from Texas, right, Ginger?" Harry asked.

"You bet."

"That's in the South. No wonder you sound like Cleatus."

"Texas is just Texas. It ain't the South. But I git it when folks lump us together," Ginger said.

"Wow." Piggy fanned his face. "And I swore you were from California, Ginger. You act like an uppity California woman."

"Yeah, Piggy. I know how you backwoods Oregonians hate Californians. You ain't running me off."

"How about you, Lieutenant?" Don interrupted. "Got any crazy laws from the great state of Arizona?"

"A few. My favorite is donkeys can't sleep in bathtubs."

"Hah!" Piggy exclaimed. "Can't imagine why they'd have that law. Lots of asses in tubs around here."

"Who would know better than you, Piggy?" Ginger threw at him.

Loni spoke up. "My second favorite is it's illegal to hunt camels." Loni turned to Cleatus. "How about you, Cleatus. Where in the South are you from?"

"The fine state of Mississip, of course, Baws. Ya'll can tell by ma' Mississip accent."

Harry grinned. "You Southerners all sound alike to me."

"You got any crazy laws?" Loni interrupted.

"One I recollect is you can't shave in the middle of the road."

"Now that is crazy."

"Harry?" Cleatus says. "How about you? I know you're from Missouri."

"Really?" Harry reacts in surprise. "How'd you know that?"

Cleatus grins. "No biggy. You related to President Truman, right?"

"What president?" Piggy asks.

Harry ignored the sniggers. "I remember you can't give beer to an elephant. Or drink beer from a bucket while sitting on a sidewalk." Harry thought a minute. "Oh, yeah. This one I did get in trouble for when I was a kid. You can't say cuss words outside your home. My older sister always threatened to turn me in. One time she got all the way to the station before my mother caught up with her."

"What'd you say to piss her off?" Ginger asked.

"Called her a hypercritical bitch." Harry snickered. "She had just called me a little shit."

"Okay, Don. It's your turn."

"He's from Alaska." Harry grinned. "This ought to be good."

"Like Harry we can't give beer to an animal only ours is a moose, but the one I like most is that you can't tie your dog to the roof of a car."

"Reminds me of that jerk Mitt Romney," Ginger grumbled. "He stuck his dog up on the roof of his car for a twelve-hour drive. The dog puked all over it. Served him right."

Piggy objected. "What's wrong with that? I voted for Romney."

"Yeah, well," Ginger carped, "I'm sure you voted for Trump, too, you dumb shit."

"Damn straight!"

"Jackass!"

"Okay, everybody," Loni said. "Enough. Time to get back to work."

"You mean everybody but Piggy," Bobbi muttered, fingers flying over her computer.

Piggy stomped over to her and flapped his wet jacket in her face. The water came off the nubby wool threads and shot everywhere.

Screaming at Piggy to stop, Bobbi nearly threw her printout at him while she dodged the splatter and hurried over to Loni. "I've got some information for you, Lieutenant." She handed Loni the printout on Carboni's bank account. "That bank account we found in Chicago? Seems the money came from a New York lab. She didn't even try to hide it." Bobbi handed her the credit card report. "She stayed in the Grand Hotel several times this year. And visited several shops on the same date."

"Such as?"

"Nordstrom, of course. Modo Boutique, Cache." Bobbi sighed. "Jeez, Lieutenant. We must be in the wrong profession."

"Thanks, Bobbi. Would you look through the hospital male personnel for anyone who fits our description of the man at her house and see if you can come up with ten or so photos to give Piggy?"

"Which is?"

"White, slender, medium height, dark hair, balding, wears rimless glasses. Loni skimmed down through the printout while Bobbi wiped the wet mess off her computer. "Also see if you can find a photo of Barelli Giovanni, Doctor Giovanni's ex-husband, and add that. She said he owned a lab in Portland as well as New York so maybe it's his car. She said her grandmother insisted he have a lab in Portland to work with the Harborville hospital. Doctor Giovanni said he was mostly in New York. He comes out occasionally to check on the Portland lab. Find out who he deals with at the hospital. He ought to have a website."

"Wait!" Piggy invaded Loni's space, complaining in a loud, whiny voice. "Them's hundreds!"

"It's a small hospital."

"Stuff it, Piggy." Bobbi demanded. "It's doable." She turned back to Loni. "Then what?"

"Bring me the photos."

"On it."

Then Piggy…Piggy! Are you listening?"

"Tryin' to, ifin' youz stop hollerin' at me."

Loni lowered her voice to a near whisper to force Piggy to listen. "I want you to get on a computer and search through DMV records for that red sports car."

Staring at Piggy, Loni added, "If you get the name of the car owner in under an hour, I'll let you off work an hour early."

Piggy grinned and rushed out her office and settled in on Cleatus's computer. Piggy's computer was always broken so he coerced anyone he could to use their computer, usually a reluctant but benevolent Cleatus. "Get your ass out here, Bobbi, and help me."

Listening to Piggy bellyache, Loni rubbed her forehead as she talked to Bobbi. "I've got a friend on the Portland police force. We went to police academy together in LA and kept in touch. She owes me for getting her through a tough course. I'll ask her do some footwork for us." Watching Bobbi leave, Loni picked up her phone, pushing speaker she dialed. "Leslie, I need your help. If I email you photos and the name of a hotel, could you see if anyone can identify them? I also want to know if any of the men were with my murder victim, Carlotta Carboni."

"How many photos are we talking about?"

"Probably ten or twelve men plus Carboni. Is that doable?"

"Sure."

"Thanks! Look forward to hearing from you."

Loni grinned as she heard Leslie say, "That's it? I haven't seen you in like forever. You could come up this weekend to party. We could go dancing."

"I'd like to do that sometime soon. I'll let you know when I can. And thanks." Loni grinned to herself as she hung up the phone and jotted down a note. Settling in, she carefully read Bobbi's report for any indication Carboni was not alone. Finding nothing, she stacked the report back on her desk just as Bobbi came in with several photos. "Here you go, Lieutenant. "Closest I could come."

Loni nodded her approval as she flipped through the photos. "Piggy?" Loni called out her door. "Come in here, please." Loni watched Piggy come in and sit in front of her as Bobbi walked to Loni's office doorway wiggling fingers at her mouthing "good luck" with a shit-eating grin.

"Hell, Lieut. Whatcha want?"

"You find the sports car yet?"

"Nope."

"Okay," Loni nodded to the stack of Photos on her desk. "There's your photos. Try to get someone identified."

"I got photos right here," Piggy answered patting his chest.

"What photos?"

"My dog. My car. My boat." Piggy cackled.

"Cute. Take these photos. I want you to ask five questions. One, do they recognize anyone, two, what time of day or night did they see them, three how often they saw the person, and four, was anyone with them."

"Jeez, boss. Of course, they'll recognize somebody. In this town, ever'body knows ever'body."

"Okay. Fifth question. Did they see the person at Carboni's house? No, make that the first question."

"Are you trying to confuse me?"

Loni waited for Piggy to stop squirming. "Let me see if I can explain this in a way you can understand me. Take these photos and get a name for the guy owning the sports car identified as the man at Carboni's house!"

Bobbi added, "Why don't I finish Piggy's search for the car. Can't be too many like it around here."

"Good, Bobbi." Loni said. "Do that. If you find the car and owner, it will give us verifiable proof."

"Damn, Lieut. Overkill as usual. I think we should just use Bobbi's search and save me the trip."

Loni stared at Piggy a few seconds before she answered, "Verifying means the same information from two sources. That's never overkill." Turning back to Bobbi, Loni handed her a slip of paper. "Here's an email address. When Piggy gets back with an identification for Carboni's lover, add it to the email to my friend in Portland along with Carboni's, Jenna and Barelli Giovanni, and the DA."

"Whatcha doing that for?" Piggy questioned.

"Just a hunch, Piggy. Why do you want to know?"

"Wait! I don't do hunches."

"Piggy! Pick up your photos and get outta here."

"Look at that stack! Jesus." Piggy ranted as he picked up the photos and trundled over to the office door. "Why you wasting my time, Lieut? The woman's one of them queers lookin' straight, and they's the worst hidin' they's nature. She's guilty as hell anyways!"

"Jesus, Piggy." Loni followed him out of her office. "I'm queer."

"Yes, and shame on you, though you a little different, Lieut. You ain't trying to pass. And you're not a mean, man-acting dyke hanging out in bars, fighting all the time."

"How do you know I'm not? And how do you know all bar dykes are bad?"

Ginger rolled her chair around to Piggy, arms crossed, blue eyes sparking, sputtering, "You often hang out in dyke bars, Piggy?"

"No. But I seen you in your leathers on that motorcycle. You a topper? Or a dominatrix? How about threezies?"

Ginger nearly lost it. Shooting up out of her chair, she went nose to nose with Piggy. "Jesus, Piggy! We're just people like everybody else."

"What about that dyke broad that nearly got the chair for killing kids?"

"Who?" Harry asked in confusion.

"Cleatus knows," Ginger answered. "Tell em, Cleatus."

"Wasn't that Jeannace Freeman?"

"See?" Piggy gloated.

"I'll give you that one, Piggy. Talking a lover into killing her children because they're in the way is god-awful. But that wasn't because she was a dyke. Straight people do that, too."

"I never heard any dyke do good in all the history of mankind."

"What about Lucille Hart?" Ginger raged at Piggy.

"Who's that?"

"Didn't you say you were a native Oregonian?" asked Ginger.

"Yeah. So?"

"Didn't you learn any Oregon history?"

"So?"

"Okay, Piggy," Ginger lobbed another at him. "How about Marie Equi?"

"What about her?"

"She helped bring unions into Oregon."

"There's your mistake right there. No damn union is good."

"What about Kate Brown?" Don joined the fray.

"Who?"

Ginger shook his head in disgust. "Our governor, Piggy. Your boss!"

"Nothing wrong with her."

"She's an out bisexual."

"No." Piggy was appalled. "She couldn't be!"

Cleatus continued with a litany. "There's Gail Shibley, first open lesbian in ta' state legislature. Don't forget Virginia Linder, first open lesbian judge elected ta' the Oregon Supreme Court."

"So what? Don't make that Giovanni woman any less guilty. Has to be with that foreign name! Giovanni. What kind of name is that?"

"Italian, Piggy." Loni answered. "And it's her husband's name. He's from a well-known family in the Tuscan Valley."

"Tuscan Valley?" Piggy asked. "Never heard of it. That up around King's Valley?"

Loni grinned. "No, Piggy. Italy. It's in Italy."

"See? Not only a foreigner, he's rich. Rich men can't get it being honest."

Loni gave up. "I think you should find the natty dresser with the fancy sports car. You ready to do that?"

"Well, no."

"Do it anyway before you go home." Loni was furious. "And tomorrow morning on your way in, pick up the plumber for a talk. I really want to know why he spends so much time at Carboni's house and what he might know." Loni watched Piggy drag himself over to the elevator grumbling about stupid orders until the squawking door shut off the sound.

Loni went back to her office and shut the door. She dialed a number and put the telephone on speaker. Sitting back in her desk chair, she said, "Hey, Jenna. Got a minute."

A tinny voice answered. "I do. What can I do for you?"

"Up to answering some questions about Carboni?"

"I thought we already covered this multiple times."

"I know. But I really need more information. I was hoping to maybe jog something new out of you."

"Is it personal?"

Loni laughed. "No. I think we covered that. What I'd like to know is anything you can tell me about her past. Any lovers, how she gets along at work, who she's close to."

"Lovers I don't know. She never said."

"When you were hanging out with her, you never looked in her drawers?"

"What does that mean?" Jenna sounded angry.

"You know. Open drawers, cabinets, closets."

"Why would I?"

"Okay. Did you know she was bisexual?"

Jenna was quiet for a few seconds. "I gather you got into her drawers?"

Loni avoided the question. "Do you know of any close friends?"

"No."

"What was she like? Easy to anger? Smart? Any talents? Family?"

"She had a temper when she didn't get her way," Jenna said cautiously.

"What do you mean, get her way?"

"Now that's a little too personal. And it's none of your business."

"Right." Loni felt herself blush. "What about the child that died? Do you think it might be connected to Carboni's death?"

"I have no idea."

"Maybe if we talked face to face you could remember more? Is that okay?"

"Like right now?"

Loni looked at her schedule. "How about tomorrow night?" After a long silence, Loni promised. "Just to talk, okay?"

Jenna finally agreed in a slightly warmer voice. "Make it five o'clock, and it's a deal."

"There's a brew pub called Topper on the highway just outside of town. They make the most amazing green corn tamales."

Jenna laughed. "Your favorite food."

"Good things don't change. You know where it is?"

"Sure. I always go by it on my way home and wondered what it was like."

"Don't be late."

Loni heard Jenna laughing when the phone went dead. It had always been Jenna's habit, hanging up without saying goodbye. She claimed the word was just too sad.

Chapter Seven

Loni arrived early enough to get some work done before the detectives straggled in one by one and grabbed the morning doughnuts she had left on the table. Ginger poured herself a cup of coffee and asked, "Whose turn is it to bring the goodies tomorrow?"

"Not me!" Harry quickly reminded everyone. "I brought Tuesday."

"I guess that makes Bobbi next." Ginger looked around. "So, where are Bobbi and Piggy this morning, Lieutenant?

"Bobbi's late. She called about some new disaster with her husband. Something about when she caught up with him, she'd kill him. Piggy's supposed to be bringing in a perp on his way to work. He must have got lost."

"Again? How many times does that make this week?"

Cleatus laughed. "Which, Ginga? Bobbi or Piggy?"

An hour later Loni was working on the Percyville paperwork with Ginger and Cleatus when Piggy stepped off the complaining elevator. Loni rubbed her tired eyes as Piggy shuffled to his desk and peeled off his wet jacket. When he threatened to shake it on Ginger, she snapped, "You do and you'll end up with your balls shoved up your nose! And cut out the cackling! You sound like a sick chicken."

Loni cringed at the image. She called out to Piggy. "You bring in the plumber?"

"Yeah. He's down stairs getting processed. I'll get him in a minute." Piggy said as he shook his wet jacket which forced Ginger to throw her body on her computer. "Stop, it, Piggy!" they all shouted in unison

"I can't see why I'm the only one what's wet."

"Where's your raincoat, jackass?" Ginger asked.

"With my umbrella, ignorant Amos. I don't own one. Why'd I want to spend my time and good money keeping up with the useless things! What good's that crap in upside down an' sideways rain, anyways?"

Loni interrupted Piggy's rant and snapped, "Just give me your report." He sauntered into her office and sat down. "He drove up to Carboni's house just as I was done talking to the second neighbor. How easy is that?"

Taking a deep breath, Loni gritted her teeth to control her temper and asked again. "Not the plumber. What about the natty dresser with the red sports car?"

"Oh, yeah." Piggy wiped his balding head with a wet handkerchief. "Belongs to Guy Murphy. He's the head of Harborville hospital. The neighbors IDed him. So did the plumber."

"No, he's not!" Bobbi corrected Piggy as she walked in to Loni's office. "He's the finance manager." Sitting next to Piggy, she apologized. "Sorry I'm late."

"Same thing." Piggy pulled the group of wet photos out of his shirt pocket. "Money's where the power is." He handed Loni the top one. "That's him." He waited a minute and added, "They also recognized the red sports car as a classic Ford Mustang. It belonged to Guy Murphy. Want me to go pick him up? It'd be fun pissing off the rich asshole."

"They say how often they saw Murphy at Carboni's? And when?"

"Yeah." Piggy fished his damp notebook out of his shirt pocket and flipped it open. "Nearest neighbor said he saw Murphy retrieve the newspaper one morning and go back to the house. He was half dressed."

"What do you mean, half dressed?"

"Half-dressed is half dressed. There's another way?"

Loni sighed. "Go on."

"They just saw Murphy on Fridays, and he usually stayed all night." Piggy flipped his notebook closed.

"You said his name was Ronnie Pierce?"

"Who? The Ford Mustang?"

"No. The plumber."

"How'd you know that?"

Exasperated, Loni stared at Piggy. "Are you for real?"

"Whaa . . ."

Loni shook her head in disbelief. "Did you check out Ronnie's alibi?"

"Why? I said before—"

"Call Ronnie's boss, Piggy. If his alibi holds up, let him go." Loni watched Piggy leave her office. "Bobbi. Adanna has a file for me. Could you go down to evidence and get it for me? Along with the crime scene photos Adanna has for me on the Carboni case?"

"What can't she send the file to my computer?"

"Said she was not comfortable with some of the information going on line for anyone to read."

"Like what?"

Loni admitted she had no idea She was disturbed by her loss of focus. "She said I'd know when I saw it."

Bobbi had disappeared down the stairs by the time Piggy hung up from his phone call. Loni stared at him, and he stared back at her. Impatient, she snapped, "So? About the plumber?"

Looking confused, Piggy said, "What about the plumber?"

Loni rubbed the bumps on her nose and hoped it would help calm her down. "Does he have an alibi? And a reason why he was at Carboni's house so much?"

"Oh, yeah. About that, Lieut. Plumber's gotta a damn good alibi. He was with his boss from seven in the morning until late afternoon plumbing a new house across town." Piggy's bulk jiggled as he did a happy dance. "Told you it wasn't him! He said Carboni had lots of plumbing problems." A lascivious expression crossed his face.

"Don't go there, Piggy!"

Ignoring the reprimand, Piggy continued, "Said the tree roots kept breaking her septic tank field lines and leaking into the ocean."

"Okay. Soon as I talk to him let him go."

"Jeez, Lieut! If'n he didn't do it, why bother?"

"If he hung around that much, who knows what he saw? I'd just like to find out what I can. And before you complain again, I need your paperwork on the Hasselbeck case," Loni said. "Get on a computer and finish it."

"What for?"

"To get an indictment for the grand jury, Piggy."

"That's Bobbi's job."

"It's your job, Piggy. Quit pawning your work off on other people." The volume on Loni's voice kept rising until she was shouting by the end of her sentence. Damn! Loni realized. There went her resolution to be more tolerant.

"Where'd Bobbi go, anyway?"

"She's down in evidence." Loni rubbed her face again to stay focused.

Piggy threw up his hands and stomped over to Bobbi's computer and sat.

Determined to block out Piggy's mutters, Loni continued to finish the notes she had started notes on Carboni's case until the rising decibels of Piggy's swearing broke through her concentration.

"Shit, shit, *shit!*"

Loni looked up in time to see smoke pouring out of Bobbi's computer.

"Unplug it, Piggy!" Ginger shouted. He just sat staring at her, until Ginger leaped up and pulled the plug out of the outlet. "What did you do?" Ginger shrieked at him.

"The damn computer was squeaking so I used WD 40 on it."

At that moment, Bobbi walked off the elevator with Jumbo trailing after her. "Piggy!" she wailed. "What have you done!"

Piggy leaped up and crab-walked away as fast as he could to take cover behind his own desk. "There weren't no computer open but yourn." He watched Bobbi stare at her smoking computer a few seconds before she turned and stared at him. "Jeez, Bobbi. It could've been worse."

"He's right." Ginger added sarcastically. "He could have burned down the whole building."

Jumbo looked around in distaste. "Looking at these puke green walls all the time, nobody would care." He dropped a stack of duplicate photos from the crime scene onto a round table by Loni's office door. "Heard you wanted to see these, Lieutenant." Perching on the edge of Ginger's desk, he watched Bobbi while she pathetically swiped at her melted computer. "Hey, Bobbi. Did you hear about the guy who hid his laptop in the oven to hide it from burglars while they were gone for the weekend? But, when they got home, he forgot to tell his wife who decided to bake a roast and turned the oven on to preheat?"

Bobbi glared at him, and Piggy tittered.

"Or how about the guy who found ants in his computer so he opened the cover and sprayed them. Killed the ants along with the hard drive."

Bobbi threw a pen at him. "You can leave right now, Jumbo. Or I can just kill both of you."

Jumbo ducked the pen. "Or how about the guy who got so mad he threw his laptop into the toilet and kept flushing."

Bobbi picked up her stapler and threatened Jumbo. He threw his hands in the air in surrender.

Loni fought a grin. "Want to borrow my gun, Bobbi?"

"Got one, Lieutenant. Still thinking on using it on Piggy first." Bobbi fanned the smoke away from her computer.

"Mine's bigger."

Ginger snickered. "You'd need a cannon to kill Piggy."

"I'm not sure that's big enough?" Bobbi's sarcasm bounced over Piggy's head.

Ginger sighed. "You're right. The Piggy's of this world are like cockroaches. Stomp one and a thousand takes its place. They're always with us."

Jumbo reacted to Bobbi's hostile stare with a faint look of concern crossing his face. He quietly slipped over to the stairs and left.

Loni turned and found Piggy rummaging through the photos. She snapped, "Piggy, for God's sake. Put those photos down before I shoot you."

Piggy looked up and noticed Bobbi stalking toward him. With an alarmed jerk, he rushed to the stairs after Jumbo.

"Where are you going, Piggy?" Loni demanded.

"To pick up Guy Murphy," Piggy answered as he disappeared.

"No, Piggy. Not yet!" Loni yelled at Piggy's disappearing back. "We don't have a warrant."

"Don't need one," Piggy hollered back.

"That just Alice rabbiting again, Lieutenant." Cleatus grinned.

"Bobbi. Call the judge for a Ramey warrant, please."

"Piggy's right. You don't need a warrant."

"I know but I got a feeling this suspect will refuse to come without one. Besides, nothing is more intimidating than being slapped with a warrant."

"What do you want on it?"

"You have his name, right? His description I gave you earlier. Address. Say he's a suspect wanted for questioning in the murder of Carlotta Carboni. And call Piggy to pick up the warrant."

The sound of the elevator startled her, and she looked up. An officer came in with a young, chubby man. "Piggy left this guy downstairs."

"Damn!" Loni tried to forget about Piggy's carelessness as she walked the plumber into the interrogation room. He almost cried when they talked about Carboni and her death. She decided he didn't have any useful information and let him go, shaking her head at Piggy as the elevator doors closed behind him.

Loni left an hour early so she would be on time to her dinner date with Jenna. Both horses and Coco were excited to see her, but the poodle started to look anxious when she threw clothes on the bed to figure out what to wear. Levis? Or dress pants? She solved her dilemma by closing her eyes and grabbing the first thing she touched. Dark green pants. She added a light green Western shirt and a bolo tie highlighted with a dark green splat of turquoise. She rubbed the stone, remembering her best friend Willie and wondering, as she often did, how she could have saved him.

The last thing she did before she left was to get a special chewy out of a jar for Coco, the signal that Coco couldn't go with her. The dog's liquid brown eyes darkened in hurt as she took it with a huff and walked off into the living room. She didn't even look up when Loni walked out the door.

Loni knew she shouldn't look forward to seeing Jenna again, but she couldn't control the thrill that went through her body as she rushed to the restaurant. A few minutes early, she waved to Abe Pickard. The owner was a tall man, bulky, nearly black hair with light blue eyes, whose baby face made him appear ageless.

"Sit anywhere," he said with a broad smile.

In a quiet booth in the back, Loni sat with her back to the wall, waiting for Jenna and watching Abe gracefully move around the room as he served, and laughed with the customers. She had met Abe the second day she started work at the Harborville Police Department because she was the only available detective when he reported a robbery at his restaurant. By the time Loni got there, the thief was long gone with six dozen green corn tamales, Abe's total day's batch. The thief hadn't even taken any cash from the register or the gun under the counter. When she asked why the robber didn't take anything else, Abe handed Loni a tamale, and she understood why someone would steal Abe's tamales. A warm feeling of home washed over her with every bite. "You gotta' be from Arizona," she said to Abe.

"Got that right." Abe said in amazement. "Globe-Miami area. How did you know?"

"Any Arizona native knows this taste." They became fast friends. Like Loni, Abe was fed up with the heat, but he was also getting tired of the rain. He couldn't make up his mind which was worse. He said that the real reason he left Arizona was to get away from the scorpions. His wife's heart condition made her highly allergic, and the last time she was stung the antidote cost him over forty-thousand dollars.

"My God, man." Loni sympathized with him. "You can get it for less than a hundred in Mexico."

"I know but I didn't have time to get down there and back before my wife died." Abe handed Loni a Coke. "Damn the drug manufacturers! They corner the market and then rob us blind." He shook his head in disbelief. "Sad to say, the free market is like religion. We're so indoctrinated into believing manufacturers should be able to charge whatever they want, that any time we actually try to do anything, they wrap themselves in the American flag and hide behind the cross, crying, 'down with regulations!' Nobody seems to care that the only reason we have rules and regulations is to protect us from the business vultures."

Loni sensed a kindred soul in Abe, especially after he became her snitch and called her any time he heard about something illegal. The week before he told Loni about how a woman he was serving was laughing about loaning her boyfriend her car for a robbery. She was thanking her friend for letting them stay with her until they could find a fence. Loni put both women in jail. The boyfriend wanted to shoot it out with them but finally gave it up.

Jenna arrived and Loni stood, waving her back to the booth.

"My sister dropped me off." Jenna said as she sat across from Loni. "I hope you can take me home."

"As long as I don't get a call-out. You might be riding shotgun with me."

Abe brought them a tray piled high with tamales, and Loni introduced Jenna to him. "Hope this is okay," Abe said to Loni. "It's what you always get.

By the time they finished dinner, the copper stained ceramic serving plate was piled high with limp pale-yellow corn husks. Loni leaned back and sighed in contentment, and Jenna smiled at her. As Loni looked around to nod her thanks to Abe, she explained that he had sold his bar in southern Arizona because, as Abe told everyone who would listen, "The four seasons on the Arizona desert were hot, hotter, boiling hot, and, put out the goddamn fire!" Another time he said, "The temperature was so high that hot water came out of both spigots." Or he'd claim, "I chewed chili peppers to cool off." Even his apron showed two skeletons in lawn chairs with one saying to the other, "But it's a dry heat." His customers heard his complaints so often that occasionally someone would shout out, "How hot was it?"

Friendly to gays, the place was a haven for Loni during her bad times of loneliness. She could always sit at the bar eating tamales and listening to Abe's stories from Arizona while she admired the dark mahogany bar that extended the length of the room and up to the high ceiling. Elaborately hand-carved pillars every few feet held shelf after shelf of bottles and glasses. Abe swore it came around the Horn in the 1800s. When the bar burned down in 1983, Abe said that people in the town pulled the bar out of the building and across the street. Half the town was destroyed that day, but the bar remained a treasured fixture. Private barrel-shaped booths circling the room's perimeter left space for a tiny dance floor, while hanging lights with squares of stained glass dropped soft-colored circles on the tables. Pool tables and noise game machines were consigned to a back room, and the bar provided a quiet space in afternoons and early evening.

Loni and Jenna were on their third cup of coffee before Loni said, "Tell me again what happened on the day the child died?"

Jenna seemed to fixate on the scene in her head. "The first thing I remember is the sound of a code ninety-nine call. When I got there with the code team, Carboni was doing CPR on a child in respiratory distress. I directed the resuscitation attempt." Jenna wiped at a tear rolling down her face before she acknowledged, "We were too late. The child had already aspirated." After a few minutes she straightened in her chair and continued in a calmer voice. "For some reason, I don't know why, I picked up a sharp container from a tray beside the bed and opened it. I found a trocar."

"What's a trocar?"

"It's used in bone marrow aspiration." Jenna sat in thought a few seconds before she continued. "Early the next morning before I went to see Carboni, I watched part of the autopsy. The hospital pathologist showed me there was not only a bruised puncture wound on the side of the child's hip, the site had also been pre-prepped with betadine. When he opened the wound, he found a puncture on the bone. I asked him if it could be caused by the grinding from a trocar. He agreed the evidence would indicate that someone had attempted a bone marrow aspiration."

"And that wasn't good?"

"The pathologist thinks the side effects of anesthetizing a child already in respiratory distress could have been lethal. Especially if an untrained person wasn't sure of the dosage. I haven't seen the tox screen test yet, but I would bet it will show excessive use of benzodiazepine."

"Benzo . . . what?"

"It's the anesthesia this hospital uses."

"Why would that kill the boy?"

"Respiratory distress combined with an excess of benzodiazepine could kill someone."

Shock rode down Loni's back. "Ah, shit. That would make it murder."

"Yes, but it couldn't be proved in a court." Jenna paused a few seconds. "There's more. After the autopsy, I went back up to the pediatric floor and grabbed another doctor to help me check out the rest of the children. We found three more with puncture wounds."

"Why didn't anyone notice them?"

Jenna flashed angry. "I assume because it was probably done in the early morning hours when the floor is the quietest."

Loni smiled to relieve Jenna's tension. "Tell me about the other three children."

"The first one is a year-old boy. He is in because of a staphylococcus aureus infection, E Coli. The second is an eighteen-month old girl with asthma exacerbation. The third is a three-year-old boy, brought in for a broken arm and renal contusion."

"What's renal contusion?"

"It's a bruised kidney."

"Child abuse?"

"Can't be sure. I'm trying to follow up on that one. Something was odd though. The kid cried about his butt hurting. I used my phone to take photos of the children with puncture marks." Jenna handed her phone to Loni and kept talking while Loni studied the photos of the purple bruising.

"Any idea who did the . . . what did you call it? Aspiration?"

"No." Jenna kept talking while Loni sent photos to her work email but seemed to be more cautious. "I can tell you this. Whoever it was, wasn't working alone."

"What do you mean?" Loni took a hard look at Jenna.

"Someone had to perform the procedure, and someone had to administer the drug through an IV so the child won't move or cry."

"I don't understand."

"A nurse could administer the drug. But it would take a trained doctor to know how to do the procedure. It's a specialized procedure in oncology or hematology but, outside of that, not a whole lot of doctors have actually been trained to perform an aspiration."

"What are you trying to tell me?"

"It had to be a doctor. A nurse isn't trained to do it."

"Do you know anyone who has been trained?"

"No. Certainly not me."

"How long would this aspiration take?"

"Maybe fifteen, twenty minutes."

"How many doctors have hospital privileges?"

"I don't know. I haven't met all the doctors."

"Could I ask where you were the nights when this was going on?"

"I probably shouldn't answer you, but I'll tell you anyway. I'm on the night shift in the emergency department and usually go home to my daughter when I get off."

"Except for the mornings you visited Carlotta Carboni."

"Yes. Except for that. You can ask the nurses to account for my time, and the doctor on the day shift following me. We always discuss any information I need to pass on about the patients."

"How many shifts are there?"

"We have a day, evening, and night shift."

"Do you know the doctor very well who followed you?"

"No. He's just out of residency. He seems very dedicated. I can't see him involved."

"Do you know what doctors and nurses were on duty on the pediatric floor during the night shift?"

"No. I only know Carlotta. I've only been up to that floor a couple of times."

"Think she was involved with the bone marrow aspiration?"

"I don't know. She was the only person in attendance when I got there. We had to have arrived within minutes of the aspiration. As the charge nurse, it's hard to believe she didn't know something."

"Maybe she saw something that got her killed." Loni rubbed at the condensation on her water glass. "Looks like it's time for me to get the names and addresses from the hospital of all the doctors and have a little talk."

Jenna agreed. "Looks like."

"And the night nurses on the pediatric floor."

"It will take a court order to get the information. We have federal laws regarding patient privacy." Jenna grinned. "My grandmother loves to enforce them."

"Okay." Loni grinned. "Hope she doesn't remember me."

Jenna grinned back. "Don't count on it. I gave her a hard time about you for a very long time."

"Did you now? Sorry I missed that."

Loni stared at Jenna until they both became uncomfortable and looked away. "Tell me about the bone marrow. What's it for?"

"A bone marrow transplant can be used to replace unhealthy bone marrow with healthy bone marrow."

"How does one usually get a hold of bone marrow?"

"It can be donated, but it's illegal to sell."

"What's it worth?"

"On the black market? It's the most valuable part of the body. It could sell as high as twenty thousand per gram."

"Is that twenty thousand dollars or twenty thousand pesos?

Jenna laughed. "Dollars."

"Oh, my God! How much could I get for my body?"

"Theoretically, up to around forty million dollars."

"Who do I see?"

Jenna laughed again. "You could always make me laugh. One of the things I never forgot about you."

"Assuming Carboni was part of it, maybe if we knew what the bone marrow was used for we could track the killer that way."

"It's used to treat a variety of things such as leukemia, severe aplastic anemia, lymphomas, multiple myeloma, immune deficiency disorders . . . or as a source."

"Whoa, whoa! I have no idea what you're talking about."

"Sick people."

"Right, smart ass. Then who would she sell it to?"

"There's an endless number of buyers beginning with parents who would pay anything to save their children."

"Got it. Where would the bone marrow go next?"

"To a pathology lab to check if the bone marrow is making healthy blood cells."

"You know of any?"

"Remember? My ex-husband has one in Portland."

"What does he drive?"

"I have no idea. Every time I looked around, he was driving something new." Jenna looked away. "He lives in New York and spends most of his time at the New York lab. It's been several months since I've seen him. He doesn't care about seeing his daughter, but he loves his toys." She pushed her blond hair away from her face and looked back at Loni. "Girl toys, boy toys, car toys, whatever."

"Would he know Carboni?"

"Maybe, though I doubt it. He does do business with this hospital which is why he has a smaller lab in Portland. My grandmother insisted on that."

"She financed him?"

"Of course."

"If he did visit this hospital, who would he see?"

"Probably Guy Murphy. Orders and payments would go through his office."

Loni recognized the name of the hospital's finance manager. "Tell me what you know about him?"

"Nothing, really. I rarely saw him and don't even remember ever carrying on a conversation with him."

"He didn't hit on you?"

Jenna didn't deign to answer.

"You trust your ex?"

"No. But I can't see him as a murderer. Especially such a vicious attack. He doesn't care that much about anything except himself."

Loni was quiet for a moment before she moved on. "What kind of security do you have at the hospital?"

"A couple of big guys I see wandering around. Security cameras at all the doors and in the halls."

"Not in the rooms?"

"No. And none on the floors. Federal privacy laws, remember?"

"Do they keep the recordings?"

"I don't know. You'll have to ask."

"I will." Loni glanced out the window at the slashing rain and at her watch. "Wow! It's getting late, and there's another storm coming in."

"I guess we better go."

Loni paid the check and jogged through the parking lot in the heavy sideways rain to get her Ford pickup. Jenna waited under the overhang at the entrance where Loni could pick her up. Dark clouds boiled in the sky and sucked up all the light as she turned off Highway 11 onto the gravel road to Jenna's house. Loni snorted, "I can't believe how the eight miles from the highway to your house never got any shorter."

"Your point?"

Loni sketched a hand in the air. "Just saying."

Jenna patted Loni's arm. "You always complained about this road. Poor thing!" Jenna glanced down at Loni's waist and continued, "I have a question for you. Do you ever go without a gun hanging off your waist?"

"Sorry, Jenna. I forgot how you feel about guns. And yes, I do. Next time I'll wear a shoulder holster."

"Is there going to be a next time?"

"I'd like there to be."

"You'd like what, exactly?"

Before Loni could decide on an answer, dim jiggling headlights came out of the trees behind them. They came up fast as she started to round a sharp corner. Loni slowed down, looking for a place to let the vehicle pass. The lights were on high, blinding her in the rearview mirrors. She yelled at Jenna to hang on the second before the truck rammed them into a spin on the rain-slick gravel road. Loni's pickup slid toward the ridge of a long embankment into a deep, running creek. The truck hurtled into the creek as Loni glimpsed the profile of an old pickup. They hit the water with a huge splash. Jenna screamed. Water filling the cab rose up Loni's legs. She fought the airbag off her face and released her seat belt. Jenna was slumped against her deflating airbag. Loni called out her name, but there was no response. She released Jenna's seatbelt and pulled her into her arms.

The sharp banks blocked both doors, and the water was at flood stage. The pickup settled to the bottom. By the time Loni pulled herself out of the seat, water was chest high. She knew they were trapped.

Pressure on both sides of the cab made it bow. In the fading dashboard light, Loni saw the windshield pop out. She pushed Jenna onto the hood and climbed out after her.

Loni saw the light of the pickup come back and stop up on the road. She heard two doors slam. Jerky lights moving toward them blinded Loni. Bullets zinging around them forced Loni into action. She pulled Jenna off the hood into the water. Jenna cried out.

"Be quiet and hang on to me, Jenna," Loni whispered. She peeked over the hood, squinted down her barrel sight, and aimed back and forth at the flights. Her volley of shots stopped their assailants' gunfire. A light dropped and rolled around.

A male voice cried out. "I'm hit. The bitch shot me."

Another male rumbled, "How bad?" The voice was familiar, but Loni couldn't quite place it.

"Gut shot. Get me out of here."

Loni heard the sounds of truck doors screeching shut and tires spinning on the gravel. Left in the deadly quiet, she flashed back to the sound of tired, unoiled doors of her grandfather's old GMC pickup. She shook her head and realized she was going into shock from the icy cold water. The night was pitch black except for the fuzzy glow up on the road. She knew they had to get out of the water immediately. The truck cab was submerged to the windows. She pushed

Jenna up to the top, crawled up after, and grabbed her cell phone. She hoped like hell that it would function.

The 911 operator answered her call. Loni's voice was so shaky from adrenalin and the cold water that the operator kept asking her to repeat the information. "She's hurt! We're a mile in from Highway Eleven on Brown Bear Road. We're in the ditch buried in water. Hurry!" Fighting panic, Loni hung on to Jenna. "How you doing?"

"I'm so cold." Jenna's quivering voice answered. "And a bad headache from hitting my head."

Loni wrapped herself around Jenna to keep her as warm as possible. Her adrenalin high was fading, and they both shivered from the icy water. She tried to distract Jenna by talking nonsense. The faint glow of the light faded away. She lost track of time.

When the ambulance arrived, two paramedics climbed down to them. Loni gently pushed Jenna in front of her and tried to climb up the bank. She felt hands pulling her up onto the side of the road. One of the paramedics checked her over while the other loaded Jenna into the ambulance. The ambulance screamed away. Loni desperately wanted to go with Jenna, but she had to stay at the crime scene.

Barely able to stand, Loni greeted the cop who had just arrived. She recognized him as someone she had ridden with when she was learning about her new town's people and places. "Hey, Hank," she said. "Could you get me the blanket out of your trunk and a ride to the hospital when we're finished?"

"What the hell happened, Loni?" Hank handed her a blanket. He walked over to the edge of the creek so Loni could pull off her wet coat, shirt, and bra. She wrapped the blanket around herself. Hank shined his flashlight on her pickup as he stared down and grunted in surprise. "Bullet holes? Only been here a few months. Made enemies already?"

Loni had been wondering the same thing. "Just lucky, I guess."

"Did you see who did this?"

"Not really. A dark, old pickup with squeaking doors. Considering how hard it hit me, the bumper's got to be dented." Loni pointed at her banged-up truck. "Should have plenty of black paint embedded. Maybe a dented fender as well."

Hank shrugged. "Must be hundreds of old pickups, Loni. Not likely to find it."

Loni sighed. "Probably not." She turned to Hank. "Can I borrow your flashlight?" She fought her shivering wet misery as she walked the area, searching in a circular pattern for the flashlight. "Here you are!" Loni shuffled back to the cop, returning his flashlight. "One of them dropped this."

"So? How you going to find the owner?"

Loni smiled. "With my favorite secret weapon. Got an evidence bag in your car?"

Hank dropped her off at the emergency department. Still wrapped in the blanket and clutching the evidence bag, Loni hurried to the desk and was directed to the first curtain. A doctor was stitching the cut on Jenna's forehead above her swollen, purple eye. They both turned as Jenna's grandmother rushed in, leaving a wake of lilac scent. Loni had never seen her long silver hair in disarray. "What happened? Did he hit you?" Jenna's grandmother grilled.

Who? Loni wondered. Who would hit her?

Not waiting for an answer, her grandmother turned a haughty stare on Loni. "Who are you?"

"Loni Wagner, ma'am. I'm a police lieutenant. I was in the accident with Jenna."

The grandmother turned back to Jenna, demanding, "Why are you riding with the police?"

Jenna groaned, struggling to answer. "She's working on a murder case. We went to an early dinner to talk about it."

The older woman turned back to Loni and snapped, "Are you drinking? Or on drugs? What's wrong with you?"

"No, Grandma," Jenna interrupted. "We were run off the road and shot at. She managed to shoot back and run them off."

"What! Wait a minute," Mrs. Davenport screeched. "You were shot at! For God's sake! What's going on?" She turned to Loni. "You first."

"Sorry, but I'm not at liberty to say."

The older woman studied her profile. "Why do you look familiar? Do I know you?"

Loni stood and turned to Jenna. "Can I give a you ride home?"

"Of course not," the grandmother barked. "She'll go home with me.

"Of course, she will." Loni turned back to Jenna. "I'll see you later."

Without glancing back at the old woman, Loni pushed aside the curtain around Jenna's bed and quickly walked out to the front desk. She showed the nurse on duty her badge and asked about gunshot victims.

The nurse shook her head. "We haven't had any gunshot victims tonight." She cocked her head. "You never know, though. The night is young."

Calling dispatch for a ride home, Loni waited until Hank drove up. She climbed in, grateful for the car heater. "Thanks again, Hank. I appreciate this."

Not until she got home and buried herself under the covers in her bed did she remember she'd forgotten to look at Adanna's report.

Chapter Eight

Tossing and turning in her bed, Loni drifted in and out of REM sleep. Her ribs and bruised shoulder ached from slamming against the seat belt and bouncing against the door during the grinding destruction of her pickup truck, and her dreams kept reliving the wild ride down into the creek, the gun fire and bullets bouncing around her in the place where she and Jenna almost died. Fighting the sheet and blanket that had twisted around her in different directions, she desperately felt the need to find Jenna. The shoulder pain increased from her frantic jerking and pulling until it became excruciating. Finally she was exhausted but free. And awake. She climbed out of bed to take a couple of aspirin and straightened up the bed covers. Back in bed, she hoped for relief that didn't come. More than pain kept her awake. Much more. Somebody wanted Jenna dead.

The aspirins eventually helped her drift into a restless sleep as a storm blew itself out over the coastal ridge. Struggling out of bed, Loni was half awake as she stumbled into a hot shower. She smelled snow as she limped out her back door in the dim light of early morning to feed the horses. The barn provided relief from the bitter cold east wind, and Loni grabbed the blankets off a hook on the stall wall to cover horses. They chewed on a half-full bucket of rolled oats, and she apologized for locking them in the barn. The empty spot where she usually parked her Ford pickup reminded her again of last night's close call. Coco watched her every move with a hangdog expression. "Yes, Coco, you're going," Loni reassured her. The dog bounded into the T-Bird, and Loni carefully climbed in after her. She backed the car out of the barn while the fuzzy poodle shoved her wet nose up against the passenger window and froze in place.

Aching, angry, and scared, Loni was on a mission to find the shooting victim. In her tired eagerness, she drove faster than usual, and the ancient car complained with every bump along the road. The tires squealed at the turns, and Coco clung to the seat with her claws.

Her first stop was the hospital emergency department. Loni hoped against hope that the man shot had been admitted during the night. Hurrying through the opening automatic door, Loni displayed her badge, explaining, "I'm looking for a shotgun victim. You get any in last night?

"Hey, Mary," the guard hollered. "Get any gunshot victims in last night?"

The admittance clerk shook her head no. "Not last night. Had one the night before. Man claimed his dog shot him."

The guard laughed. "You heard her. Must a been one pissed-off dog."

"Nah." The clerk grinned. "Just over excited to be outside. Accidently caught a claw in a gun leaning against a tree."

"Was it serious?"

"Nah. He won't be sitting down for a while though. Buckshot."

Hurrying back to the car, Loni stopped next at a large, red-brick building housing several doctors and labs. Opening the bag with the flashlight, Loni gently pushed it onto Coco's nose. Hoping she had the scent, Loni gave her a nonverbal signal for search and find.

Coco sniffed around the door and dragged Loni through the parking lot before stopping her search back at the car. Nothing. Emanating regret, Coco sat and waited for more orders.

Several hours later a very tired dog and a very discouraged woman returned home after stopping at every medical facility in several neighboring counties including talking to paramedics at fire stations. Failing at each place, Loni drove to stores that would possibly sell first-aid products. She walked the parking lots as well as around the entrance doors. Each time they got back into the car, Coco looked at her with pity and put her head on Loni's shoulder.

Chapter Nine

Loni woke up slowly, reveling in the wisps of a soft dream about Jenna and the feel of Sunday in spite of the deep hurts and aches that reminded her of Friday night. Sun rays streaking through the trees out her window warmed her face until she crawled out of bed. Her only concern was wondering if Jenna was okay. When she called, she got the answering machine and was unwilling to leave a message. A hot shower made her feel better, and she pulled on Levis and a heavy hooded sweat shirt. Coco danced around her as she yanked on her riding boots. "Yes, Coco. You're coming too," Loni reassured the large poodle. She grabbed a piece of tired sour dough bread, smeared a hunk of peanut butter on it, and wandered out into the brisk morning air with Coco bounding around the yard as she sniffed at everything in her path.

Both horses enthusiastically greeted her, and Loni apologized to Gladys while she saddled Roani. She settled into a comfortable seat as the three of them picked their way through the forest floor. Reaching the fore dune, they flew through the beach grass, hooves and paws scattering sand down to the ocean lapping at the long, empty beach. Roani joyfully splashed through the waves as Coco barked and snapped at the water spurting up from the horse's hooves. Two hours later, hunger, a cold wind, and two very weary friends herded Loni home. The long-string like mares-tail clouds scudding out of the southwest foretold a coming storm, and she didn't want to get caught in a heavy squall.

They picked their way homeward, and Loni rubbed Roani's wet neck. She knew she should not have allowed him to push so hard, remembering how he had once danced around the wild half Brahma desert steers for hours to hurry them along. His old age had made him stiff, and she slowed him to a running walk to cool him down. There was a time when he would dive in to nip a rear and spin away from a sharp hoof as they followed Willie and his paint horse tracking half Brahmas who only wanted to go home back to Old Mexico. The worst of Roani's aches came from when off-shoot tribe of the Cocopah would borrow him without permission. Roani always came home injured and crippled from the wild runs along the southern Colorado River. That finally ended when Loni promised to shoot the next person who kidnapped Roani.

Coco bounded ahead of them in a zig-zag pattern as Loni talked quietly to Roani as she watched Coco. Padding atop the soft needles of the forest floor and the give of the beach sand were much easier than the long desert rides of the past. Home again, Loni rubbed Roani down and bedded him before she crawled back into bed and let her tired, aching body rest until she got ready for dinner.

Loni hoped she wasn't lost again as she searched for signs guiding her to the Judge's house. So far, she had been lost twice along the old, long vacated, forest lumber road. Her GPS was worthless on the back roads, and she thought back to the time when she chased a speeder into a dry Arizona river. His GPS didn't work there either. He climbed out of the car that he had half buried in the river sand and stood, cursing his GPS and the missing bridge.

A faint light shone through the trees in the settling dusk as she arrived at the house that had mostly disappeared in the hanging fog along with the tree tops. She couldn't tell either the building's size or color as she picked her way onto a wrap-around porch. The judge opened the door before she knocked, and Loni handed her a bottle of red wine, hoping it was good. She never knew what to get, but she had paid enough for it. A women Loni assumed was the judge's wife, Helen, came up from behind the judge. She grabbed Loni's hand and pulled her into the foyer. "The infamous Loni Wagner. We meet again. Of course, the last time we met, you were still in diapers. I held you once and fed you your bottle. Welcome. Charlie's already here."

"Oh, no! Am I late?" Loni was startled at how much the two women looked and dressed alike. Except for the hair. Helen had straight, dark brown hair combed back from her forehead and shaped around her face like the 1920s flapper look. The judge's hair was its usual bun of sliced salt and pepper streaks. They were the perfect androgynous couple, both model tall and thin.

Loni felt overdressed and uncomfortable as she looked at their casual designer jeans with pink tee-shirts sporting outrageous sayings. Helen's read "It isn't going to lick itself." Compared to Helen's shirt, the judge's was much more sedate. "All women are lesbians except those who don't know it." As Loni listened to them, she began to single out their differences. Helen exaggerated everything in a highly expressive and joyful voice. The judge corrected almost everything Helen said with a shake of the head and a smile or a quiet laugh.

"No, no. Charlie's always early." Helen quickly told her. "I think he would move in if we would let him."

"Don't you dare!" the judge warned as Helen continued to pull Loni into the living room. "I got enough to do keeping up with you." The judge turned and stared at Loni's black eye. "Heard you got in a bit of trouble Arizona style. You alright?"

"A few bruises. Jenna got a scalp cut and a slight concussion. My truck took the brunt of it."

The judge laughed. "Boys and their toys. Butches in this case. Bet you had a redneck F150 Ford, right?"

Loni grimaced. "Not anymore."

Helen let go of Loni's hand, gave her a quick hug, and slapped the back of the judge's head as she passed behind her and headed off to the right. "Be nice and fix Loni a drink while I finish dinner."

"What'll you have, Loni."

"Diet coke would be great, Judge."

"You sure? That fake sugar only addicts you to wanting more sugar."

"Don't judge that child," Loni heard from the kitchen. "I burned your robes this morning."

Laughing, the judge hollered back, "Message received." She grinned at Loni. "It's a social occasion. Why don't you call me Marlene."

"Got it. Marlene." Loni said, stumbling over the name. She greeted Charlie with a nod and wandered around the living room while the judge disappeared in the same direction that Helen had gone. The flickering light from the fireplace blended with soft lights gave a warm glow to the room. The combination of ornate collectables and Quaker plain furniture worked for Loni. "Really nice in here."

Charlie laughed. "A little eclectic for my taste."

"What taste, Charlie?" Marlene said, walking into the room and handing Loni a regular coke bottle. Loni grinned at the "Made in Mexico" label. A touch of home. Arizona restaurants always used the good Coca-Cola from across the border. Marlene continued in her judge voice, "You haven't had any taste since your first girlfriend."

"That's because she was the only one you liked."

"Yes, and you should have married her."

"I would have if you hadn't asked her first."

Marlene broke out in laughter, pounding on Charlie as she astonished Loni with the change in her. Marlene turned to Loni. "I remember your grandmother's antique furniture. My family used to visit your grandparents on holidays. I played with your dad. He was a few years older. I'll never forget how kind he was to me. He had an Erector set, and he would help me build the most amazing things."

"Soup's on!" Helen called from the dining room. "Marlene Dietrich! Do your job."

"Helen Keller! I am doing my job! I'm entertaining our guests."

"Helen Keller?" Loni asked Charlie as they moved toward the table.

Marlene began to explain to Loni. "Our mothers were married to cousins. They were the best of friends so they named their children after their favorite people."

"I get it. Your sister, James's mother, was Ethel Merman."

Charlie laughed. "Should have named Marlene that. She was the dyke."

Marlene laughed. "Don't tell me you never saw Marlene Dietrich in the movie *Morocco*?"

Loni grinned. "I read where she liked girls more than boys."

"See, Charlie? Marlene was a really hot butch, especially in her tux."

"Oh, God!" Loni fanned herself. "I remember that scene. Especially when she kissed that girl."

Charlie's mouth dropped open. "A woman dressed in a tux kissed a girl in an old movie?"

"Yup," Marlene said. "Right on the mouth."

"Amazing thing?" Helen said. "That was Dietrich's first movie. It's a wonder that scene didn't kill her career."

"I gotta see that."

"Look on the internet, Charlie. It's all there in living black and white."

"And Ethel Merman?" Loni asked as she sat at the table, admiring the ornate gold trim on white china setting.

Helen spoke up as she carried in a large platter of baked salmon surrounded by scallops and shrimp. "Ethel fit her name. A true butch bitch."

"Any others?"

Helen laughed. "My oldest brother was Bruce Barton." Responding to Loni's confused expression, she continued. "My mother's favorite writer at the time." Helen grabbed Marlene's hand and pulled her out of the room. "You're supposed to help me carry in the food."

Loni couldn't remember Bruce Barton and when the two returned carrying the rest of the meal, Loni asked Helen. "What's your last name?"

"Barry."

"Oh, my God. Your brother's name was Bruce Barton Barry? That's funny."

Loni followed Charlie to the table that was lined with ten chairs and watched him sit at the head of the table.

"That's my chair, Charlie," declared Marlene, "And you know it. Move your ass."

"Hey. I'm the guest of honor."

"Since when?"

"Every time I'm here I honor you by my presence."

"Oh, bullshit. Move it, Charlie, before I throw you out on your pointy head."

Charlie laughed and traded chairs. "Sit across from him, Loni. He's left handed."

Loni grinned. "So am I."

"Sit next to him at your own peril."

Helen hurried in with a large soup bowl and gave it to Charlie. As it was passed around, Helen rushed back and forth until the table was full of food. Finally she sat with a relieved whoosh and looked around with a pleased grin. "Hope you all like vichyssoise," she said as she picked up her spoon. Loni was too embarrassed to ask what it was, but the soup tasted like cold onions and potatoes in milk.

Charlie passed the lima beans to Loni as he went back to their conversation. "I knew a family whose last name was Cotton so they named their kids after cloth. Terry was the oldest. Then there was Velvet, the boy was Silky, another boy was Gunny. Then there was Poly Ester."

"Gunny?"

"That's what we called a burlap sack. Gunny sack."

"Enough!" Helen intervened.

Loni couldn't resist. "I knew a family who named their four sons after medieval weapons. Dirk, Lance, Mace. I can't remember the fourth."

Helen groaned. "Oh, God. Here we go again."

"I like Rapier or Sabre."

"I think it was Pike." Loni decided.

"Or Catapult." Charlie said.

"What's that?" Helen asked.

"It throws things over walls," Charlie said.

"No. That's a trebuchet."

"Is not!"

"Is."

"Not!"

"Look it up."

Charlie pulled out his phone and typed away. "Says here they're the same thing. Specifically, a trebuchet is a type of catapult."

Marlene refused to admit defeat. "Bet the mother's name was Battle Axe."

"Enough already!" Helen cried. "I hurt from laughing. Somebody change the subject."

"Okay, then." Marlene obliged. "Helen, please explain why that ridiculous ceramic rabbit is in the middle of the table. Last time I saw it was outside in the flower bed sunk in the mud next to those old decoy ducks."

Loni stared at the colorful ceramic statue and grinned. She loved things that made her smile. This one was holding out a bouquet of wild flowers with a shy, hopeful grin on its face.

Helen blushed bright crimson. "I felt sorry for it."

"Charlie. Did I hear right? She brought that filthy thing in from the yard and sat it in the middle of the table because she felt sorry for it? You did witness that, right?"

"No, no, no. You're not getting me in the middle."

"But I washed it," Helen defended herself. "In the dishwasher."

"Loni?" Marlene demanded.

"What rabbit?"

"When does your next case come up for trial?"

"Gosh, Marlene. I think that lovely rabbit should go home with me."

Charlie grinned. "If you really want one, Piggy's sister Martha has her house full of rabbits. Damnedest thing I ever saw.

"What do you mean Piggy's sister has a house full of rabbits?"

"They're everywhere. I swear it."

"What were you doing in Martha Washington's house anyway?"

"Wait, wait. Martha Washington?" Loni was stunned.

Charlie laughed. "You ever ask Piggy what his name is?"

Loni sputtered, "Don't tell me it's George."

Charlie pointed his finger at Loni. "Bingo!"

"No wonder he goes by Piggy!"

Laughing, Marlene continued questioning Charlie, "You haven't answered my question. What were you doing in Martha's house?"

"Campaigning. Don't you remember? I always visit every house I can the month before election. She dragged me into her house for fear of letting rabbits out."

"At least they shit dry."

Loni laughed. "Not always."

Charlie groaned. "Cute. Ever step in it? I did. Shit is shit, crunchy or not."

Helen was curious. "Didn't the house smell?"

"Nah. They're vegans."

"Martha?"

"No, the rabbits!"

"For heaven's sake! What's she going to do with them?" Helen was fascinated. "Sell them, eat them, breed them, what?"

"No. Seems Piggy convinced her she could make a fortune selling their eggs."

Marlene stared at Charlie for a few seconds and with a straight face asked him, "Sold any yet?"

"Not yet." Charlie burst out laughing. "I understand she's waiting for Easter."

"How long . . . no, no, no." Marlene broke down laughing. "I'm not continuing this conversation."

"Hell, why not?"

"Because it's too much like talking to Piggy." Marlene shifted into serious. "Sad thing is she's doomed to failure and heartbreak."

Helen sat quietly for a few seconds. "My dad was one of those. Always doomed to fail."

"What are you talking about?" Marlene asked. "I remember him as the sweetest, nicest man I knew. Certainly, nothing like mine." Bemused, Marlene argued. "He was so accepting and loving toward us. At least you didn't have to leave home like I did."

Helen passed Charlie a large bowl holding something that resembled a very thick stew.

"What is this?"

"Rabbit." The judge said with a straight face.

"No shit!"

"No, it's not," Helen giggled. "It's Mexican Stewed Chicken. I thought you would enjoy a touch of home," she told Loni.

"Thank you," Loni took the bowl and heaped her plate. "One of Bahb's favorites."

"Who's Bob?"

Grinning, Loni corrected Charlie. "It's Bahb. B A H B. Means grandfather in Pima."

"Thought you were Apache?"

"That was my grandmother's side."

"Did your grandparents attend the Indian School in Phoenix?"

Loni frowned. "You mean the white man's torture prison for Indian children?"

The judge studied Loni. "Did your grandparents tell you much about their experiences?"

Finding herself in a place she didn't want to be, Loni's answer was vague as she attempted to wave the question away. "A comment here and there."

The judge wasn't dropping it. "Like what?"

Loni lifted her eyes from her plate and met the judge's soft stare. "My grandmother was five when they jerked her out of her mother's arms. She never saw her again. They took her from the high plains of the San Carlos reservation to the summer heat in Phoenix. Shaved her head. Dressed her in heavy clothes. Left her to sit in the sun. Fed her strange food. Let her cry herself to sleep every night. She said many of the people there tried to be kind, but they had too many children and too much to do. She wanted to be friends with the other children but they were from different tribes, different languages, and none of them spoke English. Years passed before she could make sense of that world."

"And your grandfather?"

Loni smiled as she thought about her grandfather. "Bahb told a different story. They didn't catch up with him until he was in his early teens. He knew enough broken English to get by, but, according to my grandmother, would never talk to anyone but her. My grandfather became her protector from their very first meeting when she was twelve. That never changed." Loni paused, thinking. "He was tall for his age and desert wild, unpredictable. My grandmother said nobody messed with him, or her. He was wonderful with animals so they left him to work the horses. That never changed either."

"I remember. He was famous for the horses he trained. Everybody wanted to own one." The judge saw the tears shimmering in Loni's eyes and changed the subject. "Helen. We were talking about your dad earlier."

"Yes. Unlike your grandfather, Loni, my dad had the Sadim touch."

"What the hell is the Sadim touch?" Charlie asked.

Marlene patted Helen on the shoulder in empathy and answered Charlie. "The opposite of Midas touch. You know. Instead of everything turning to gold, it turned to shit."

"Stop it, Marlene. You know I hate gross images when I'm trying to eat!"

Helen sighed. "No matter what he tried to do. He opened a café for the lumbermen to get a square meal, and they banned tree cutting. Too close to the watershed for the town, they told him." Helen turned to Marlene. "Remember when you and I left, he was trying to farm cotton but by then India was growing cotton a lot cheaper. Remember we helped them move? In fact, all the years you knew me, we moved seven times, every time because he failed at something. The last time Marlene and I went home he had driven a truck all summer. Mother was so proud of him until on the last day he ran the truck into a ditch and it cost every dime he made to pay for it."

The judge nodded. "I remember you moved back to Caliente every few years and we were able to be together for a while before you left again. Broke my heart every time you left."

"Awww." Helen leaned over and gave the judge a light kiss. "We had to move back in with my grandfolks every time my dad went broke. Just as soon as he begged and borrowed a few bucks, we were off again."

"Until the last time. I wouldn't let her leave me again. I was in my second year of college at ASU. We moved off campus. Both got jobs as we went to school."

"At least he was always smiling, happy until the day he died."

"I know. He never gave up."

Charlie poked at Helen. "Everybody loves a happy loser."

"Bite me!"

"Speaking of sweet, how's my nephew James?" Marlene asked. "He was such a sweet child."

"You kidding me?" Loni sputtered. "James was a spoiled brat whose sole goal in life was to figure out how to behave just barely good enough to get away with hiding how cruel he really was. Nothing sweet about him. I had to save his sorry ass twice before he would even look me in the eye and speak to me." Loni's face softened. "I guess we finally made our peace."

"How'd you save his life?"

"The first time we got a call he was in trouble at the Oasis Bar. When I got there, I peeked in the window and saw a Mexican on each side with a gun in his ribs. I got a serape out of the truck of my car, threw dirt all over me, messed up my hair into a tangled mass, and pretended to be a whore. I walked into that bar hollering "*Puta. Alguien quiere un puta?*" Loni laughed. "The only taker I got was old man Lester asking how much? I said a dollar, and he said it was too much. Maybe a dollar if I throw in a beer. Didn't exactly help my ego."

"Wait a minute." Helen stopped Loni. "Is old man Lester still alive? He was a hundred years old when we left."

"I heard he died just before I moved up here."

"Of what, for God's sake."

"I don't know. Congenital old age?"

"Ignore her, Loni," Helen said. "Finish your story."

"One of the Mexicans told the barkeep to give me a beer to shut me up. And to make sure he kept me down wind. That really pissed me off so when they pulled James off his stool, I hit one of them with the bottle while I kicked the other in the balls. But here's what got to me. We loaded the two of them in James's car and he drove off without even a thank you and took credit for the arrest."

Marlene groaned. "Takes after his ma."

"You said you saved him twice?" Helen asked.

"The second one was just carelessness on his part. He turned his back on a perp, and she nearly got his gun before I pulled her off him. She turned on me then, and he stood there laughing while I got the shit beat out of me until I got her under control."

"Sorry about laughing," the judge finally contained herself. "After all that, how did you ever make peace with him?"

"When we were trying to catch a coyote at the 'Well That Minnie Dug' and ended up catching his own partner working with the coyotes. His partner's greed and callousness was really hard on him, and we sort of ended up bonding."

"Minnie dug a well? What does that even mean?"

"The wells across the desert all had names. The one called Minnie hadn't worked in years. Unfortunately, the windmill fan could be seen from one of the main trails out of Old Mexico. It attracted too many border crossers thinking they could find water." Loni's voice hardened. "So many lives lost at that well."

"Why didn't they fix it?"

"The owner was a large corporation in New York and wouldn't even respond. I tried to help my Uncle Herm fix it a couple of times but our version of the Bundys kept destroying it."

"Don't tell me you had them in Arizona."

"Those the same that got off scot free here?"

"The same. Several extremist groups have volunteered themselves using armed vigilante tactics against anyone they find near the border."

"That's terrible," Helen cried. "Doesn't anyone help them?"

"A group called Humane Borders leaves blue water barrels on the desert trails. I always wanted to cry every time I saw one of their tall blue flags. They saved so many lives." Loni acknowledged. "Some also say the barrels convince more people to try crossing."

"But that's not the point, is it?" Helen said.

"No," Loni nodded at her, grateful for her understanding.

"Do you have a girlfriend, Loni?" Helen asked.

"She does," Charlie answered for her. "But she won't admit it."

"Really!" Marlene stared at Loni. "You didn't say."

"Shut up, Charlie!" Loni turned to Marlene. "He's referring to some girl I ran into the other day. She was my first love a hundred years ago."

Helen's eyes teared as she reached across the table and tweaked Loni's cheek. "The first love is the hardest to lose. Always devastating, often damaging, impossible to let go of."

"Hey!" Marlene interrupted. "I was your first love, and you've still got me. I don't see any damage."

Helen turned to Marlene with a soft smile. "I was referring to every time we had to be parted and I never knew if I'd ever see you again."

"How sweet." Charlie sighed in light mockery. "Loni's girlfriend is also in big, big trouble."

"You know I can't discuss a case with you, Loni, but I can say I'm worried about Jimmy. He's cancelled two grand juries, blown off several arraignments, and won't return calls. Everything's backing up and out of control. I need to find out what's going on. Either of you know anything?"

Loni and Charlie looked at each other. Loni answered, "I've got the same problem. I can't find anyone who knows anything."

"If you hear anything, let me know?"

"Sure."

The judge turned to Charlie. "I knew I was forgetting to ask you something, Charlie." The judge changed the subject with a loving look at her wife. "Where's your latest?"

"Ah ha. Wondered when you'd notice. We got in a fight yesterday and she went home to think about it."

"So she had a brain. Not your type anyway."

"Wait a minute! I enjoy smart women. That's what I always look for."

"Hah," Helen laughed. "What was it Joan Rivers once said? Something about she never saw a man reach up some woman's skirt looking for a library card."

Charlie groaned. "That's harsh."

"Where is home, anyway? I thought she moved in with you last month?"

"She did. Then she moved out again. Back to Phoenix."

"Arizona?"

"No, no. Phoenix, Oregon."

"Why didn't you stop her?"

"You know those theories on how to argue with a woman? I'm here to tell you they're all wrong."

"Too bad," Helen said. "She was a cutie. Can't you ever compromise?"

"Like when?"

Marlene ragged on Charlie. "Like when you got hair sticking out your nose and ears, but not on your head, got a beer gut with skinny legs, dirt poor, and you still try to convince us you're not only sexy but also the best catch in the world because your male entitlement says so. No way can women compete with that attitude."

"Point made. Where's the dessert?"

Loni looked around realizing everyone had sat back and away from the table. "Wow. I laughed so hard I don't remember eating." She looked around for a bathroom.

"You, too?" Helen got up to show her as she informed the table. "If anyone makes me laugh one more time, you'll be cleaning it up. And the guest bathroom's down the hall."

By the time Loni got back, dessert was on the table, a beautiful Mexican sopapilla cheesecake pie. "Perfect," she said and grinned. "Is that really what I think it is?"

"It is," Helen verified. "Marlene's favorite dessert."

"Mine, too. Who gets to cut?"

"You do." Helen handed Loni a knife. "Enjoy."

So full she ached, Loni felt mostly warm inside as she found her way back home. Just a little piece felt lonely and restless, thinking how Marlene and Helen had been able to keep each other all these years. She remembered how long she lived with the wrenching loss of Jenna. Not ready to go to bed, Loni opened her computer to email Sandi.

TO: Sandi@gmailyahoo.com
FROM: Loni Wagner
DATE: December 12
SUBJECT: Greetings

Hey Sandi,

How's my favorite sister-in-law? How's Mama? I appreciate that you want me to move back to L.A. I do plan to get back to visit soon, but I can never move back. I still have too many bitter memories. Even more, I don't think I want to live in a city again. So many people moved to the big city to find anonymity and freedom from the prying gossips of their small towns and lost what was the most valuable. All I learned from being a cop in the big city was that I should tell newcomers don't trust anyone, have several locks on all the doors, keep a close eye on everything they owned, and take advantage of anyone's vulnerability. And, of course, never look anyone in the eye.

When I moved back to small town living, what a high! Everything is open and unlocked. Even people's hearts. No one is afraid to park anywhere or leave a house open when they leave. And they can walk anywhere, any time. Obviously there's no privacy so you can't do everything you might want to like you can when hiding in the anonymity of the city, but you learn to accept there is a good reason for that. Living with all those social rules that guarantee a safe but boring life is okay with me.

I do understand that the loss of privacy is a problem for some. There was the time that this guy from out of town came looking for a friend who had a job here. He called the Chamber of Commerce, and the person working there said that the friend was shacked up with a woman who lived up Hay Creek Road. He was so upset to be found where he was, he left town the next day.

Then there was this new librarian who was scared spitless when people spoke to her by name wherever she went around town. Her picture had been in the newspaper and everybody recognized her. She left town the same day and mailed the library key back when she got fifty miles away.

My granddad always said small town living is like living with a family that doesn't always get along. Sometimes it's fun, and sometimes it's painful, but you're always surrounded by people who care and who always help through the hard times.

Sometimes, however, the quiet allows me too much time to think. Sometimes I feel like time has curved in on me, reminding me how much I lost, especially the other day when I ran across my first girlfriend. I don't know which is more painful right now - looking backward or forward. But Jenna is another story for another day.

Love to the family,

Loni

Chapter Ten

Loni worried about not having her Monday morning report ready for the chief as she climbed the stairs into the squad room. At the entrance, she shook out the rain from her long black leather coat and glanced around. Everybody there was busy, but Piggy was missing as well as Don and Harry. She nodded to two of her detectives in response to "How come you look like shit this morning?" from Ginger and "Yo" from Cleatus.

Ginger studied her with concern. "Hell of a shiner you got there. You get in a fight?"

"Somebody ran me off the road into a creek Friday night. Then shot at me."

"How rude," Ginger said, a stunned expression settling across her freckled face.

Cleatus laughed. "How rude? That's it?" He turned toward Loni and asked, "You okay?"

"Don't have a hole in me if that's what you're asking. Just a lot of bruises. Someone else does though. I spent all day Saturday looking everywhere for a gut shot victim."

Bobbi had her headset on and didn't notice Loni until she finished talking. She stared at Loni's clothes. "Still practicing how to eat, I see." Bobbi reached up and brushed croissant crumbs off Loni's red wool vest in an attempt to mother her.

"Hey, careful there. Them's private parts."

Bobbi snickered. "Not the right parts for me, Lieutenant. I do this all the time for my three-year old."

"Really? She's already got private parts?"

"Shut up and stand still. I swear to God you got more food on your front than in that potty mouth."

"I know. I was in a hurry to get here and I ate on the way."

"Right. Nothing's messier than a flaky croissant."

Loni grinned and put Bobbi's hand back on her computer. "First thing I need you to do is to call around asking for a man with a gunshot wound, probably a gut shot. Somebody shot at me Friday night, and I want to know who. I need you to call any trauma center in the state for a possible gut shot male victim." Getting a nod of acknowledgment from Bobbi's worried face, Loni continued on toward her office, brushing herself off a bit more.

"Wait a minute!" Ginger ordered Loni. "You can't just walk away and not tell us what the hell happened. What do you mean you got shot at?"

Loni ducked her head, sighed and turned around, facing her detectives. "Not that much to tell it happened so fast. I was taking a friend home when this pickup ran me into a creek. When I crawled out of the cab and pulled my friend out, whoever sideswiped me started shooting. I fired back and hit someone, and now I'm looking for them."

"Who's the friend?" Ginger asked.

Loni shook her head at Ginger.

"Give it up, Lieutenant. You know you want to." Ginger prodded.

"Jenna Giovanni. And that's all I'm saying on the subject."

"You datin' a suspect?"

"Ginger! Drop it!"

"Not smart."

"It's not that. She's an old friend, in fact, a roommate for two years at Lewis and Clark."

"How come you're not a law'ya then?"

"Life got in the way. Can we move on now?"

"Oh, by the way, Lieutenant," Bobbi grinned as she changed the subject. "Chief called and said he couldn't see you until this afternoon." Relieved, Loni headed into her office when she heard the faint ding of the elevator and looked up to see Piggy. She met him halfway, hearing his chatter. "Turned the loot into evidence" was somewhere in his mutterings.

"Did you get the warrant for Guy Murphy?"

"Nope."

"Did you get Bobbi's message?"

"What message?"

"To pick up the warrant."

"Yup."

"Don't bother taking off your jacket, Piggy. Get the warrant. Then go to the hospital and bring Guy Murphy in for questioning."

"Can't."

"Why not?"

"Damn, Lieut. It just keeps coming. I can't be everywhere."

"Start by dealing with one thing at a time."

"That's what I'm doing."

"In the time that you've been standing here complaining, you could have solved four crimes. Now, go pick up Guy Murphy."

Loni was still at her computer an hour later when Piggy led Murphy into the interrogation room and walked into Loni's office still complaining. "I'm never going back to that hospital no way ever again. Just like last time, he lawyered up. Told you so."

"Crap, Piggy! Check out his alibi."

"Now?"

"You got a better time?" Loni lobbed back at him. Turning toward the interrogation room she added, "Let me know as soon as you find out."

"What for?"

"Tells me whether to arrest him or let him go." Loni moved toward the interrogation room.

"Where you going? Told you he lawyered already."

"I'm going to go watch him."

"What for?"

"Everybody's got a tell, Piggy. Would be good to know his."

Through the one-way glass, Loni watched Murphy circle the gray metal table. Loni figured he knew he was being watched. At every pass around the room he stopped at the mirror to pat his perfectly-layered blond hair and check his teeth. *He was a pretty boy who walked straight out of an Armani catalog*, she thought. She smiled to herself as she compared her own rough-out walking boots to his shoes, so shiny he could see himself in them. A few minutes later he started showing signs of stress. He'd sit down and immediately stand up to pace, circling like a hurting dog who couldn't settle. Loni watched as he pulled on his fingers like milking a cow. Maybe his tell. Suddenly, Piggy was beside her.

"What'd you find out?"

"Nothin'. Nobody home."

"Piggy. Go in and ask Mister Murphy some questions."

"Told you, Lieut. He lawyered.

"Do it anyway. Tell him we're not accusing him of anything. Tell him we hope he has information that can help us solve a murder. Ask him if he knows

Carlotta Carboni. If he says yes, ask him how well. Does he know Doctor Giovanni? If so, again, how well? Does he know her husband? Then ask him about his job at the hospital."

Loni watched Piggy walk into the room and explain to Murphy that he wasn't a suspect. The bite of Murphy's angry voice bouncing around the room triggered loud squawking from the speaker in the room where Loni watched. "I'm suing this police station and you for everything you got and will ever have," Murphy screamed.

"You're damn sure welcome to what I got which ain't nothin." Piggy sniggered. "Just sit a minute, answer a couple of questions, and you can go."

Loni carefully watched Murphy's eye movement and the way he pulled his fingers as he talked about not knowing Carlotta Carboni or Jenna's husband. He left his fingers alone as he talked about how important his job was and how he singlehandedly kept the hospital doors open.

The longer he talked about his job, the more he lost his jitters. He sat quietly in his chair and folded his hands on the table, not moving. He didn't blink. One cool character, Loni thought as she walked in to confront him. Wondering why he was so calm now compared to earlier, she sat down across from him, frowned, and dropped a folder on the table. Pulling out photos of the crime scene, she scattered them in front of him and, matching his cool, asked, "Did you kill her?"

Murphy blanched as he looked at the bloodiest photo that she had deliberately put closest to him. He turned the pictures over and, pushing them away, stared directly into Loni's eyes. "No I did not kill her. Yes, we were lovers. Like I said, I want my lawyer." He began to fidget and sweat, but he didn't touch his fingers. Nor did he utter another word. Disappointed, Loni let him go, reluctantly accepting he might be innocent. Loni stepped out and watched him hurry down the stairs.

"That went well, Lieut," Piggy said sarcastically.

"Yes, it did, Piggy." Loni told him. "For him anyway."

Piggy stared at her quizzically. "You loony?"

"Nah, Piggy." Cleatus said. "She's just pissed. Some sorry idiot tried to do her in last night."

"Do her in? What does that mean?"

"Ran her off the road, Piggy. In a ditch."

"Really? Do much damage? How 'bout the other guy? He have insurance?"

"Didn't have a chance to see who it was, Piggy. I was too busy ducking bullets."

"Really? See the car?"

"Sort of. Like a ghosting silhouette. It reminded me of my grandfather's old GMC."

Piggy cawed like an old crow. "Know thousands of people own old pickups. Even the DA has one like you described. He even leaves the key in it for anyone to borrow so's they don't bother him."

"You know what? I still want to talk to the DA. How about you and I take a ride?"

"Why?"

"Because I don't know where he lives, and you do. Since he's never in his office, I figure maybe he's home." Turning to the other detectives, Loni said, "As for the shooting, I'd like you to stop talking about it and concentrate on your own cases." Loni struggled back into her coat walking back to the stairs. "You coming sometime this century, Piggy?"

Loni drove five miles north trying to ignore Piggy's incessant whining. She stopped the car and stared at a manufactured home on a corner lot in a neighborhood with other places. More manufactured homes, stick homes, trailer houses, big and little, old and new, cheap and not as cheap. The house that Piggy pointed to felt abandoned and unkempt with a yard overrun with weeds. "You sure this is where he lives?" The house was well designed with bump outs on both ends and an attractive porch, but it was still a manufactured home, not the big, expensive home she expected. "He doesn't live rich, does he."

"Jimmy? It's a nice house, Lieut. He's just not home much."

"So, where is this pickup?"

"Looks like it's gone. So's his car."

"Piggy, go knock on the door, just to be sure."

Piggy grumbled and climbed out of the police car. He slogged his way up to the door and banged on it with his fist. "Jimmy! You in there? Get your sorry ass outa here! Jimmy!"

A chubby woman hollered from her yard next door, "He's been gone the weekend, like usual."

"You know where?"

"Not my business where any foreigner goes. He's nice enough though."

Loni and Piggy drove back to the station in silence and separated at the elevator. She turned toward the stairs and bumped into Molly.

"Geeez, Lieutenant. How come you look so tired?" Molly grinned. "Lucky late night, I hope."

"Not kind, Molly."

"Struck out again, did you."

Loni stopped and turned back to Molly. "Don't you have some case to help us solve?"

"Just taking a break for a cuppa," Molly said. "Know what? You should've come out with us last night. We saw a great movie. I keep inviting you. We straight girls can be fun, too." Molly kept prattling as Loni started up the stairs.

"One night, Molly. One night," Loni promised without looking back.

Nodding to Bobbi, Loni ignored Piggy as she walked into her office, hung up her coat, and picked up the phone. She called the lab and put the phone on speaker. While she waited for an answer, she watched Cleatus through the window into the squad room and admired the way that his fingers flew over the computer keys. "Hey! Got time to meet me at the hospital later this afternoon?" Loni said when Adanna picked up the phone.

"You buyin' lunch?"

"Sure."

"Now?"

"Raincheck? I have to see Chief for my Monday report. He postponed it until now. Wish I knew how ill he really was."

"Wish I did, too. See you at the hospital."

By the time Loni hung up the phone and stood in her doorway, she realized she had no more time to prepare for Chief's report. "Okay, people. Before I go down for my Monday report to the chief, anybody got anything new to add?"

Ginger looked up. "Nope. Did find a hungry child with one of our perps in Percyville. He was raising the kid alone. She was so adorable I wanted to take her home with me."

"Yah," Cleatus joined in. "Took her to the shelter. Ginger cried all the way back to the station."

"There you go," Piggy scoffed. "Finding ways to waste tax money."

"Jesus, Piggy!" Ginger spurted. "It's a child in need!"

"You bleedin' hearts so busy putting wasters on welfare and food stamps, you're destroying our country!"

"Yeah?" Cleatus said, "Onlyst time a conservative ever gave a crap 'bout any of us, Piggy, is when we're in our mama's belly."

"Cleatus, why can't I understand a word you say?" Piggy said, complaining about Cleatus's thick Southern accent.

"Probably 'cause you be home schooled."

"Ginger? What'd he say?"

Ginger buried her face in her hands, muttering for patience. "He said the only time you conservatives gave a damn about any of us was when our mother was pregnant. Once we popped, none of you conservatives gave a rat's ass what happened to us."

With a brief grin, Loni turned back to Bobbi. "Seen Harry or Don? They should be in by now."

"They were on their way but got caught in a dispute of some kind."

"Dispute? That sounds ominous. What kind of dispute?"

"You know what I know, Lieutenant."

The elevator door opened, and Harry and Don emerged, still arguing as they headed for their desks. "Come on, Don. Admit you were too hard on her."

"What's going on?" Loni interrupted.

Don turned to answer her. "We stopped for coffee when Harry here watched his teenaged neighbor park in the handicap zone next to our police car and hang up the blue handicap tag. He rushed out of the shop and arrested her before I got to them."

"She deserved it, Don!"

"She's sixteen years old, Harry!"

"Never too young to be taught a lesson."

"What's the problem?" Loni demanded to know.

Rubbing his craggy face, Harry turned to Loni. "My next-door neighbor was using her grandma's tag. We buried her grandma a month ago."

"Tell her the rest, Harry."

"When I took the tag away from her, the girl went ballistic so I cuffed her. Said it was a gift from her grandma, the only memento she had. Said the aunts had seized the house and gutted it and sold it. She didn't even have a place to live."

Loni cringed. "Boy, does that sound familiar."

Bobbi's voice penetrated Loni's consciousness. "Lieutenant! Lieutenant!"

"What, Bobbi?"

"I got a call on the line. It's a cat thief's owner."

"Say what?" Piggy snorted. "A cat on the phone? Good one, Bobbi."

"No, Piggy. The owner of a thieving cat."

Cleatus laughed. "Lettin' the cat outta the bag is a whole lot easier than putting it back."

Ginger snorted. "I've heard of cats stealing, Lieutenant. Lots of animals steal things."

"Lord, yes." Harry jumped in. "Bears, foxes, monkeys, squirrels…"

"Some animals even trade." Don laughed. "One time camping, a trade rat visited me. "Got my pocket change and left me its turd."

"Better than bird shit, Don. I had a crow that was always bringing me stuff to thank me for the food. If there wasn't any food there, he would shit on my windshield."

"Y'all know that there crow's the smartest animal in the world? Even smarter than most of us."

Piggy groaned in annoyance. "Come on, Cleatus. It's just a stupid bird."

"Just think on this. There's over one million species on earth. Of those, two hundred and eighty-four use tools. Of those, forty-two can make tools. Of those, five can make different kinds of tools. But only two species can make hooked tools. We humans and the crow."

"Bullpucky, Cleatus."

"Piggy. Just once, try educatin' yourself before you speak."

"You're just full of crap, Cleatus. Birds ain't smarter than me."

Loni agreed with Cleatus, but she knew she'd better get their argument stopped. "People! Can we move on? Please?" Loni waited for the snickers to settle before she turned back to Harry. "Mark the sticker invalid and give it back to the girl." Turning to Bobbi, she demanded. "What's the problem?"

"Yeah, Bobbi," Piggy said. "Tell the owner to make the cat take it back."

"Yeah, Bobbi," Ginger asked. "Why do we even care?"

Bobbi turned back to the phone and rephrased the question. "Ma'am? Is there a reason why your cat's thievery is important?" Loni watched the expression on Bobbi's face change from a smile to amazement as she took notes. "Really!" Jotting notes as fast as she could, she thanked the caller, told her someone would be around soon and hung up.

All eyes focused on Bobbi as she looked up from the phone and shook her head. Her short dark hair scattered in all directions, and she gulped like a fish, trying to get her breath. The group stared back at her dark brown eyes that had grown large and round. Loni clamped a hand onto her shoulder, and waited until Bobbi could finally give an explanation. "The woman decided to wash the cat's bed. She has an opening into a cabinet in the washroom and a cat door to the outside." Bobbi stared down at her notes. "You won't believe this. The woman found three watches. One of them a Rolex. Several pieces of women's jewelry including a four-carat diamond engagement ring. Sixteen unmatched socks, nine pairs of men's shorts, a queen size purple sheet, eight towels, and eighteen pieces of women's underwear. Apparently, the cat's favorite, the sexier the better. Most were G-strings." Bobbi looked up. "But the strangest was the dildo she was cuddling like it was her baby. And none of it belonged to the woman."

Loni took a deep breath to keep from joining the laughter around the room and nodded at Piggy. "You're up. Go take pictures of everything and collect the valuables, especially the Rolex and diamond ring. Ask around the neighborhood for missing items. Tell them they need to bring proof of ownership to collect the expensive items from the lost and found at the station."

"I ain't returning no dildo."

Harry laughed. "Don't think that's considered a valuable item, Piggy."

"Maybe not to you." Ginger giggled.

"Why can't I just give them back their things?"

"If someone stuck a Rolex in your face, what would you say?"

Piggy opened his mouth to answer but Loni cut him off.

"Do it, Piggy. And tell the owner to lock the damn cat door."

"Jeez, Lieut. How come I always get all the hard cases? I already got a murder case now!"

"Piggy!"

"Just saying."

"Hey, Piggy." A devious expression crossed Ginger's face. "If you stuck that dildo up your ass, maybe you would smile once in a while."

"Don't say it, Piggy!" Loni warned.

"But, Lieut!"

"Just don't!"

Piggy jerked his limp brown-checkered jacket from the coat tree and grumbled all the way into the elevator. Once the door closed and the elevator squeaked and squawked its way down, Loni joined the group in whooping and hollering. After the noise settled down to an occasional chuckle, Loni asked Bobbi to enter her phone call as a new case.

"What'll I call it?"

"How about the Dildo Caper?" the usually quiet Don tossed out, bringing on another round of chuckles.

Loni was running late to see the chief. She rushed downstairs and stopped short at the door to his office, shocked at how much worse he looked. The dark bags underneath his eyes were highlighted by his sallow skin, and his clothes seemed to hang on his frame. Under his tan sports jacket, his white shirt was wrinkled, and his red and gray striped tie was stained with egg yolk. He seemed to make an effort to stand before he fell back in defeat. Loni perched on the edge of a chair across the desk from him. "You okay, Chief?"

Chief waved her off. "Can't seem to shake this bad cold. Usually spending the weekend at the lodge cures me of all my ills."

"Guess you better go back next weekend and try again."

"Maybe so."

"What kind of lodge do you have, Chief?"

"Just a small one up in the Cascades. Mostly my buddies and I escape from the wives and play a little friendly poker. Sometimes, if we get around to it, fish and hunt." Chief grinned as he picked up his half full coffee cup. "Join me?"

"No thanks. I'm jittery now. Is that Fiesta ware you're carelessly waving around?"

Chief snorted. "You're as bad as my wife. She's still ticked off at me for taking this cup from her collection. Keeps saying I'll break it. She keeps finding god-awful ones at garage sales to trade me. I refuse." Chief held it up. "It fits my big fingers."

Loni grinned. "Bet she sneaks in one of these days and liberates her cup."

A half-suppressed laugh bumped out of Chief's mouth before he got serious again. "What have you got?"

"I'm sure you heard about the depressing one from Percyville." Loni wiggled around in Chief's uncomfortable wood spindle chair.

"I heard. Tell me the details."

"The boy, Malcolm Beloat, did the shooting. He's ten years old. The victim was his brother Buford. He was fifteen." Loni shook her head unable to speak for a moment. "Seems the ten-year old got mad at his brother because he wouldn't let him ride the ATV so the ten-year old went in the house and got a loaded rifle from behind a door. He came back outside and shot his brother. Then he dropped the rifle, got the ATV key out of his dead brother's pocket, and rode around on the ATV until his dad got home. His mother was at the hospital with her mother. She'd had a heart attack that morning and left the older brother in charge."

"Who's working on it?"

"Ginger and Cleatus. It's going to be a messy one. Before he disappeared, the DA couldn't decide whether to schedule a grand jury or a preliminary hearing.

He wants to try the boy as an adult and prefers to do it in court." Loni looked up at Chief Alden. "Can he do that?"

He rubbed his bald head. "I doubt it. According to Scots Law, children have to be fourteen and over to be convicted under adult law. Although children under fourteen can still be subject to an arbitrary punishment. Still, it would be hard to convict them in an adult court."

"But they could be punished if the court thinks they know right from wrong?" Loni argued.

Chief grimaced. "True. Except for children under seven who can't be subject to any punishment."

"You mean like the case of the seven-year-old whose father bought him one of those new colorful children's rifles and he shot his sister?"

Chief gave a heavy sigh and looked up at Loni. "Your case is not our call. Next case?"

"Same one. Ginger and Cleatus are out asking questions of the neighbors and people who knew Malcolm. Did he torture animals? Was he a bully? Does he wet his bed? You know the kinds of questions head churners want. Ginger says the boy has no remorse for what he did. She's calling him a psychopath. Cleatus says the child hasn't reached his age of reason and he doesn't know what he's doing. He maintains that the kid needs to be carefully handled because someday he'll figure out what he's done and suffer tremendous remorse."

Chief gave a grim laugh. "Of course. Ever looking deeper. That's our Cleatus. I think Ginger might be right on this one though."

Loni flipped to another page. "We still haven't been able to arrest anyone in the case about the teen who was beaten so badly. Ginger and Cleatus are also on that one. Four boys were witnesses along with the perpetrator, but they won't talk, and I don't want to arrest all of them. Sometimes I consider it. The boy had a broken jaw, three broken ribs, a damaged kidney, a broken wrist. Nearly lost an eye."

"Did you find out why?"

"According to the boy, he was interested in a girl who lived in Percyville and drove out to see her. It seems that outsiders are not welcomed."

"I know." Chief smiled. "It's a guy's town.'"

"What do you mean?"

"Junk cars stacked in the weed-infested yards, paint worn off beat-up salt houses, blue tarps on roofs, cardboard in windows with signs saying things like,

'If you can read this, you are within range,' and every house has at least fifty guns."

Loni laughed. "Power of love does you in every time." Loni watched the chief's expression change to one of deep sorrow. She wondered why he was so upset by what she said and moved on to another case. Flipping another page, she continued. "Harry and Don finally finished the murder case to be prosecuted. That's the one where this shirtless, screaming drunk, stood in the middle of the highway shooting a pistol until he managed to kill someone."

"That Percyville again?"

"Yup."

Chief laughed for the first time since Loni had come in. "I asked Harry once if he was related to the Harry Truman who got covered in ash when the top blew off Mount St. Helens, but he said not. That's when he joked about being related to President Harry Truman."

"At least he does look like him."

Chief sat back and rubbed his head. "He does, doesn't he." A serious expression settled on the chief's face, and he continued. "Looks like the crime in Percyville is getting out of hand. Maybe we should get the state to send a patrol out there more often."

"Maybe an officer should move there."

"Maybe you're right. Wonder who we could get."

"Piggy would fit right in."

Chief laughed. "Any other updates?"

"Those are the serious ones. I just got started. You're going to love these." Loni flipped another page. "A man was arrested for beating his wife with a very large dill pickle. She said she preferred it to him and he lost it."

Chief groaned. "That's awful, Loni. Next."

Loni flipped another page. "Got a call to a break-in. Front door was unlocked so the owner called 911. They found the loot in a pile on the living room floor and the perp in the Jacuzzi in the master bedroom. That one needs to go to the grand jury next Monday, but I can't find the DA anywhere."

Chief's blank stare at Loni told her that she wasn't going to find anything out from him about Jimmy Lange. She kept on talking about the cases. "This perp robbed the Shell station down on the corner last night. The one that stays open all night? Wore a ski mask. Handed them a note rather than speak. Only problem is he didn't change his service shirt with his name on it. And the company he worked for. The boys in blue have already picked him up."

"Last one for this report. Caught a thief that turned out to be a cat that made off with some rather valuable things."

"I'm not in the mood for a joke, Loni."

"No, no. All true."

"What'd the cat steal?"

"Along with clothes and other shit, the cat took a Rolex watch and a valuable engagement ring." Loni flipped her notebook closed and started to her feet. "That's it."

"Wait a minute. How about the Carboni case?

"Nothing to add, Chief. Piggy's still interviewing."

Chief nodded acceptance. "Heard you had a dustup. Anything there?"

Loni shook her head no. "Not yet. Nothing at the scene except a flashlight to tell me anything. Turned it over to Adanna. Bobbi is checking trauma centers for a shooting victim. Let you know what I find." Loni ducked her head. "I can tell you it scared the wholly crap out of me. Been a while since anything got that close."

"Got a call from the DA. He thinks you're too close to the case, Loni. Maybe even interfering." The chief sounded resolute. "He wants you to back off and let Piggy handle it."

"Is the DA finally back in his office? I need to see him." Loni wondered why he hadn't said something earlier.

Chief answered. "Guess so. He didn't say where he was."

"I'll talk to Piggy," Loni said. "I already set up a trip to the hospital as soon as I'm done here. When I'm done with that, I'll give Piggy more of a free reign."

Chief turned and stared out the window. Feeling dismissed, Loni went upstairs where she found Piggy rifling through the top drawer of her desk.

"Piggy! What the hell!"

"Just looking for a pencil, Lieut. Don't get bent outta shape."

Loni considered asking him what he was really look for but figured she wouldn't get an answer out of him. "Why aren't you out on the job I gave you?"

Piggy stuck his chin out. "Found a couple of uniforms to do it." He grinned. "Should've heard how excited they got."

"Piggy!"

"It's just a goddamn cat, Lieut."

Loni groaned as she pulled on her coat. Out in the squad room, she yelled back, "Come on Piggy. We're going to the hospital."

"Why? You sick, Lieut?"

"Not yet."

"I'm driving."

"Like hell!"

The second they climbed into the police car, Piggy suddenly started the loudest hiccupping Loni ever heard. "Would you stop that?"

"Can't help it. Never could (hic) stop (hic) it."

"How long does it last?"

"Some (hic) time (hic) for hours (hic)."

"Put your head down, chin as close to your chest as you can get it, and keep it there until they stop or you stop breathing."

"What (hic) for?"

"Do it!"

Loni waited a minute until Piggy stopped hiccupping. "Done?"

"Wow, Lieut. How'd you know about that!"

"Old Indian cure, Piggy. Learned it from my Apache grandma."

"Thanks, Lieut. It can really start hurting after a while."

Adanna was standing in the hospital parking lot as they pulled in. Loni and Adanna skirted puddles as they walked through the mist, and Piggy splashed through the water. Watching Piggy, Adanna grinned at Loni. "Beaut of a storm last night, Lieutenant. Flooded my place."

"Yeah," Loni agreed. "Had a tree come down that nearly blocked me in getting to work. You have any damage?"

"Some. My back bedroom's carpet got wet. Washed my boyfriend's boat right out of my carport and out to sea. Pray I never see that ugly thing again. Always a blessing in everything. Right, Lieutenant?"

Loni laughed at Adanna's chatter. "And I got some firewood." They paused at the hospital entrance and Loni opened the large glass door for Adanna. "Don't know how you do it, but you always make me feel good. Somehow you turn sour lemons into lemonade. That's a special talent."

"You got that right. That feel-good high is one of the ways we keep going, looking forward for the next high."

"I think you got something there. Certainly, the reason for drugs."

"And sex."

"And eating good food."

"And holding a child." Adanna smiled at that one.

"Or hurt an animal because they could. I've seen too much of that. And, sometimes, some men beat on their wives to get that high."

Adanna grimaced in pain. "Had an ex-husband like that. He would get this shiny gleam in his eyes like he was really happy. I knew to either duck or run."

"What does your boyfriend think about his boat being gone?"

"He doesn't know yet. He's a truck driver on a long haul. I figured when he was next due to get home that I'd leave him a note with the sad news and visit my mother."

Loni laughed again. "Good thinking." At the desk inside, Loni introduced the three of them to the hospital guard and showed him their search warrant. The squat man had the thick neck of a weight lifter, and his skin matched his brown uniform. "Benny," Loni said, reading his name tag. "Do you have a map of the locations of your security cameras?"

"Jeez, Lieutenant. Don't need one. They're everywhere. All the hallways. Entrances. Exits."

"And the pediatric floor?"

"On the door entering the floor."

"No cameras in the rooms?"

"Nope. Invasion of privacy."

"Right. We were warned to be careful. Benny, we need two things. First, take us to Carlotta Carboni's locker. And anywhere else she might have left something." Loni looked over at Piggy standing off to the side and unusually quiet. "Piggy. You okay?"

All she got was a reluctant nod. "After you finish, help Detective Washington access your security recording on the pediatric floor door for the night shift of the seventh through the tenth and email the images to our office computer. Can you do that?"

"We might can do that." Benny turned to the young woman sitting next to him. "Joyce, show them where they need to go, okay?" The young woman gracefully moved her bulk out of her chair and rounded the corner into a long hallway, her long, dark brown hair swinging about her massive shoulders as she waited for them to follow. Another weightlifter, Loni decided, watching muscles ripple through the heavy dark blue uniform.

"Thanks." Loni said turning back to Benny. "Piggy, you know Bobbi's email address. Get the images downloaded to her."

"Jesus, Lieut. I know how to do my job." Piggy nodded his round head at Loni as he stood, seemingly stuck in place.

"It would help if you followed Benny."

Piggy's head weaved back and forth as he finally admitted, "My daddy died here. Choked to death. God, I hate this place. You got a cure for choking?"

"Only with swallowing wrong. Stick your arms in the air over your head far as you can. It opens the airway."

Piggy shook his head. "Wouldn't've saved him."

"Didn't you learn the Heimlich maneuver in your first-aid classes?"

"Couldn't remember it."

Loni decided to leave him alone. She turned back to the security officer, hoping his big, square open face meant that he had lots of patience. "Are you okay with that?"

"Sure. You planning on taking stuff from Miss Carboni's locker?"

"Yes. Don't know what else."

"How long you gonna keep the stuff?"

"Until the case is solved, probably."

"I have to notify the head office."

Piggy managed to follow behind the security officer and disappear through a door behind the counter before Loni followed Joyce down the hall. Falling behind, Loni listened to the scraping sound between the woman's thighs from the rough cloth on her uniform mixed in with the clicking of her boots as she walked in front of her and Adanna. Loni stayed behind, giving the woman space to swing her body down the hall through a door marked "Employees Only." They thanked the guard and watched her leave before inspecting Carboni's locker. "You have any idea what we're looking for?" Adanna asked.

"No idea."

Loni hoped they would be lucky enough to find a smoking gun, and it took the rest of the afternoon to bag and tag everything from Carboni's locker. Along with extra uniforms and shoes, an assortment of notebooks, files, and messy makeup filled the locker. Loni was still trying to decipher the notebooks when Adanna finished collecting the last of the fingerprints from around the door.

Rain was coming down in buckets when they approached the hospital exit. "What do you think, Lieutenant? Would I get less wet if I ran or walked to my car?" Adanna asked.

"Couldn't tell you. The last time I was at the Shell station, I asked an old timer there how long it would take me to get to Wilsonville. She said, 'It takes two hours. It don't matter whether you drive fast or you drive slow, it takes two hours.' Might be the same for the rain."

"Wet is wet, huh. Glad this stuff is in plastic bags." Adanna studied them. "Think they'd make a good umbrella?"

Loni grinned at her antics. "Do me a favor and process them as fast as you can. I've got a gut feeling that something really bad is about to go down. Hopefully this," Loni pointed at their evidence, "will help us figure out what's going on before the bad happens.

Adanna nodded in agreement. "We'll find out soon. As Cleatus would say, 'Lord willing and the creeks don't rise.'"

"Did you find anything useful in Carboni's house?"

"Not really, Lieutenant, although I must say it's been an eye-opener. You remember her toys?"

"Hard to forget."

"We got an office pool to guess what some of them are. You're welcome to take part."

Loni ducked her head to hide the blush. "Maybe next time."

"You get extra for the best descriptions." Adanna grinned. "You blushing, Loni?" Laughing, Adanna pushed out the door with the plastic bags swinging over her head and waved goodbye just as Piggy waddled up to Loni.

"Got 'em, Lieut. Sent the stuff to Bobbi's email." Piggy reported as he watched Adanna run off through the rain. "Hell of a mess out there. You ready to brave it?"

"I'll stand here just a minute to see if it lets up."

Piggy snorted. "Newbie. I can see our car from here. Why can'tcha unlock it for me so I can get outta this place."

Loni grinned and used the remote to unlock the car doors. "Go for it!" Piggy lurched into the rain after Adanna.

Before she could follow Piggy, Benny call out to her. "Got a minute?" He shuffled his feet a few times and stared down at the floor before he could speak.

"I hate gossip but I just want you to know, I seen Guy Murphy and Carlotta Carboni making out in his car a couple of times when I was patrolling the parking garage."

"Thanks. I appreciate the information." Loni tapped the stocky man's shoulder. "Anything that helps solve a murder isn't gossip. Okay? Let me know if you think of anything else," she said before she ran into the rain.

Chapter Eleven

"Come on, Coco," Loni called. "You might be useful this afternoon." The fuzzy brown dog leaped around her with joyous yelps as Loni walked to her loaner pickup truck from the police department salvage lot. She promised to have it back in two days for the police auction, hoping it would last that long. The paint had been chipped so badly the actual color was no longer discernable, the jeep fenders that didn't quite fit rattled at every bump. Even worse was the camper shell with its ripped-out screens. One window wouldn't close, and the back door needed a crowbar to pry it open. No matter, Loni was glad to have something until her insurance paid out. Maybe she should rent a loaner.

Coco rode shotgun with a doggy-smile the entire way to the police station. Loni always felt guilty when she didn't pay more attention to the dog. Everywhere else she had worked, Coco had worked with her to find drugs. In Harborville, she didn't need Coco's skills because the Drug Investigations Unit had their own dogs.

The dog followed close at Loni's heels as they walked into the squad room. The detectives were busy, but Coco got their attention, wandering among them and shoving her nose under their arms. Coco made a wide circle around Piggy as she headed for Cleatus. Making a long swipe with her tongue at his chin, she crawled under the desk and refused to come out.

"Leave her." Cleatus smiled at the dog. "If'n we're goin' to work together, we best be friends."

"Fine." Loni snipped at the dog as she walked away. "Bobbi, in my office, okay?"

"Sure."

"Shut the door," Loni told Bobbi. "I need to work on the Carboni case but I don't want the DA to know. Seems he told the chief to tell me to leave it with Piggy. You okay with doing this on the QT with me?"

"Of course, Lieutenant. I don't like the way Piggy's investigating this either. Sometimes he's so back-hill bigoted against everything but white men. His folks came from the Ku Klux Klan that settled in southern Oregon, you know. They moved up on Lackly River when Piggy was a kid which wasn't much better. I don't think he'll ever overcome it."

"Or want to, I'm afraid. We're all bigoted. It's a protective instinct against the unfamiliar." The frown on Loni's broad forehead accented her high cheekbones and midnight black hair from her Native American heritage. "It's fighting that instinct and overcoming our biases that separates us from animals." Loni shook her head in disgust. "The DA's not the only one resisting my working this case. How's it going with research on Carboni? Anything I can use?"

"Just the usual education for nurses. Her grades were average. There's also some indication she partied big at school with no obvious income to pay for it. No inheritance. No indication she was from a rich family." Bobbi checked her notes. "Just the opposite, in fact. Went to school on scholarships. She was whip smart. Came from trailer trash from what I found. Must have been hard to dig out of that."

"Damn!" Loni leaned back in her chair and thought a few minutes. "Anybody else show income discrepancies?"

"Yeah. Remember those money transfers from that Chicago bank? Looks like they came from a New York account that apparently belongs to Doctor Giovanna's ex-husband, Barelli Giovanni. The interesting piece is his large amounts of money in foreign banks. And somebody else is looking through his books."

Loni's mind raced. Damn. She hoped Jenna wasn't part of that! "Do you know who?"

"Might be the IRS. At least that's who keeps poking back at me."

"Maybe we better back off Giovanni's banking for now," Loni suggested. "Before they block us doing anything else." Worried about Jenna, Loni spun her desk chair around a couple of circles before Piggy burst into her office. She motioned a warning to Bobbi and changed the subject. "DMV still hassling you on the printout of possible owners of that Ford?"

"Really?" Piggy laughed. "You got one of those too?"

"Cute, Piggy. No, I don't."

Piggy perked up. "What Ford?"

"Hit and run this morning," Loni said. "Witnesses described a king cab black Ford pickup."

Bobbi caught on to the change in subject. ""Yes, the jerks. But I'm not giving up."

"What truck?" Piggy asked again.

"I just said. A black long bed, king cab Ford pickup." Loni answered.

Piggy doubled up in laughter. "You have any idea how many rednecks around here own that kind of pickup? They even beat out them stupid lesbians driving sporty SUV's like Ginger out there. Highway patrol has one. Even we have one." Piggy cackled again. "Why don't I go arrest it and bring that one in?"

"Straight women got sporty SUV's, too," Bobbi informed Piggy. "I drive one. What do you drive?"

"I did drive a souped-up Charger that we picked up in a drug bust."

"What do you mean 'did drive'?"

"I totaled that one a week ago."

"Really? How?"

"Chasing a big honker Humvee when I sort of hydroplaned down a hill. Both of us went into a telephone pole. Caught them though. Drugs everywhere, even in the exhaust pipe." Piggy laughed so hard he had to hold on to his belly. "That's what slowed them down and made it easy to catch em."

"The Charger got totaled on a telephone pole?"

"What'd I just say?"

"I'm not sure anymore."

"I never heard about that case. Why didn't you turn it in?" Loni asked.

Piggy shrugged. "Didn't want to do the paperwork so I gave it to drugs."

Loni spun in exasperation. "Just . . . oh, hell, Piggy. Have you finished checking out who the cat stole from?"

"Give me a break! I ain't had no time."

"Why not?"

"Just ain't."

"Piggy? What do you want?"

"A cop brought up a teen that robbed some woman."

"Did you search the teen?"

"I ain't feeling around nobody's woohoo."

"Not there, Piggy, for Christ sake! Her purse and pockets!"

Piggy huffed and stalked out. Loni watched him hand the teen off to Ginger who gently wrapped the sobbing girl in an arm as she walked her to the interrogation room. Watching them, Bobbi sputtered about Piggy's laziness as she stood up to leave.

"Wait, Bobbi. Come back and close the door. I'm not quite finished."

Bobbi closed the door again and waited.

"I want to go through the hospital images. Can you set it up in the conference room now?"

"Sure." Bobbi opened the door again.

Loni followed Bobbi out of her office and walked over to Harry and Don. "Boys? We need to finish up your drug case. How's the girl who got shot?"

"Stopped by the hospital on our way in, Lieutenant. She was lucky," Don reported. "According to the hospital, the bullet just clipped the fatty part of the side of her chest next to her elbow. A through and through, the bullet so hot it nearly cauterized the flesh."

"Have you asked her who shot her?"

"She said it was her boyfriend. We're just waiting for a search warrant before we go pick him up. If we can ever find him."

"Can't you use probable cause to arrest him?"

"The DA hates it when we use probable cause and usually throws it out."

"Anyway lieutenant," Harry continued the conversation. "Can't find the DA anywhere."

"Then get a Ramey warrant."

"What! Wait a minute!" Ginger interrupted. "Her own boyfriend shot her? Why?"

"You surprised?" Piggy said. "Ain't it always the husband or boyfriend? She be deserving, I'm sure."

"According to the hospital report, he stole a batch of cannabis plants from her father, and she tried to get them back. He was so scared of her father he shot her. Then he told her he didn't mean to hit her. Just wanted to scare her off so she'd go home. She countered that he was a good shot and knew exactly what he was doing."

"Huh," Piggy said. "It's just wrong for illegal pot to be so much cheaper."

"You got a point there, Piggy. Why bother legalizing it."

"That's what I just said."

"Okay, okay." Loni over-rode the chatter. "You need to go out there and make sure the place is clean. Cleatus. You're our agricultural expert. Go with Harry and Don. Coco can help you."

"Sure Boz." Cleatus reached down and petted Coco's head as he baby-talked her. "You be good girl, yes you are, yes you are."

Shaking her head, Loni watched them packing up with a stern warning. "Cleatus? If you bring that dog back covered in mud, take her through a hosing downstairs before you bring her back up here. You hear me?"

Cleatus grinned, his teeth gleaming in his beautiful black face. "Hee, Coco. You my girl. I expect a good time, hear? Ya raddy to go?"

Coco stood, staring at Cleatus, unmoving, as she canted her brown head.

"Cleatus." Loni started laughing. "She doesn't understand your dialect. Try to use plain English when you talk to her."

Loni waited until they disappeared down the stairs before she turned back to Piggy. "Where's your report on the cat thief, Piggy."

Piggy responded indifferently. "Haven't heard from my boys yet."

"Maybe you should go find them."

Piggy ignored her again. "I still got a murder case to work, remember?"

"Okaaay, then. Go to Guy Murphy's house and ask him about his alibi." Loni didn't move from her office doorway as she stared at Piggy. "Why are you still here?"

"Ya see that storm out there? I think that big one predicted is arrived. Look at that!" Piggy pointed to the rain slashing at the windows.

"Damn it, Piggy. That's just a little Oregon dry rain. The big one's not due 'til Wednesday night, now get your ass out there and find those owners!"

Ginger broke up in giggles as Piggy squirmed for a while before getting out of his chair. Dragging his jacket, he slogged to the elevator and faced the door. It took a long time for it to open, and Loni waited to continue with Bobbi until she heard the elevator squawking away.

"While you're finishing up your report, Ginger, pick up the calls, will you?" Loni said, "Bobbi and I are going into the conference room." With her computer, Loni followed Bobbi into the conference room in the back of the squad room. The long room had a white board on both ends, a magnetic board across the back, and a table holding eight chairs in the center. The walls were totally blank. No windows anywhere. Not even a clock. Loni spread out the photos identifying the night shift staff in the pediatric floor while Bobbi retrieved the hospital files from the computer.

Loni opened a note pad and said, "What we need to find out is who entered and exited the pediatric floor during the night shift on the times following the children's admissions to the hospital. That should tell us who maybe worked with Carboni. Assuming it was her."

"If we list everyone, we should know something."

"Something is right." Loni fidgeted. "So let's list what we do know. We know the first child was admitted on the seventh, two of them on the eighth, and the last one on the tenth. That makes four nights to watch."

"Sounds doable," Bobbi replied. "We can line up the photos from the hospital personnel in front of us to identify who comes and goes."

"Good idea." Loni arranged the pictures. "We'll put anyone on duty and likely suspects in the front row. That includes workers such as security staff and cleaners."

"In other words, anyone assigned to the pediatric floor."

Loni stood and began pacing back and forth at the blackboard as she wrote the names Bobbi gave her across the top. Suddenly Ginger appeared waving a phone in front of Loni who kept writing. Finally Ginger grabbed Loni's arm. "Stop, damnit!" Ginger insisted. "I need to tell you. That alibi for Guy Murphy you been trying to get? There's a patrol cop on the phone. He said Piggy sent him to get an alibi? He's at Guy Murphy's apartment now. Said to tell you that Guy does have an alibi for Carboni's murder. The woman he's living with said that Guy was in bed with her the morning Carboni was murdered. He didn't leave for work until ten o'clock. Adanna said she called his office. He was in a meeting after that. His secretary said he didn't even leave the meeting to pee. And she's sure because she had a bet going with a co-worker. Apparently Guy has a really big bladder. Wish I had one. I have to stop every five minutes. It was even worse when I was pregnant. How's your bladder, Lieutenant?"

Loni sat down in utter disappointment. "What the hell do we do now?"

Bobbi interrupted. "We keep going, Lieutenant. We still need to know who kill the boy. Maybe that's the murderer."

Ginger stood, watching them. "Whatcha doing, anyhow?'

"I'm going against orders, Ginger. I could use your help, but you could get in trouble."

"You kidding? That's what I live for." Ginger leaned over Loni's shoulder.

"Stop breathing down my neck!"

Ginger laughed and blew on her ear. "Enjoy it, dear. It'll be a long time before you feel that again."

Loni groaned. "I'm sure you're right. Move your ass anyway." Loni watched Ginger sit beside her.

"Careful how you talk to a pregnant woman, Lieutenant."

"Wait! I thought you were a lesbian."

Ginger guffawed a big laugh. "Lesbians don't get pregnant?"

"Not players."

"I'm not a player, Lieutenant. I just like to flirt. So does my wife but we always go home together."

"Know what, Ginger? That's incredible. Congratulations. Your first?"

Ginger grinned. "Nope. Got a little two-year-old girl named Tulip and a mother-in-law that loves to keep our Tulip."

"Tulip? You named a kid Tulip?"

"Don't ya love tulips?"

"I love Bat Face Cuphea's, too, but that's . . . oh, hell. Bobbi, play the surveillance images."

"Wait. What are we doing again?"

Loni said, "We're going through the hospital surveillance files along with these photos to find the persons who extracted bone marrow from four children. If you want to help, look for anyone who was on the pediatric floor at the same time as anyone else. We need two people working together to do the aspirations. We think someone was helping Carboni but we can't prove it." Loni pointed at the photos lined up on the table. "Most of these photos are from the hospital's staff directory of those assigned to the pediatrics floor. The rest are those with possible knowledge of bone marrow aspiration."

Ginger's bright blue eyes sparked her anger. "Gotta tell ya I don't give a crap about this Carboni woman, but I'm really upset with the child's death. If that had been my beautiful Tulip."

Bobbi echoed Ginger's rant. "Me too, Ginger. Me too."

"I agree and understand, ladies and that is our highest priority but we got to start somewhere and I think finding who killed Carboni will likely be the person or person's responsible for the child's death."

"Sounds good. What can I do?"

Bobbi explained further. "We sorted them according to administration, doctors, nurses, and maintenance."

"The uniforms and general clothing should help us there," Loni noted.

"Yeah," Ginger added. "If they got pretty ties, they're important shits." She pointed at a photo of one of the doctors.

"Most ties are pretty, Ginger. What are you talking about?"

"You know. All them Ivy League schools where those doctors and administrators go have their own tie. Tells everybody how important they are."

"Wait! What schools?"

"You know. Like Harvard, Dartmouth, Cornell, Princeton, Penn, Yale, Columbia. Like that."

"How do you know all that, Ginger?"

"My older brother went to Yale. When he came home, he showed me pictures of the clothes they wore and made me learn the ties so I'd think he was important." Ginger giggled. "Jerk! He flunked out before he could get one. Still, it was a lesson I never forgot."

Bobbi laughed. "Good thing for us they don't have visiting hours on the night shift. Hate to have to identify all those visitors."

"In this hick town?" Ginger questioned. "I doubt it."

Bobbi chuckled in agreement.

"Okay," Loni turned back to the job. "First. What do we need to know?"

"How long an aspiration takes?"

"Got that, Ginger. Around fifteen to twenty minutes. What else?"

"Tools needed, where they got them, did they sign them out?"

"Good. What else?"

"How often a shift are the children assessed or looked in on?"

"Look for routines. Good." Loni paused a few seconds. "Okay. We'll look at the night shift files on November seventeenth, eighteenth, nineteenth and twentieth and note how long each person stayed, who was there together, and how often. We know it takes at least two people. Okay, Bobbi, forward it nice and slow."

After three grueling hours, Loni summarized their notes on the blackboard. "Let's start by listing all the people who entered the pediatric floor on those dates. We found six in all. Carlotta Carboni. Doctor Giovanni. Two nurses, two cleaning women, and one maintenance man. According to these photos, the nurses are Alba Arnold and Mike Kenyon. The cleaning ladies are Marge Kern and Virginia Makay. The maintenance man is Elmore Leaky."

"Okay. Let's start with Carboni." Loni wrote her initials on the board. and drew a line from her initials to the bottom of the board. "Give me the rest of them." Loni continued until all six initials were listed. "Okay, Bobbi, give me the times and duration."

"The first time we see Carboni entering the pediatric floor on the seventeenth is at one am for an hour. Then again at three-ten am for twenty-five minutes. She also enters on the eighteenth and nineteenth at one am for one and a half hours and three am for nineteen minutes and on the twentieth at one am for an hour and three-twenty am for nineteen minutes."

On a vertical line Loni wrote in the dates and times when Carboni was seen entering the pediatric floor.

"Right. Next is Doctor Giovanni."

"She went in on the twentieth at three-forty with her crash team when they responded to the emergency call. They were there for forty-three minutes and left together."

"The two nurses?"

"Alba Arnold appeared with Carboni at one am all four nights, the beginning of her shift and left with Carboni. According to the records that was the time they assessed the children for medication, temperatures, blood pressure, and whatever."

"Have we got a record of her doing that?"

"No," Bobbi answered. "I'll make a note to check it out."

Ginger added, "She appeared again at three-fifteen all four nights. She stayed for an average of thirty minutes."

Loni turned to Ginger and saw Piggy looking over her shoulder. "What the hell, Piggy. Back already?"

Piggy attempted to look over Loni's shoulder. "Couldn't find my boys. Out on a call somewheres."

"Damn, Piggy," Loni blocked his view and pushed him toward the door. "I told the chief we would have that case turned in by the end of the work day. Go find them or you'll be spending the night working on it."

"Know what? You're mean." Piggy complained. "Whatcha doing in there anyway."

"Not your purview, Piggy. Now, go!" Loni watched Piggy until the elevator doors closed before she went back to the room and the board. "Where were we?"

"Alba Arnold appeared again at four every night for a half hour."

"That it for her?"

"Yup."

"Who's next?"

"The other nurse, Mike Kenyon."

"He entered the pediatric floor on the seventeenth at three-ten am and five am. He also entered on the eighteenth at three am and five am, the ninetieth at three am and five am, and on the twentieth at three am and five am."

Loni looked at Bobbi. "Three's the same time Carboni was there. Did you check any background on him?"

"Nope."

"I think we need to know more about Mister Mike Kenyon." Loni turned to Ginger. "And the cleaning crew?"

"That'd be Marge Kern and Virginia Makay. They came together at midnight and were gone by one."

"And the maintenance man?"

"He went in at one-thirty am with an arm full of light bulbs and was out ten minutes later."

"Probably routine maintenance replacing light bulbs on all the floors."

"What happened to the doctor on call?"

"Never entered the floor."

"Anybody find out why?"

"No."

"Ginger. Aren't you friends with one of the guards?"

"Yeah."

"In the morning, go to the hospital on the low down and ask her. Can you do that? And find out what you can about Mike Kenyon?"

"Sure. You won't dock me if I'm late?"

"Have I ever?"

Loni studied her chart on the blackboard. "Looks like the only two people entering the floor at the same time each night is Carlotta Carboni and Mike Kenyon."

"And the two cleaning women."

"Right. Better not assume they're innocent." Loni turned back to the board. "Doctor Giovanni appeared only once, and that was the last night when the child died. No other doctor showed up until Doctor Giovanni answered the emergency call."

"Looks like." Ginger agreed

Loni rocked back in her chair, mulling. "If the child died close to aspiration, that would indicate Carboni was involved. Assuming autopsy will tell us time of aspiration and time of death, we can also assume Carlotta Carboni and Mike did the aspiration. What's still bothering me is where Guy fits in. I think we need to talk to his ex-wife. Let's see if she knows anything."

"I can do that in the morning on my way in to work," Ginger volunteered.

"Thanks, Ginger but you got the hospital, remember? I think I'll do that on my way home tonight." Loni turned to Bobbi. "We also need to know more about Mike. Would you look into his background?"

"Sure."

Loni had just finished erasing the blackboard when the cell phone in her pocket vibrated. She answered it. With a "thanks" she quickly hung up. "That was the mayor's office. The town's shutting down Thursday for the storm."

A loud explosion of voices burst into the room from the stairs with Cleatus, Harry, and Don trying to talk over each other as Ginger scooted to her desk. Loni and Bobbi were right behind her. Coco barked, adding to the cacophony, and loped over to Loni who got down on her knees and hugged a damp dog. The elevator expelled Piggy as she listened to the report on the cannabis farm.

"Holes everywhere from plants pulled up, but we couldn't prove anything." Harry reported. "Coco found bits of leaves and seed everywhere but nothing big enough to bring them in."

"But they ain't sitting in high cotton now." Cleatus smiled. "Like a tornado just went through and left a real pretty sight."

"Signs of a big fire made it look like he had to burn what the kid didn't steal," Harry added.

Loni raised an eyebrow. "You find the kid who did the shooting?"

"Nope." Cleatus answered, "He'd left outta there faster tha' green grass through a goose."

Harry grinned at Cleatus. "Last time his mother saw him he was hightailing it out a town in his beat-up truck. She said he took most everything he owned with him and said he wouldn't be back. She said good riddance."

Piggy said, "I didn't have any better luck with my case either. Still can't find my patrol boys." Piggy turned to Cleatus. "I think you should have left that pot farmer alone. It's legal now, you know."

"It's the job, Pigs."

"But it's cheaper to buy the stuff on the street!"

Don spoke up. "Problem with street cannabis is that you don't know what quality you're getting."

"Hell," Harry asked, "is it even a good thing to legalize it? It's just another dangerous drug."

"Better for you than booze," Don argued.

"I'd admit Don is right," Cleatus said. "There's no definitive evidence cannabis makes a body crazy or dumb. Or plagued with psychotic attacks. Or messed up performance. Or any lasting effects. And it's much easier on us than road sody."

"What'd Cleatus say?" Piggy asked Ginger.

"Jeez dimwit. It's having open booze outside." Ginger answered.

"Somebody tell me what name to put on this file?" Bobbi demanded.

"Otis Fama." Cleatus told her.

"Sorry, Cleatus. What was that name again?" Bobbi asked.

"Otis Fama."

"Otis What?"

"Fama! Didn't y'all know? Corn shucking and winnowing."

"Spell it."

"F-A-R-M-E-R. Fama."

"Oh." Bobbi laughed so hard she was gasping. "Farmer!"

"That's what I said," Cleatus insisted. "Otis Fama."

"See! Cleatus already said, Bobbi," Piggy flung his arms around in exasperation. "Pay attention for once."

"Sorry, Cleatus."

On her way home Loni stopped at Guy's house, not looking forward to the conversation with his ex-wife. She knocked, and a woman opened the door. From the expression on her face, Loni decided not to invite herself in.

"We heard you wanted to ask me about my ex," the woman snapped.

Loni nodded in surprise.

"Only strange thing I heard was a conversation with the DA. Guy wanted to borrow his pickup truck."

"That seems to be a common thing. Borrowing his truck."

"Guess so. He said everybody did it. Guess the DA didn't care who took it. I asked him what for, and he said to go fishing. Really? Guy didn't fish. He didn't even own a fishing pole."

"And yes, I saw him spending lots of money. He said he was winning in card games, but I don't know where he was getting it from. I can tell you I didn't get any of it. Said he also won at the horses but I didn't believe him. He hates horses."

Loni tended to accept her story. Especially when she talked about how much she despised him. Most interesting to Loni, however, was that Carlotta broke up her marriage. "Mind telling me where you were on the morning Carlotta was killed?"

"Working my ass off." Guy's ex-wife stuck her finger in Loni's face. "Don't you come in here accusing me of her murder. It's not that I wasn't grateful to her for taking the lying, cheating, sonofabitch off my hands anyway."

Chapter Twelve

Loni tapped a pencil on her desk in an uneven drumbeat and ruminated about what to do with the information on who might have aspirated the bone marrow. Half-pissed, she grumbled to herself about how the DA would ignore anything she sent him. "Oh, hell!" She threw the pencil down and spun her chair as if she were trying to run from the mind hounds baying in her head. At the sound of a ringing phone, she jerked and grabbed her desk to stop the spin. She noted the caller's I.D. and snapped into the phone, "Check's in the mail."

The deep bark of a laugh was loud enough that she pulled the receiver away from her ear and pressed the speaker. "Charlie Orville, here. Morning to you, Lieutenant. How much?"

Loni grinned at the booming voice. "Wow! A call from the mayor himself. How'd I get so lucky?"

"Must be that clean living you brag about. Never understood how you can live without a shot of good old aged mellow bourbon every morning. Only way to start the day right."

"Hard to miss what you never had."

"Don't know where you got that piece of shit euphemism. But we can debate that another time. You working on the child death case?"

"Sort of. DA's got me hogtied."

"Meaning?"

"He has the wrong killer, but he won't believe me. So I'm working on the QT."

"You know who the killer is?"

"Got a suspicion but not enough proof."

"You know how you're going to get the proof?"

"Not a clue."

"Okaaay. So, the pathologist listed the child that died at the hospital as possible negligent homicide. Tell me what you know."

"When did you become my boss?"

"Humor me."

Loni groaned to herself and attempted to explain, "The pathologist did a tox screen and found a possible lethal trace of benzodiazepine. The hip was prepped with betadine, and there was a puncture wound plus evidence on the bone from the grinding of a trocar aspirating bone marrow. I asked the pathologist how close was the death of the child to the aspiration. He went vague."

"Translate for me."

"Somebody took out bone marrow which could have killed the child."

"But you can't prove anything?" Charlie asked.

"Nothing for sure about the death. The pathologist said he was sick enough that the benzodiazepine in his system could have caused respiratory arrest which is what killed him."

"In other words, even if you knew who did it, you couldn't prove anything."

"That's about it."

"Do you have a copy of the autopsy yet?"

"No. And I don't know what the hang up is, exactly. Seems the DA is holding on to it."

"When you get a copy, fax one to me."

"Sure. But I still want to know why you are interested."

Charlie ignored her comment. "You said there were other children?"

"So far as we know, three other children have signs of bone marrow aspiration. Why are you asking?"

Charlie huffed. "The chief's worried about having a murder in our town. Bad for our reputation as a vacation spot. He's not sure you should be the one working this case. Didn't say why. You said you got a suspect?"

"Getting there. Problem is we found our main suspect dead. So badly brutalized I can't tell if it's related to the child death or a crime of passion. I'm looking at one of the nurses as someone who may have helped Carlotta Carboni with the aspirations. If it was Carboni. Maybe he murdered her because she caught him. Maybe he didn't. Maybe one of her lovers did it."

"Hidey ho, cowboy. Go get 'em."

"Golly gee, Mister Mayor. Go piss up wind." Loni hung up to Charlie's laughter.

The phone rang again as soon as Loni hung up. She picked it up and said, "Morning, Mister DA. You're a hard man to find. Heard you were finally back in town. Welcome home." A frown crossed her forehead as she listened a few minutes before slamming down the receiver. "Shit! Shit!" she yelled. She thought for a few minutes before she got up and walked out her office door. "Piggy, we have to gather up all our paperwork on the Carboni case and take it to the DA." Loni turned around. "Bobby. Help Piggy pack. When you finish, send the DA the hospital files."

"Why, Lieutenant?"

"DA says hospital's claiming we got it without the hospital's permission because we didn't have a warrant. He also said he didn't need them anyway."

"Says who?"

"Apparently, the DA had an epiphany. He's arraigning the alleged killer as we speak."

Piggy turned to Bobbi. "What the fuck's an apiff—"

"Ya see, my main man," Cleatus said, "don' piss on ma' leg and tell me it rainin'."

Piggy turned to Ginger. "What the fuck does that mean?" Throwing his arms in the air, Piggy yelled. "Never mind. I don't even care."

Loni helped Piggy and Bobbi repack the box including all the financial printouts and photos from the crime scene. Struggling with the box, Piggy left. Loni turned back to Bobbi. "Keep a copy of the hospital files before you send them on."

Bobbi grinned. "They're already in the cloud. You can download them whenever you want."

Within a few minutes, the phone rang again. Loni frowned, "What now?"

The Chief said, "Hey, Loni. The DA wants your paperwork on the Carlotta Carboni's case."

"I already sent it with Piggy. What do you know about this?"

"Only that the DA wants to talk to you about the case."

"On my way." The phone was dead before Loni even finished. She stretched, popping a few joints as she groaned. "Headed to the DA's, Bobbi. Hold down the fort."

Loni walked into the DA's office and found Piggy sitting next to the desk with the file box at his feet. The DA was on the phone. He was about five foot five with thin dark hair skin so smooth that Loni couldn't begin to guess how old he was. A huge number of degrees, awards, trophies, certificates, badges, and memorabilia related to winning anything from fishing, bowling, and shooting covered all four walls. Some were even taped to the back of the office door. She had never seen him smile. "Afternoon, sir," Loni nervously greeted him as he hung up the phone, nodded, and perched on the edge of a short couch.

"I've notified the media we have the killer."

"But—"

"Is this all the evidence you have?" The DA nodded at the box at Piggy's feet.

"No, and—"

"Get it now. Send everything you have and get back to your other cases."

"But—"

"Don't make me repeat myself."

"Just like I told her, Jimmy," Piggy said. "The doc did it, but she won't listen."

Loni frowned. "Are you trying to circumvent me, Piggy?"

"Whatever the hell that means," Piggy spit back. "The DA ought to know how wrong you are."

"Piggy!" Loni said in disgust. "Anytime I'd agree with you, we'd both be wrong."

"Children!" Jimmy Lange barked. "Play nice." He pointed to the box. "Is this everything? Including any exculpatory evidence?"

"Everything we have on paper."

"I'm indicting her this morning on two counts of Murder One and one count of Criminal Negligence. I need everything you have for the preliminary hearing."

"Who are you indicting?"

"Doctor Jenna Giovanni. She has an arraignment scheduled for eleven. I have enough for a conviction."

"But that's not true, sir," Loni blurted out. "She didn't kill Carlotta Carboni and I can prove it! Even more to the point, somebody out there is trying to kill her. Like maybe the real killer?"

"I'm not referring to the Carboni case. I'm talking about a new murder."

"New murder?"

"Yes. Guy Murphy was found in his car with a hose in his face."

"Sounds like suicide."

"Not according to the coroner." He nodded at the phone. "That was him on the phone, changing his earlier findings from suicide to murder. He's still at the scene."

A sliver of fear sliced through Loni at the DA's next words.

"I have a unit picking her up and arresting her as we speak."

"What?" Loni carefully modulated her voice, hiding her fear and anger.

Piggy cackled. "Told you I always knowed Doctor Giovanni were guilty. Now it's three murders. Should've kept her in jail and throwed away the key."

"I gave you evidence that proved she had nothing to do with Carlotta's murder. I can also prove she had nothing to do with bone marrow aspiration or the child's death. Whatever information Piggy has given you he pulled out of his ass."

Piggy jumped up and stuck his face close to Loni. "Who cares about Doctor Giovanna or Carlotta Carboni. Those queer sluts deserve ever thing they get."

The DA interrupted Piggy's diatribe. "Piggy, that's enough." He turned to Loni. "You can't prove her innocent of Guy Murphy's death because she doesn't have an alibi. As to the child's death, I've been told a nurse and even most doctors aren't trained to do the aspirations. Just drop it, Loni, and do your damn job!" He stared at her and changed the subject, "Did you check on that explosion on the Lackly River?"

Loni had to sit a few seconds, not willing to drop her argument. "Of course. I sent Piggy."

"Piggy's on the Carboni case. Why did you send him?"

"Because it was clear who the perpetrator was. It was an easy arrest." Buying time to calm her shattered emotions, Loni turned to Piggy. "You need to finish that report."

The DA turned to Piggy. "Well?"

"Did it yesterday."

"It's not on my desk, Piggy."

Piggy shrugged indifferently. "Oh, well."

"Piggy!" the DA warned him.

"The guy was a fisherman blowing off steam. He thought it would be funny to set dynamite sticks in a baby carriage to blow up the bridge."

"Wait a minute. A baby carriage? But won't that—"

Piggy interrupted. "They float, don'tcha know?"

"Wait a minute. They expect babies to float around in a buggy?"

"Of course, don'tcha know? This fisherman dropped it off his boat. He got a mile away afore he fired off the detonator. By the time he blew it, the buggy got caught in a current and sped toward the docks. It sank a couple of fishing boats and blew out a buncha windows and stuff."

"Anybody hurt?"

"Didn't ask."

"Why not?"

"Why would I care? I got the perp. It wasn't easy either, Jimmy. Had to crawl in a crappy kayak with holes in it and paddle way the hell up one of them river sloughs where that there butthole lived. Get this. There's hundreds of them up there, huge, huge family, and all of 'em big, big-time mean." Piggy shivered. "It rained the whole way. It rained so hard I had to shovel water out as fast as I rowed. I never been more miserable my whole life." Shifting in his seat, Piggy ran a pudgy hand over his face before he grinned. "When he saw me, he jumped butt-naked into the river and started swimming until he came eye to eye with a croc." His last word turned into a cackle. "Should've seen him, Jimmy. Turned around and crawled into my kayak, nearly feeding both of us to the crocs." Piggy stopped laughing. "Damn, Jimmy. Nearly broke my paddle on that croc's head tryin' to beat'm away. Then that croc had the unmitigated gall to take ma paddle. Had a hell'a time getting' it back from him."

"Piggy." The DA held up his hand for Piggy to shut up. "That's the biggest lie I ever heard you tell. That story's about as useful as a trap door on your kayak. You know there are not crocs around here. Alligators either as that's what you really should say. Gators eat people, not crocs."

"You kidding me? Ever'thing's around here is dangerous as shit."

"What? That's another crock, Piggy. You live on the coast of Oregon. That means no poisonous snakes. No poisonous plants. No poisonous crawling bugs. Not even cockroaches. And the mosquitoes are blown away faster than they can hatch. So, please, cut the shit."

"Semantics, Jimmy. Semantics and blarney."

Loni stared at Piggy. "Do you even know what that word means?"

"Which one?"

"Never mind. I don't care." Already stressed about Jenna's arrest, Loni grabbed the arm on her couch to keep from running out of the office. Or flattening Piggy.

The DA almost smiled at Loni. "Piggy grew up on Lackly River up one of those Deliverance sloughs. His mother wouldn't let him off the river until he was big enough not to get shot at or raped by a cousin. Nobody hides from him." Seemingly as an afterthought, the DA asked Loni. "You ever visited Piggy?"

Loni shook her head no. She fought to focus on the nonsense because she didn't care what they were saying.

"I have the misfortune to visit his house every time I go fishing. You ever heard the word 'hoarder'? He puts them to shame." The DA turned to Piggy. "How many boats sank?"

"Just the two. The explosion from the carriage hit 'em just wrong. They was those old wooden boats made before we's born, Jimmy. They were dry rotted sitting on the bottom almost anyways. Did those fisherman a favor, I say, an' whatcha mean, hoarder. Ever'thing on my place is valuable."

The DA shook his head and returned to the point of conversation again. "Before you tell another lie, tell me about the dynamite the fisherman used? Where'd he get it?"

"You don't want to hear about how useful my stuff is? Lotta good stories."

"No, Piggy. Tell me who had the dynamite."

"That was Pete Rader. He has a little land down around Percyville. Ya know? Love that town. Somebody allays beating somebody up."

"Piggy!"

"I'm getting there. He was blowing up stumps."

"Okay. That explains the dynamite. Did you really say he was trying to blow up a bridge?"

"He was drunk again. When he comes in off that ocean he always gets drunk. Said all he could think of was how much he wanted to blow up the new bridge over the Percy river, don' you know. He missed the old bridge that always welcomed him home. Says looking at the new bridge wasn't the same. Said it wasn't appealing whatever the hell that meant. Didn't even remember pushing the buggy out on the water. No different than when those ignoramoses in Florence tried to blow up that dead whale on the beach. Did you see the pictures of it. Sent pieces of blubber into space. Hurt cars and people. Ever'body cussing as they tried to dodge those hunks. Stank up the town for days. Check out the YouTube, Jimmy."

"Piggy! Shut up!" the DA said sharply. "You're wasting my time!"

"But Jimmy, blubber's valuable. Remember that fisherman what weighed four hundred pounds what fell off his boat ten miles out? He stuck floats in his shorts until they found him hours later. See how fat pays? He would've been dead if he weren't fat and a fisherman hadn't told the Coast Guard how he must have fell out where he was fishing. Any idiot would know it's hard to fall out of a pilot cabin when your underway back home, don'tcha think?"

"What's your point, Piggy?" the DA demanded.

"Which one?"

"Out!" The DA made shooing gestures at Piggy. "Take that box back to evidence. *Now!*"

"See if I take you fishing again anytime soon, Jimmy." Piggy picked up the box and huffed out the door.

"God help me," he said as he closed the door behind Piggy and returned to his chair. "As for you," he turned to Loni, "I want an update on your other cases ASAP. Especially the Hesselbeck case. It should have been on my desk yesterday. Also make sure Piggy gets that dynamite case written up. I'd like to arraign Pete Rader this morning. And the Carboni case. Do you understand? Or do I need to call Chief again?"

Holding her anger in, Loni nearly ran out of the DA's office as she fast walked on down to the parking lot and climbed into her pickup. Loni began to wonder if it was the DA protecting Piggy's job, but that didn't make sense. She was sure it was a bigger power broker than the DA or any town official. Still, it was small enough to suss out. She spun out of the lot and took a few corners at a dangerous pace. Mentally smirking, she knew the pickup could take it. She'd driven it for two days and learned that the good parts hidden under the beat-up body made it a power house. The others bidding at the auction only cared about how it looked, and she'd gotten it for $400.

The garage door was open at Guy's apartment, and the coroner was removing the body. Loni nodded to the officers as she walked up to the coroner.

"Glad you're here, Lieutenant. I thought this was going to be a slam dunk suicide until I took a look at the victim. You see what I see?"

Loni studied the scene. "If this is carbon dioxide poisoning, the victim should be cherry red."

"That's right. You've seen carbon dioxide poisoning before."

"Once or twice," she acknowledged. "Seemed to be a favorite way to die where I come from."

"Interesting. A gun to the head is favored around here."

"If it's not carbon dioxide poisoning, then what is it?"

"I'm not sure. Have to get a tox screen."

"You got a guess?"

"Nope. Do you?"

"No. I've only seen three deaths by poisoning. That was ricin from castor oil seeds. Even though it can't be stopped, it takes hours for that to kill, though." Loni leaned against the garage door jamb, fighting off a stress headache from lack of sleep as she remembered the case in Arizona. "Trash from smashed castor oil seeds had been accidently mixed in with meth cooking. Several people were killed, including a very special and talented teen who didn't even know he ingested the drug." Loni attempted to remember what the victim looked like as she continued thinking out loud. "The boy's death was especially sad. A really good kid who was tricked into eating spiked brownies."

"Yes, I thought of that one. Takes it a while to wipe out your kidneys and liver though. I also thought of others. Water Hemlock, Wolf's Bane, Belladonna. Strychnine. But they all take a few hours and usually cause vomiting or convulsions that leave visible symptoms on the victim."

Adanna joined them earlier, listening. "How about Doll's Eye?"

"Possible. I remember from my poison seminar it's a sedative relaxing the muscles. It brings a quick death." The coroner stared at Adanna. "That's not common around here. How'd you come up with that?"

"Chief grows it in his greenhouse."

Loni gave Adanna a strange stare. "You spend much time in Chief's greenhouse?"

"Not really. He calls me over there sometimes to get his extra sugar beans and cabbage. We both love sauerkraut. I always give a few jars to him when I fix a batch. That's when I saw this crazy plant that was full of eyes staring at me and I asked him. He said not to touch it because it was poisonous. But he loved the staring eyes and couldn't resist growing it."

"Would you know if the DA ever visited Chief?"

"Never saw him there but, then, I'm not there that often myself. He's got a lovely wife but she's a tad jealous of any woman hanging around her husband."

Loni turned back to the coroner. "Got any estimate on time of death?"

"Not until I determine what killed him. Under normal circumstances I would estimate twelve hours based on rigor."

"Can you put a rush on this, Doc?"

Loni returned to the court house in record time and rushed downstairs to the jail to talk to Jenna.

Jenna immediately jumped into Loni's arms and began to cry. "Get me out of here, Loni. They took my daughter from me. Please help me find her."

"Who? Who took her?"

"These two cops brought a case worker with them and said a sicko like me had no business raising kids."

"Damn! I'll get her home, Jenna. But I can't get you out of here just yet. Tell me you have an alibi."

Jenna's eyes reflected her fear. "I was home all day with my daughter on one of those rare days when nobody else was in the house. My sister had taken her brood Christmas shopping. Grandmother went back to New York."

"I don't think a four-year old can give you an alibi." Loni sighed and walked Jenna over, sitting her on the cot. She sat beside her. "I'm so sorry, but I can't get you out this time. You're getting arraigned this morning and on the docket for your preliminary hearing."

"I know. My lawyer says on a murder charge I can't even get bail."

"Do you still have that hospital lawyer?"

Jenna shook her head in disgust. "He's the one my grandmother insists on. Seems they're old bridge playing buddies."

"If I got you a criminal lawyer, would you hire her?"

"You know a good one?"

"The best."

"Tell her she's hired."

"I'll call her then."

"Can't you get me out of here?"

Loni sadly shook her head. "Probably no bail. They consider you a flight risk because you lived overseas." Loni lifted Jenna's chin. "Listen to me." Jenna's eyes started to focus on Loni. "I can't come see you until this is over. We can't even be seen as friends so I can't go to your arraignment. But you need to listen to your lawyer. I promise I'll be working on your case, and I will get you out. Hear me?"

"Please!" Jenna cried. "My daughter! The storm! I really need to be there for her. Storms frighten her so badly she only wants my sister or me."

"I promise to get your daughter back to your sister. Do you think your sister would be willing to give you messages from me?"

Jenna cringed. "She didn't approve of us but I'll make sure of it."

"I'm sorry."

"Hold me?"

Loni reached for Jenna and brought her close in a tight hug.

"God, you feel good!" Jenna clung to Loni.

"Time to leave, Loni." Janson stated as she opened the cell door. "Before you get us both in trouble."

Loni suddenly realized she never wanted to let go. Until she had to.

Chapter Thirteen

Loni spent a sleepless night feeling helpless, scared, and angry. Exhausted, she dragged herself up the police station stairs the next morning to find Piggy on the phone with a big shit-eating grin on his face. He hung up and crowed, "Hey, Lieut! You're gonna love this one. Caller said he had rustlers."

In no mood for Piggy's crazy stories, she snapped, "He had what?"

"I said we got rustlers now.

"What rustlers?"

"How would I know?"

"What'd they rustle?"

"Caller just said rustlers came and took 'em all."

"Took what?"

"Caller didn't say."

"Shit, Piggy! Call them back!"

"Ain't that up your alley? You're the one with horses and all. And that freak dog you call a tracker."

Totally fed up with his stupidity, Loni said, "Sniffer, Piggy. She finds drugs. And call them back to find out. It's your job."

Cletus laughed. "Hey, Piggy. You might ask Inuktitut where they'all went."

Don agreed. "Good as anything I can think of."

"What's a unic?"

"Inuktitut! That a spirit that finds what's lost. That two-legged glued rock pile on your'n desk." Cleatus pointed at the rock sculpture.

"This?" Piggy picked it up and stared at it. "My girlfriend gave it to me. Said something about I was always losing her."

Shaking his head, Harry mimicked John Wayne dialect. "Say there, fella. Why don't you go catch us some rustlers."

Harry's antics cheered up Loni enough so that she could be civil to Piggy. She turned to him and asked, "Did you get the evidence box back to Adanna, Piggy?"

"O'course. What'd you care? How many times I got to say it? We got our killer, easy-peasy."

"Just don't want evidence compromised."

Cleatus snorted in disbelief. "Piggy, y'all be obtuse."

"Whaaa?" Piggy looked around. "Where's Ginger when I need her?"

Loni's mood dropped again as she thought about Jenna in a jail cell. "Piggy, while you're at it, take your case notes on the dynamite case, and put them on my desk. Then check at the hospital to see if Dale Hesselbeck is conscious yet. If not, stay there until you can interview him. Get it signed and go pick up the kid who beat on him."

"Why, Lieut? I hear he deserved the beating."

"For visiting a girl?"

"He didn't belong there."

Loni turned toward her office to hide her disgust before she answered Piggy. "That's not the point. If it wasn't self-defense, and it sounds like it wasn't, and the boy is seriously injured, and it sounds like he is, then it's a crime. And while you're at the hospital, have them send the files to the DA." Loni looked around. "Why are you answering the phone, anyway? Where's Bobbi?"

"She's late again."

Piggy huffed as he opened his drawer to get his gun. He grabbed his coat from the rack and got to the elevator just as the door opened and Bobbi walked out.

Bobbi watched the elevator door close behind him and grinned. "Alone at last."

"Aaaw, Bobbi," Don said. "You do love us after all."

Bobbi giggled. "I do. But only when he's gone. He has such a huge negative essence it suffocates me. It's so peaceful around here without him I can think."

Loni laughed and then remembered her conversation with the DA. "Join me?" she said somberly.

Bobbi hung up her rain jacket and followed Loni into her office.

"Lange's indicting Jenna Giovanni this morning. Her arraignment's at eleven."

"Jesus, Lieutenant!" Bobbi said. "Does he have any proof?"

"I don't know, Bobbi. Jenna doesn't have any alibi for the latest murder. Our only chance to free her is to find out who did the killings."

"I still can't find a man with a gunshot wound anywhere in this county. What do we do now?"

"What we been doing, Bobbi. Maybe broaden your search? Something stinks. The DA has been over the top in pushing this off on Doctor Giovanni, and we need to find out why. Maybe it's all tied in together with where he disappears all the time. Search his phone records and credit card purchases along with any travel time he listed."

"Wonder if he was staying with Carlotta at the Grand. When are you going to hear back from your Portland friend?"

Loni had no answer so she changed the subject as she walked to her office door. "Listen up, everybody," Loni said in a tired voice. "I'm sure you've heard by now that the town is closing down tomorrow. Along with hurricane force winds, landslides and severe flooding are expected. Schools are closing. Only a skeleton crew will be available to handle emergencies. We need to talk about our jobs during the storm." All eyes were on Loni as she talked. "Who lives in or near town?"

"We do." Bill said. "Harry and I live next to each other over on Taylor."

Ginger laughed. "No wonder I keep confusing you two for Frick and Frack. Same kind of house. Same kind of car. Did you marry twins?"

"Ginger? Where do you live?"

"What do you think, Lieutenant. I'm a lesbian. I'm in a rental on a few acres in the country up Bear Creek Road."

"I'm just outta town in Alderville." Cleatus turned to the crew. "That's a suburb to Harborville, don'tcha know. Built when Harborville still had the sundown laws."

"What are those?" Bobbi queried.

Ginger huffed an answer. "Just what they sound like, Bobbi. All the black people had to be out of town by sundown. They had to live somewhere, so they built Alderville."

Loni intervened. "Back to the storm. Those of you who can, hang out in town to help any way you can and maybe prevent looting. If you've got chainsaws, make sure they work. Prepare for electric outages. Anybody who doesn't live in town, try to take any emergency call in your location. You got this afternoon and maybe this evening to get ready." The room emptied before Loni had time to put on her coat.

Loni picked up her phone again. "Charlie. Can you meet me for lunch?"

"Sure. Port Bar?"

"Is there any other place?"

"Nope.

Charlie was in a booth across from Judge Wentworth when Loni looked about the bar. Sliding in on the hard, red vinyl bench beside the judge, Loni appreciated Marlene's wide smile and hug. Plus her whispered warmth to "hang in there."

"How'd the arraignment go?"

"Loni!" the judge cried.

"Not even a small hint?"

The judge laughed. "I wouldn't know anyway. I don't do arraignments."

"Who does?"

"We have a young woman new to the bench covering the arraignments for now." The judge gave Loni another good squeeze. "Stop worrying! Good things come to those who wait, my child. Patience." She left her arm around Loni's shoulders as she turned to Charlie's voice.

"It still strikes me as how strange it is that you were both born and raised in Caliente, Arizona and both ended up here."

Marlene stared at Charlie with her poker face. "I don't think it's strange." Turning to Loni she asked, "Do you think we're strange?"

Loni blinked. "Define strange."

The big grin came back, and the judge gave Loni a hard squeeze and let her go.

Charlie cocked his head in cognizance. "That why you talked Chief into hiring her?"

"Good to see you jump right on that, Charlie." Grinning, the judge turned back to Loni. "I understand you heard from your cousin James."

"He called me about coming up for a visit. Along with his wife who's eight months along in her pregnancy."

"Wow. Last time I saw James he was still in diapers. His dad had just hit a good streak of gold." The judge seemed lost in her memories. "Ethel was beside herself with finding ways to spend the money."

Loni grinned. "James must have inherited that from his mother. I remember when I taught him how to find a perp's tell. Seems he used it for gambling and won a lot of money. The other players decided he cheated and wanted their money back so he had to find a place to hide out." Loni threw her arms in the air. "Surprise! My lucky day."

The judge grinned. "But of course, he didn't have the money any more."

"You got that right. He even asked me to send him plane fare."

"You turned him down, right?"

Chagrined, Loni ducked her head and admitted, "Well, no. Haven't seen him yet, though."

"But he'll pay you back." Charlie stated.

"Never has before," Loni admitted.

Charlie laughed. "How much does he owe you?"

"I lost count. It's family, right?"

"It's also genetic. My sister did the same thing to me until I cut her off. She never spoke to me again."

"Lucky you."

The judge agreed. "It was for the best." She put her glass of apple juice back onto the paper coaster and smoothed her eyebrow.

Loni nudged her with an elbow. "I'd like to play poker with you. You got a great tell."

"Crap," Charlie complained. "Don't tell her! I been winning off her for years, and you're blowing it for me."

"It's okay, Charlie. I'll whisper your tell to her, and you'll be even. Better yet, I won't say anything about either one of you if you invite me to your next poker night."

"Okay," the judge laughed. "It's on the first Friday night of the month. My house. Seven o'clock."

"Don't be late," Charlie warned Loni. "And bring lots of beer."

"No, no, no. Don't bring anything." The judge turned serious. "Maybe James should stay with me. Helen would be beside herself to have someone from home she can gossip with."

"If he shows up, I'll be happy to send him over," Loni promised.

"So tell me, Loni," Charlie asked, "did you really own a ranch?"

"I did. Sold it to Thomas Moor."

"I remember the Moor family." Marlene frowned in thought. "My granddad talked about helping them cross the Salt River. They had come over from Texas in a beat-up wagon and sad-looking mules too tired to pull the wagon any further. One of the brothers moved on up to the Agua Fria and put in a ferry."

"Yes. And my uncle Herm said no woman dared cross alone with him for fear of being molested."

The judge laughed. "I heard that, too. Although I understood driving by the ostrich farm was scarier. Good thing it didn't last long."

"What were they doing with ostriches in the middle of the Arizona desert." Charlie asked.

"They brought them in to herd cattle. This rancher heard they could outrun the fastest cow, ate nearly nothing, traveled a long way without water, easy to saddle, taste like chicken, and laid eggs big enough to equal a dozen. What's not to like? Perfect to sell to other ranchers and make a fortune."

"Sounds good. What happened?"

"Just one problem. The ostriches scared the crap out of the cattle, and they scattered so bad nobody could round them up. The rancher gave up on that and went around the country betting his ostrich could outrun any horse alive. It worked until everybody lost a bundle and caught on."

Loni joined in the laughter. "That's one of the reasons why everybody was happy to see the railroad built. My granddad talked about seeing the first train that came when he was eight years old. He said it turned around at the end of the track on the east bank of the Hassyampa."

"I think you two make up these stories just to mess with me."

Loni laughed. "Charlie, anyone ever tell you what Hassyampa meant?"

"Not recently."

"It meant if you drank the water."

The judge grinned. "You would never tell the truth again."

"Just how close to that river did you two get?"

"Can't count the number of times I swam in it. How about you, Judge?"

"Me neither."

"So, Judge, when you were a prosecutor in Tucson, did you have Kirk in your court? I remember he was always in a court on some infraction."

"No. I wasn't the prosecuting attorney, but I heard about one of his cases." The judge frowned in concentration. "He was part of a claim jumping case. Something about Kirk sending James out to prove up on a claim and he got bushwhacked by an old prospector who swore James was a jumper. Nearly shot him. The story was that he peed and pooped his pants, and the prospector thought it was so funny he had to sit down to laugh. James jumped at the opportunity to grab his gun, shoot the old man in the leg, and run. Kirk sent James with an ambulance back to get the old prospector. They said the prospector cussed James the whole way back to the hospital. That the one?"

"Never heard that one."

"Who won?" Charlie asked.

"Kirk. The old prospector was trespassing although he didn't know it at the time. He was several miles off where he filed his claim."

"He die?"

"No, but he limped for a while."

Loni and the judge were laughing so hard that tears were running down the judge's face. Wiping them off, the judge sighed into a reflective silence as she studied Charlie's solemn face. "Sorry, Charlie. You had to be there." Shrugging, the judge turned to Loni. "You heard from anyone else from home?'

"My aunt Mae calls me every couple of weeks or so to check up on me. They're coming up to visit this summer. You and Helen will have to come have supper with us."

"I will. It would be good to see Mae again. She and your Uncle Herm were good friends to Helen and me." The judge paused a few seconds. "You said James was as big an asshole as his mother. How so?"

Loni chuckled. "Not so much anymore. Doesn't mean I still didn't want to kill him sometimes." Loni sipped her coke. "Even Uncle Kirk finally stopped looking at me as if he wanted to scratch dirt and cover me up. Aunt Ethel stayed the nastiest woman I ever met."

"I want to know more about James. But before you start, how about a refresh?"

"Good luck with that," Charlie nodded to a table on the other side of the bar. "Doreen just climbed in that cute cop's lap, and I don't think she's going to get up anytime soon. So let's hear it."

"James." Loni settled in her seat, leaning back on the vinyl cover. "I didn't have Daniel to protect me my last year of high school, so James made it a living hell."

"Like what would he do?"

"Outside of a lot of Indian war hooting and war dance around me, he would sabotage my car, spray paint my locker with words like lesbian half-breed, and pull other dirty tricks. He threatened to beat on me a few times but he knew our cousin Daniel would come after him for that."

"But now, James actually accepts you as a lesbian?"

"After I saved his life a couple of times. I told you about that. But that wasn't his biggest problem. His biggest problem was I ended up with the ranch and left it to my Indian mother's parents to run."

"How did that happen?"

"Our granddad on my father's side gave my dad, who was oldest, the ranch because he was the only one who wanted to work it. He gave his next son, my Uncle Herm, airport land and money to build it because he only wanted to fly and work on planes. He gave Uncle Kirk all the mineral rights, especially the gold mine because he loved rocks and digging in the dirt, which made him rich." Loni turned to Charlie. "That's how the judge here and I are nearly related. My aunt Ethel was her sister."

"Older sister. I was sixteen last time I saw her." Judge Wentworth stared quizzically at Loni a few seconds. "I suppose you want to know what happened."

Loni smiled, shaking her head. "Yeah. How come I never heard of you when I was growing up?"

"I left town when you were still little. I was caught in bed with Helen, kicked out of the house and promptly disowned."

"Oh, God! And you were only sixteen. What'd you do after that?"

"She and I moved in with her aunt in Tucson." Nostalgia settled on the judge's face. "I worked through school at the university in criminal law. After that I lawyered several years in Tucson. Helen went into school counseling. Whenever we could, we helped kids caught up like we were, trying to save them some of the pain from family rejection that we had. Finally, we got tired of the heat, and moved here." A look of surprise crossed the judge's face. "Good Lord! That was thirty years ago!"

"And Helen still puts up with you," Charlie chortled.

"Helen's from Caliente too?"

"Yup. Getting as far from my dad was one of those events that got us here. He was a mean son of a bitch. And now, I wouldn't have it any other way."

"Yeah, but to get kicked out at sixteen?"

"I don't think my dad would have been so hard on me if Ethel hadn't got herself pregnant and had to get married."

Loni grinned. "That explains why James was such a bastard."

"Hey, Marlene!"

Loni turned around and looked up into piercing blue eyes and flaming red hair that was cut short and slicked back into a duck's ass. The judge stood up and grabbed a short woman in a long hug. Loni stared in amazement as they turned toward Charlie.

"Sally." Charlie nodded to her, a slight frown on his face.

"This is Sally Harper," the judge said to Loni. "A good friend and the best damned defense lawyer I know. If anyone can help Doctor Giovanni, she can."

The woman's poker face expression changed as she smiled at Loni. "I just came from talking with Doctor Giovanni. I gather you're the one I need to talk to about evidence you found?"

"Oh, hell, yes. And thanks for taking the case."

Sally smiled at the judge. "Marlene can be very persuasive. You can thank her. And by the way," Sally demanded of the judge, "who is that cute young thing you've got handling the arraignments?"

"She's new to the bench and doing a bang-up job. Don't you go giving her a hard time."

Sally laughed. "That wasn't what I had in mind. Unless that's the way she likes it."

Charlie clamped his hands over his ears. "La la la la la la. You done yet?"

"Loni?" The judge put her hand on Loni's cheek. "You still look a little rattled. Take some deep breaths." Loni breathed so deeply that she felt dizzy and light headed. "You good to go now?" The judge waited for a nod.

Loni voice came out weak. "I think I can handle it now."

The judge held Loni's chin, forcing her to look at her. "I'll defer the preliminary hearing until next week. That gives me time to find out what's going on with Jimmy, and that gives you seven days to clear Doctor Giovanni before she comes before it. I can only defer it once." She gave Loni a piercing look. "You better be right." Hugging Sally one more time the judge beckoned Charlie. "Charlie and I are leaving now. Loni needs to talk to Sally about your problems with Jimmy."

Grinning from ear to ear, Loni stood and kissed the judge on the cheek. "That doesn't include the weekend, right?"

"Take what you can get, you little shit. Now sit down and help your girl."

Loni stared in surprise. "How did you know? Am I in trouble with the evidence I collect now?"

"Did I hear you say you were dating Doctor Giovanni?"

"No, you didn't hear me say it."

"Then you better get to work."

Loni watched them walk out the door before she turned back to Sally as they scooted back into the booth. "Oh, hell. I don't want to get the DA into trouble, but I'm really tired of his jacking me around. Tell me what you need."

"Here's what my discovery request of the DA's office produced. According to them, Doctor Giovanni has no alibi for the child who died or for Guy

Murphy's death. Your DA insists Doctor Giovanni's guilty, and apparently your boss the police chief backed him up."

"Not quite true. I cleared her of both Carlotta's and the child's death."

"You tell the DA that?"

"Yes, but he won't listen." Loni fought the forming tears. "Do you know what else they got?"

"The DA says she had access to the children and was there when the child died. She could have messed with the monitors. And that it couldn't have been Carlotta who did the aspiration because only a trained doctor can do it. He says Jenna was the doctor and Guy helped her because they were lovers. That they used her husband's lab for processing. She killed Carlotta because she was blackmailing them and then killed Guy because she found out he was in on the blackmail."

Loni shook her head through Sally's entire explanation. "I can't understand what's going on with the DA. His evidence is based on her arrest papers, and those were all Detective Washington's inventions. The DA didn't even look at the actual evidence. He ignored the information we got on both Carlotta's and Jenna's bank accounts. He didn't ask where the bone marrow was sold or who else might have helped Carlotta get it." Loni opened a folder, pulled out a photo and laid it on the table. "This is a picture of Doctor Giovanni's clothing from the murder scene. You can see where she kneeled in the blood at the victim's head trying to help the victim. At least that's what she said. She also wiped the blood off her hands down the sides of her pants. Her pants and shirt don't have any cast-off blood, and there wasn't any in her hair or anywhere else on her body."

Handing her another photograph, Loni continued. "The smaller shoe prints belong to Doctor Giovanni. You can see that the blood was almost dry before she stepped in it. The coroner said Carlotta had been dead for at least an hour before Doctor Giovanni walked in the blood around the body." Loni pulled out a copy of a receipt slip. "The stamped date on this is after the victim's death. It's from a store twenty minutes away. The clerk remembers her because they've had long talks about wine in the past." Loni pointed at another photo. "You can see the shoe prints of the actual killer that were in fresh blood."

Loni put the pictures and receipt back in the folder. "Guy Murphy also has an ironclad alibi for Carlotta's murder. He was in a meeting all day with witnesses. Then there's the child's death. At first we thought Carlotta had to have a doctor partner because aspirating bone marrow needs a trained medical doctor. The hospital files from the nights in question show that Doctor Giovanni was never there when it happened. The most likely suspects were Carlotta and Mike Kenyon."

"What did you find out about Kenyon?"

"Nothing yet. We're tracing his work and criminal history now and checking to see if he was sexually involved with Carlotta."

"Do you have any suspects?" Sally quizzed.

"No one for sure. Might be Kenyon. We can't find him for questioning. He didn't show up for work last night, and his apartment's been cleaned out. I think a third person must have partnered with Carboni and Keyton, and I think it's Guy Murphy."

Spreading her hands over the top of the folder, Loni mused, "The question is whether the DA's as weird as he's acting. Or if he's protecting the murderer. He has no proof against Jenna. No money trail, no forensics, no witnesses in either murder. But he's determined to convict her."

Loni paused to organize her thoughts. "Proving Doctor Giovanni is innocent of Carboni's murder was easy. And the child's. Finding out who killed Guy is harder. We know that Carboni was bisexual and had two regular male visitors. We identified one of them, and he's probably harmless. A plumber with a pregnant wife who maybe needed a little affection off and on. Although we aren't sure of that. She did have legitimate plumbing problems. We identified the other lover as Guy Murphy. Adanna found his DNA on a toothbrush."

Before Loni continued, she took a deep breath. "Three different sources told us Carlotta Carboni was having an affair with Guy Murphy. A security guard at the hospital said he saw them necking in Murphy's car in the underground parking. His ex-wife claimed Carboni broke up her marriage, and several neighbors claimed they saw him at Carboni's house. His car was there overnight on several weekends when she wasn't working and Doctor Giovanni wasn't there."

"Do you know where the bone marrow is going?"

"We are still investigating a couple of labs belonging to Doctor Giovanni's ex-husband, Barelli Giovanni. He's on record as having done work for the hospital and Guy Murphy. We found hidden bank accounts, but we couldn't investigate him further because the IRS is also interested in him. I don't know why."

"You're following the bone marrow now, right?"

"Yes."

"Anything else?" Sally asked.

"Not yet. I only have a week to find the killer."

"Keep me apprised?"

Loni nodded. "Can you get Jenna out on bail?"

Sally smiled. "Of course. She should be processed out by now. If she disappears, you'll be taking her place."

Loni nearly ran her way back to the courthouse to find Jenna at the processing desk retrieving her personal items. Loni pulled her into the first empty space she could find. "You know we have to stop meeting like this."

Jenna's dimples appeared. "My sister said you got Loni Lyn to her. I can never repay you enough."

"It would be enough if you stopped getting yourself thrown in jail."

"Didn't I tell you? Orange is becoming my favorite color, and jail is now my favorite leisure time activity."

"Don't get too used to it. I'm running out of friends." Loni grinned.

Laughing in relief, Jenna grabbed Loni around the waist and held her close, laying her blond head on Loni's shoulder before she gave her a quick kiss of gratitude and let go. "Can we stop for something to eat?"

"We could but I'm not sure how much we should be seen together until you're cleared."

"But I'm hungry now." Jenna pleaded.

"How about Billy Boy's?"

"I remember Billy Boy's. They had the best wineburgers."

"Don't forget the hot crispy corn chips."

"Is it really still there?"

"It is. I stopped in right after I moved here. Felt like déjà vu all over again. Everything just the same except it wasn't Billy Boy at the counter anymore. Seems he married an old butch and taught her how to cook. They say they fought so much his heart gave out. Loni grabbed Jenna's hand as they climbed the stairs to the outside. "Other than that, the time I was there…those memories of you sitting at the counter slammed me hard enough I turned around and walked out. I haven't been back."

"Is it okay to go now?"

"We probably shouldn't be seen together. Just a quick in and out, okay?"

Jenna grinned in agreement. "Do you think the wineburgers will be just as good as we remembered?"

"Hope so. It'd be really wonderful if some things never changed."

"Do you believe that?"

"Working on it."

Billy Boy's was a sled-roofed add-on to his brother's car repair shop. Measuring fourteen feet deep and forty feet long, the only seating was on stools attached to the tall counter that ran the entire forty feet. Behind the customer counter was a grill, coolers, racks of glasses and dishes, and a little counter space. More glasses were stacked on shelves against the wall. Billy's wife took the orders as customers called them in as she continued to cook.

Loni and Jenna walked in and Jenna grinned at her. "You're right. Except for no Billy, it hasn't changed."

"Hey, Lieutenant!" An older man greeted Loni and moved down a seat to give the two women a place to sit together. The short, pudgy, older man looked familiar. She nodded her thanks and slipped onto a stool beside Jenna. Watching Billy's wife work distracted Loni as she wondered why Billy would marry a woman he complained all the time about how much he hated. Hollering without turning around, the cook took their orders and tossed burgers onto the fire. "Drink?" she hollered again.

"Coke," Loni called back.

"Beer for me. Bud Lite?" Jenna said.

By the time the cook placed a basket of hot chips and the drinks in front of them, the hamburgers were ready.

"Oh, yeah!" Jenna groaned. "Almost as good as sex." The older man beside Jenna laughed, and she blushed in embarrassment. "What can I say? It's been a while." She smiled in apology as she returned to her hamburger, moaning her way through every bite. Satisfied at last, Jenna climbed off her stool thanking the cook who winked at her in reply. "Anytime sweet thing."

Loni grinned as they walked out the door. "Ready to go home now?"

Jenna stopped and studied Loni a minute. "I'm scared, Loni. Really, really scared. I want to feel safe for a while. Can I go home with you?"

"I promise. I won't let anything happen to you."

"I wish I could believe you."

When they left the burger hut, the night was pitch black, and a hanging mist drifted in delicate white swirls in her headlights. At Loni's gravel road, her headlights seemed to hit a black wall just beyond the mist. Loni wove through looming tree trunks abnormally enlarged by the fog along the familiar twists and turns of the road. They had been quiet for most of the ride. Jenna reached for Loni's hand just before they got to the house. "I once believed you were my soulmate. When I got married, I thought you were forever lost to me, and it didn't matter who I married. I was tired of fighting my grandmother, and I wanted children. I'll never regret it because I have Loni Lyn."

"And then you found Carlotta Carboni."

"Don't remind me. That was another disaster." Jenna sighed. "It was never serious."

"It's okay, Jenna. I think we weren't meant to be together during those years. We still had things to do, and we couldn't do them together."

"And now?"

Loni was silent a few minutes. "It's been so many years ago. I don't know how much what we are feeling is residual or real anymore. I think we need time but I would like to find out."

Jenna sighed. "Me too." She looked over at Loni. "Did you ever fall in love with anyone else?"

Loni stumbled with her words as she pulled into her yard in front of the barn and stopped. "I told you about Maria." Loni turned to Jenna and took her hand. "But no. I never fell in love again the way I did with you."

"Oh, God! I'm so sorry I brought it up." Jenna apologized. "She's the one who was shot."

"It's okay."

"Any others I should know about?"

"Maybe one more. I moved back to the ranch to heal and got a job as highway patrol at night. I met Lola at work. She was the dispatcher. It didn't last very long before she dumped me." Loni stopped in front of her barn and parked. Turning to Jenna she tilted her head for a soft lingering kiss. Loni feathered her hair with her face and took a deep breath as though swallowing Jenna's essence. "I would love to find us again if you are willing to try."

Jenna's smile was pensive in the reflection of the outdoor light hanging above the barn door. "It may be much harder than you think." They were quiet for a few moments, absorbing each other. "I do remember all the reasons I loved you."

"They still there?"

"Most. Some have been rough chiseled, others smoothed out. A few faded. A few are gone."

"Like what?"

"Like your sense of wonder. I can't find it. Or your joyful exuberance over the smallest things. The things that kept me warm during endless cold nights after I lost you."

Loni understood what Jenna was telling her. "Life does get in the way and change you."

"Like?"

"Like losing everyone I loved. Like being so totally alone it didn't matter which way I bounced. Or what got chipped away. Or lost. Starting with a heart. Crushing pain changes you."

"But you survived."

"Like I said before. You get up, brush off what you can, move on."

Loni leaned in to kiss Jenna again, this time deeply and passionately. When they finally separated, Loni smiled in joyful contentment at the discovery of the connection with Jenna that made them into one, made them whole and complete. "I need to get out and open the barn door. Just stay here." She hurried out into her headlights and pushed the huge door to the side and turned on the barn light. Jumping back into the car, she pulled up beside her beat-up pickup from the police compound auction.

"Wow." Jenna laughing at the appearance of Loni's new pickup. "Nice. Even a four-wheel drive. With a camper shell. Now don't that beat all!"

Loni loved Jenna's teasing. "Go ahead and make fun. This country changes lots of things I need, like getting through mud when pulling a horse trailer."

"Where'd you find it? Our local junkyard?"

"Yup. Last one on the lot."

Jenna laughed. "It's a lovely mud-bogger. And don't think I didn't notice the gun rack in the back window." Loni grinned at Jenna's gentle ribbing as she followed Loni out of the car through the barn and watched her let Coco out of the house before she settled the horses for the night. At the house, Loni opened the door for Jenna as Coco shot through before them, circling when Jenna reached for Loni's hand. "Which door is your bedroom?"

Loni nodded to the door on the left and Jenna pulled her into the room, shutting the door in Coco's face. "You want to undress me first, or do I get to undress you first?"

Loni couldn't stop grinning, even when Jenna leaned into her and kissed her dimples, one by one before she kissed her mouth. "God, have I missed you! All these years the longing for you never let up." Loni pulled Jenna into her, kissing her, holding her as tight as she could as she walked her toward the bed. She couldn't let go and they tumbled together onto the bed so tightly intertwined, it was impossible to tell when one began and the other ended.

The sound of a ringing doorbell and pounding on the door startled both of them. Loni groaned as Jenna laughed. "You expecting someone?"

"Absolutely not. Unless your grandmother's after me."

Jenna groaned. "Does sound like her."

The pounding on the door continued. "I know you're in there, Loni! Open the fucking door!"

Loni frowned. "Oh, my God. I do not want to answer that door."

"You know who it is?"

"Oh, hell yeah. My ex-girlfriend Lola. The one who dumped me over a year ago. The one I haven't heard from since."

"Doesn't sound like she's going to go away."

"No, I guess not."

"Looks like you need to deal with this." Crawling out of bed, Jenna pushed Loni away as she quickly redressed and held out her hand. "Give me the keys to your car."

Reluctantly, Loni reached in her Levi pocket and handed Jenna the keys.

"Give me a call when she's gone."

"What if I can't get her to leave any time soon?"

Jenna snickered. "Then I own a T-Bird. Thank you very much!"

Jenna opened the door, slipped by a surprised Lola standing on the porch, and disappeared into the night. Loni heard the T-Bird start as Lola pushed by Loni rushing into the house madder than a stirred-up hornet's nest. She circled the room around Loni, and her loud haranguing went on for what seemed forever. Loni couldn't keep from staring. Lola looked just the same in her sexy multi-colored dress showing off plenty of cleavage and her four-inch "come fuck me" heels. Her reddish hair still curled down her back, and her green eyes still flashed bright. Loni knew that Lola's blend of temper from her Irish ancestors and the stubbornness of her Mexican heritage made a force to be reckoned with. "Didn't take you long to replace me, huh?" Lola said, forcing Loni to focus on what the other woman was saying.

"It's been over a year since you walked out, Lola. Not one word from you in all that time. You said you were through with me and I believed you. You said you wanted to go back to a man and I believed that, too."

"True love waits forever," Lola flung back at Loni.

Loni moved Lola's suitcase so that she wouldn't trip on it, sat down on the couch, and settled back as she folded her arms across her chest. She knew she'd have to wait a while longer. Lola stomped around the house, picking up objects and immediately putting them back down. Loni hoped she wouldn't start throwing things. She carefully watched Lola and sensed a deep-down sadness in Lola, one that Loni knew she couldn't fix. Lola had changed, and so had Loni. "What brings you here? A warning call would have been nice."

"After what I just walked into, I bet. How long have you been involved with this one?"

"Fifteen years."

"You screwed around while we were together?" Lola screamed.

"Of course not! I knew her before that and just met up with her again."

"Shit! Don't tell me that was Jenna!"

"Yes."

"Oh, God. Oh, God." Lola flopped down beside Loni. "The one you never forgot. Don't tell me I'm too late!"

Loni didn't answer.

"Pretty woman."

Loni nodded, relieved that Lola seemed to be calming down.

Lola half smiled. "You can say it. Not as good looking as me."

Loni had to laugh. "Nobody is as beautiful as you are, Lola."

"Damn straight." Lola wiped away her tears as they kept on falling. Loni moved over and held Lola for a long time while she cried. "I couldn't take it anymore. My bastard ex-husband started stalking me again. He sucked up to my brothers, and they wouldn't help me. They thought we should get married again and have a house full of children. That way I'd never go back to you. I really hoped you'd get me away from him." Lola sat up straight, wiping her eyes. "Guess that's not going to happen now, huh?"

"Come on. I'll take you back to the airport."

"That would probably be best. I don't think that taxi driver would come back."

Loni pushed Lola's suitcase through the broken door of the pickup's camper shell and helped Lola into the front seat. The trip to the Portland airport was long and subdued for Loni. Lola filled in the quiet by entertaining Loni about what had been happening in Caliente since her absence. "Carl loves his retirement and Tully filled in until a new sheriff was elected. James has his name in the hat. So far, no competition. Who would want that godawful job anyway! Nobody appreciates you. People get shot at. Anybody shot at you yet? My dad took a bad spill and broke the middle finger. Looked like he was…you know, giving everyone the finger all the time. My mom wanted to strap his arm to his body. Manny's in trouble again, and you need to come home and fix it. Jesus, my oldest brother, has a new baby girl. She looks just like me. Lucky girl, huh? You remember Margarita? She got caught making out with Lulu and broke her girlfriend's heart. Moved in with Lulu and brought all five kids with her, too. Met the new owners of your ranch. Nice people. Say they're making lots of changes. Tore down the old barn. And the cabins. And the house. Don't know what's left. Or who."

"What happened to Russell after they tore down his home?"

Lola stared at Loni in confusion. "I don't know."

"Damn! Could you find out? Maybe I could move him up here with me."

"But not me." Lola's voice wavered in her grief.

"Listen. You tell Manny to get rid of your ex-husband, or I will find a way to put him in jail forever."

"You really think any of my brothers will help me?"

"Talk to Manny. I promise he will. He knows you were the one really responsible for motivating me to get him out of the murder charge. Then talk to James to get your brothers to back off. I promise he'll help. He knows I can hurt him."

Lola was silent as Loni turned off the freeway at the exit for the airport. They both listened to the powerful noise of the large jets taking off as Loni pulled into the departure lane to let Lola out. Loni came around to help Lola get her suitcase, but before she could reach for it, Lola grabbed her and wouldn't let go.

"Please!" Lola begged.

Relief washed over Loni when a guard came up and told Loni to move her pickup. Lola glared at the guard and finally let go enough so Loni could pull her suitcase out of the truck. Lola yanked her suitcase out of Loni's hand and walked into the airport without a backward look.

During the long drive home, Loni watched the light show from streaking lightning, the harbinger of supercells. Memories buffeted Loni along with winds from the predicted storm. She recalled Lola's kindness from the first day she went to work when Chief took one look at Loni and bellowed, "She's a goddamned girl."

Lola had said to Loni, "Don't worry. I'm his eye-candy. He'll do what I say."

That wasn't the last time Lola protected her from the chief's wrath. Together she and Lola worked with people in the town to convert an old motel into a refuge for undocumented immigrants until she and Lola could get them papers and jobs. Lola hadn't said a word when Loni wanted to name the refuge Maria's

Casa, after Loni's dead girlfriend. There were also the times when Lola protected her from James's and his partner Chui's cruel antics. Loni shed a few tears for the pain she caused Lola as the rain pelted on the windshield. As wild and volatile as Lola was, she had been a loyal friend.

A mile from home, the rain from the front of the strong Pacific near-cyclone storm lashed at the pickup, pushing it around like a lurching drunk and pounding the windshield in its fury. With a heavy heart, Loni pulled into her driveway just before midnight amid crashing rain and flying debris. Worried about the hail breaking her windshield, she struggled to open the barn door to park her truck, and straw from the stacked hay flew around the barn like missiles. Startled horses hopped in short stomps, and the roosting night owl in the loft let out a shriek as Loni fought the gale wind that forced the door to stay open. She struggled to breathe as she drove the pickup into the barn and jumped out to shove the door closed again. Sighing in relief, she leaned against the closed door to rest.

The storm was predicted to last for at least twenty-four hours until the early hours of Friday morning, and Loni dearly hoped the barn would last that long. She fed the horses extra hay and oats for the morning just in case it was too tough to leave her house. Slipping through the side door on the barn, Loni used the lightning flashes to light her way to the house as she bent into the wind and dug her boots into the mud for traction. Loni struggled to her back door and pushed her way in. A brown wiggling dog slid by her and was back, soaking wet, in less than a minute. Loni grinned at Coco as she locked them in for the night.

Loni dragged herself into the bedroom and flung her clothes on the floor. Stark naked, she fell into a dreamless sleep in seconds.

Chapter Fourteen

The shaking and rattling of her house joined with the sound of speeding freight trains overhead crashed into Loni's deep sleep. Jesus! The barn! Loni leaped out of bed, surrounded by pitch dark. She wasn't prepared for the power to go out. She searched in the headboard for her powerful flashlight. Stumbling toward the window, she saw the leaning outline of the old barn barely visible through lightning flashes in the thick rain. The barn was still standing. Thank God! The lake of water around the house made her wonder how long she had until the barn was flooded. Or the house.

With the help of the flashlight, Loni found candles. Music from her portable radio partly blocking the sound of screaming wind and crashing thunder helped overcome an overwhelming sense of loneliness and isolation as she dressed for the day. She started a fire for comfort and hoped the chimney cap would hold under the powerful onslaught. By the early morning hours, the barometer had fallen to 28.93, and the huge cumulonimbus clouds and heavy rain blocked most of the light from the rising sun.

Slowly, as she sat by the fire, light filtering through the storm and trees showed the barn clearly enough to convince Loni that it was still standing. She knew, though, that she'd be busy the next few days clearing the wreckage from fallen trees. Worrying about everything, she almost missed hearing her cell phone. Out of habit, she pushed it on speaker after she answered it

"Loni?"

"Jenna?"

"Can you come and get my grandmother?"

"Where is she?"

"On the road about three miles from home. She's been there for hours. She got caught in downed trees and called me. I got just enough bars on my phone to call you. Can you come?"

"What happened?"

"She was trying to beat the storm coming home from Portland."

"She didn't make it," Loni stated.

"She said trees fell all around her. They landed in front of the car and one in back. One hit the car. She said she can't move."

"Is she hurt?"

"She says she's fine."

"What about the tree that hit the car? Was the damage serious?"

"She said not. The top of the tree fell, so the limbs only dented the car. Can you bring a chain saw?"

"Jenna. I'll do what I can." As usual, Loni was left with a dead dial tone. She checked the barometer again and gratefully realized it had risen to 29.32. If I take Roani, she thought, maybe I could make it.

Loni dressed in a yellow hooded rain coat and pants and pushed out the door, leaving Coco inside. The wind was at her back as she ran to the barn and slipped in the side door. She rummaged around in her safety gear box for her safety glasses, cut a short string to wrap onto the ear pieces, and tied them onto her head. It took her almost twenty minutes to throw the chain saw into the pickup, get the horse trailer connected, and saddle Roani. Worried about damage from flying debris to Roani's eyes, Loni sorted through the tack hanging on the barn wall and snatched the horse-racing goggles she remembered hanging there among other horse racing paraphernalia the previous owner left behind. She strapped the goggles onto the horse, rubbed his nose, and apologized to him for what she was asking him to do. It took another twenty minutes to get the large door open, drive out of the barn, close the door, and be on her way. Scattered limbs and flying debris slowed her trip, and she struggled to hold the steering wheel against the gusting wind. Loni knew Roani would be nervous with the jerking of her trailer with every gust, but he was the gutsiest horse she had ever known. He would deal with it.

Her trip to Jenna's road took three times the usual thirty minutes before she reached the huge blowdown where dozens of trees were totally flattened by the giant foot of the storm. A bow echo, she thought Cleatus called it. Loni watched the long, dark bands of heavy moisture fly over her and took a deep breath to increase her resolve before she climbed out to unload Roani. She ducked from the frenetic wind, tied the saw on the back of her saddle, and climbed onto the dancing horse. Leaning low, she turned Roani loose and wrapped her arms around his neck, fighting the wind and slapping tree branches that were determined to knock her out of the saddle. A flash of lightning slammed into a tall pine tree at the edge of the blowdown, close enough that Loni could smell the sulphur and feel the pelting of flying splinters. Roani jumped at another ear-splitting thunder boom, and Loni tightened her grip on Roani's neck. A short calm in the storm let up enough for her see the white town car ahead of her among the trees.

Loni slid off Roani and tapped on the driver's window. "Are you alright?" she shouted.

The crusty old woman left her window up and shooed at Loni with waving hands before she pointed at the tree limbs. Wildly swinging tree limbs slapped welts on Loni's face and neck no matter how hard she tried to dodge them. With Roani's butt turned into the wind, she managed to untie the saw from his back. Giving the rope a good pull, she started the gas motor and slowly cut the larger limbs from the driver's side before working her way to the front. Three of the biggest ones from a huge fir had slammed directly in front of the car. Loni tied the limbs to the saddle horn for Roani to pull them out of the way enough for the car to get through. Just as they pulled the last of the limbs, the storm roared back in. The old lady gunned the car and shot forward. Huddled off to the side, Loni watched the car drive away as Jenna's grandmother looked straight ahead. "And you're very welcome!" Loni's yell was lost in the wind with the retreating vehicle.

With the wind pushing her, Loni loped back and loaded Roani in the trailer. Back in the pickup cab, she called Jenna. "Hey, your grandmother should be there any minute."

"I see her coming now. I can't thank you enough."

"Tell you what. I'm glad someone did."

"What can I say." Jenna hung up with an embarrassed laugh.

Loni grinned, but before she could start her pickup, she got a call from Bobbi. "Where are you?"

"I'm on Brown Bear Road about two miles from Highway Eleven."

"What are you doing there?"

"Rescuing Mrs. Davenport."

"Okaaay." Bobbi moved on. "I need another rescue. A pregnant woman got her car stuck, and she's having the baby. She ran into a landslide and got half buried. Can you handle it?"

"Where?"

"On Happy Valley Road. About three miles in from Highway Eleven. You're not far."

"Got it." Loni was back on the road with the storm in full force as she dodged her way to the slide on the road that looked as if half the mountain had come down. The top and part of the side of the car were beyond the mud and rocks, and Loni struggled through the muck. The driver's door could open just enough to get the woman out, but Loni had to figure out how to get her to the truck without getting knocked down by the wind gusts. Loni nodded to the frightened woman, who looked no older than a child. "I'm going after my horse to use him as a shield against the wind. Can you hang in there a little longer?"

"Please! Hurry!"

"Your water broke?"

"Yes."

"How far apart are your contractions?"

"Maybe ten minutes.

Closing the door on the huge eyes in a sweat laced face, Loni hurried back to Roani. Unloading him, she led him back to the car. "Come on out and hold on to the stirrup. Let the horse take the wind."

The three of them slogged through the mud and around the boulders to the pickup, and Loni helped the woman up into the cab. Loading Roani again, she was back on the road to the hospital.

An hour later Loni called Bobbi from the hospital. "It's a girl!"

"Congratulations." Bobbi teased Loni. "May you have much happiness."

"Alright, smartass. Need another rescue?"

Bobbi groaned. "Got a car and driver in a sink hole. He can't climb out."

"Leave him there until the storm lets up."

"Probably shouldn't. It's still sinking. He could end up in Russia."

"Who is it?"

"Piggy."

"Oh, shit! I guess we don't hate Russians that much."

Bobbi laughed. "Guess not."

"How'd he end up in a sink hole, anyhow?"

"Says he was headed for Alderville to help Cleatus's mother-in-law."

"What happened to her?"

"Looks like her house slid down the hill in a landslide and ended up in the middle of the main road. It really needs to be moved but Cleatus is claiming that it's the city's responsibility to move it because it's on city property. The city claims they don't own the house and it's the owner's responsibility. I'm thinking Cleatus is right. He always is, huh Lieutenant?"

"Is his mother-in-law okay?"

"Yeah. She was staying with Cleatus and his wife until the storm was over. Cleatus says he's sorry she wasn't in the house. He would love to make her city property, too."

Loni laughed. "Guess I'll go haul Piggy's ass out of that hole. Maybe after that I can go home."

"Don't count on it."

"Do you always have to have the last word?"

"That's why you love me."

Chapter Fifteen

Loni was an hour late getting to work because she had to stop twice to clear her road enough to get through the downed tree limbs and debris. She still beat most of her detectives. Grateful for the quiet, she wondered where she could find a couple of aspirin as she watched them arrive, loudly holding a one-upmanship contest about who had the worst time getting to work.

Bobbi swore at her galoshes that refused to let go of her shoes. "I saw the saddest thing. Had to drive around this poor dejected dog just sitting in the middle of the road in pouring rain. Head hanging with water dripping off his nose. I honked but he refused to move. Didn't even look up. Looked like he had been waiting for a very long time."

Piggy snorted. "Least you didn't drag him with you for me to smell. I hate wet dogs."

"I hate muddy dogs," Ginger added. "I hate mud, period, especially mud splatter. Hit my windshield and smeared so bad I couldn't see nothing. Time it cleared enough to see, I found myself heading into a honking semi! Had to go back home and change my pants."

Don looked up, shaking his head in sympathy. "I heard that really happened once not long ago. Two people from here died. Nothing left of the car after that semi got done."

Piggy jumped back in, "I had to dodge a bear."

Ginger snorted. "Really? I never know when you're telling the truth."

"Not as big as a semi, doofus!" Ginger scoffed.

"Yeah," Don agreed. "Doesn't anybody use a crosswalk anymore? I almost wiped out a jaywalker."

"I hate them, too," Piggy joined in again. "Tried to arrest one, but the lieut jammed me."

"Anyone hear yet?" Ginger asked. "Anyone killed or badly hurt?"

"Apparently not," Bobbi reported. "I just checked. Lots of flooding and loss of livestock. Some asshole dairyman left his barn locked and lost all his herd. Barn, too."

"There were several wrecks. Mostly sliding into each other."

"Yeah. And it was only cars. Trucks shouldn't travel when the wind hits sixty miles an hour."

Shaking her head, Loni got up from her desk and wandered over to Bobbi. "You got anything on Mike Kenyon yet?" she quietly asked.

Bobbi was equally quiet when she answered. "Just some work history, but it might be what we're looking for. Seems he spent several years back in Chicago assisting physicians in an oncology practice doing bone marrow aspiration."

Nodding in acknowledgement, Loni went back to her desk. The voices were white noise as Loni read through her notes over and over. Each time she hoped for a miracle that would prove Jenna innocent of Guy's death. Needing a break from her burning brain, she leaned back and began organizing in her mind what she needed to know about oncology to see if it were possible for Mike Kenyon to do the procedure. Harry's voice finally filtered into her brain as she realized they were discussing Guy Murphy's death.

"Murder huh, poisoned. Does the coroner know what?"

"Adanna said maybe a poison like Doll's Eye or Baneberry that can paralyze," Ginger reported.

"What the hell's that?" The whine of Piggy's distinctive, high-pitched voice always penetrated Loni's consciousness.

"Plants, dummy." Harry's deep rumbling calm voice was the opposite of Piggy's. "Wonder where they would get any of that?"

"Lots of plants are poisonous." Ginger continued. "Adanna said the chief grows Doll's Eyes plants."

"It might not be a plant," Don added. "You can get poison from milking a snake like the taipan from Australasia. I hear you don't survive its poison."

"What's Australasia?" Piggy scoffed. "Ain't no such place I ever heard of."

Don said, "It's Australia and the countries around it, like New Zealand."

"So why didn't you say Australia?"

Don ignored Piggy. "Or fish like the puffer. There's no antidote. Paralysis creeps over you, leaving you fully aware until you die in a few hours,"

Ginger groaned. "I would hate to die like that."

"I'd love to watch it." Piggy laughed.

"Piggy! Why don't you eat shit and die!" Ginger hurled back at him in disgust. Ducking her head, Loni grinned, glad to hear that Ginger was back and in her usual fine form.

Harry snickered at Ginger's outburst. "I read about a South American frog. An amount as small as two grains of sand can kill you dead."

Don shook his head. "Too hard to get. Here's an easy one. Ricin. Just takes a few castor oil seeds."

"Heard of that," Don agreed. "But it takes too long, like days sometimes. I remember reading a story about some dissident getting killed by a jab from an umbrella. The ricin was on the tip."

"Know what?" Ginger chimed in. "You don't have to leave home to find a poison. Forget about what's stored under your sink. All you have to do is leave food out and voilà! Botulism. And you don't even realize it until paralysis sits in."

"What's voilà?" Piggy asked.

The other detectives groaned in unison and continued to ignore him.

"Don't forget the poisons we make such as dimethyl mercury," Don said. "I read where some chemist spilled a drop on her hand and died nearly a year later. Or if you want fast-acting nerve gas, there's sarin and VX. All of them kill in less than sixty seconds."

"Jesus! What do you read?" Ginger demanded.

Don laughed. "I wondered what would work best for suicide so I've been studying about it."

His comment worried Cleatus. "You think about it much?"

"No. But if I were ever in great pain . . ."

"What about the Death with Dignity law in this state?" Ginger asked Don.

"Might not always live here, Ginger. Thinking of retiring to Texas."

"Hell, Don," Harry told him, "I've got an easy one. I read where a California woman sold clear plastic hoods and vinyl tubing hooked to tanks of helium to people who wanted to kill themselves. She sold thirteen-hundred for sixty dollars each before anyone stopped her."

"Where would you get the helium?"

"Damned if I know. Can you imagine? She was ninety-one years old and said she needed the money because all she had to live on was Social Security."

"There's always eating your gun." Piggy reached into his drawer and pulled out his pistol. He pushed the gun in his own mouth.

Shaking his head, Don said, "As long as you don't miss. I read this one time the bullet only went through a woman's eye and blinded her. Piggy? You do have the safety on?"

"You said that wrong, Don. You're supposed to say Piggy! Take the safety off and pull the trigger." Ginger laughed at Don's expression.

Loni leaped out of her chair as Piggy brandished his gun. At the office door, she said, "Piggy! Put the gun away!" A flash of pain crossed her face. "I interviewed a girl who had been dumped and she considered suicide. She shot herself in the leg to see if it hurt."

"Did it hurt?" Piggy asked as he put the pistol back in the drawer.

"She said 'like a somabitch.'"

Don grinned. "There's an idea. Might tell a potential suicide to try shooting a safe place first. Maybe the best way to change their mind."

Piggy cackled. "I heard about this kid stuck a cherry bomb in his mouth when he found out his mom was a queer. Lost his lips, teeth, and part of his tongue."

"That's just disgusting, Piggy!" Ginger snapped at him.

"Back to what we were talking about," Don interrupted. "At least we've got death with dignity now."

"Like Don said, I might not always live in the Northwest either." Harry reminded Ginger. "I'm thinking about living down on the Mexican coast when I retire. It's really cheap, and lots of people from the U.S. live there."

"When it's your time, you could always come back to Oregon," Ginger reminded him.

"If I'm able."

Loni walked over to Bobbi. "Are you about ready?"

"Just finishing up."

"Okay." Loni turned back to her detectives. "Listen up. As interesting as you think your conversation is, we've got a new job." She took a pointer to a map of the city posted on the far side of the squad room and said. "As you know, we've been plagued with a number of unsolved robberies lately." She gestured at a group of marks. "Bobbi found a cluster where most of them happened. They were especially busy during the storm. Last night was the worst. They tied up a woman and left her in the closet."

"That's horrible! I heard about these robberies. They even steal brass vases from graveyards. Those shits! Who could do a thing like that?" Ginger asked.

"She wasn't supposed to be home which tells me they're a local gang and casing the places in this area." Loni drew an imaginary circle on the map. "I'm thinking it could even be kids living in this area. This afternoon, I want all of you to go out, knock on doors, and blanket the area with questions. Find every snitch you can and see what's new on the street. Look up any fence you know." Loni turned to Ginger. "I don't want you out walking that much yet. Cleatus. Drive Ginger around to the pawn shops and see if any of the missing items are there."

"Good!" Ginger complained. "It's too hot in here. Be good to get out in the sunshine. You see that glorious day out there?"

"Wait!" Piggy interrupted Ginger. "You mean besides the thieving cat and the Carboni murder, I gotta go canvassing?" Piggy whined, "I don't need another job."

"Piggy, ya still ain't done squat yet." Cleatus's big smile showed all his white teeth.

Loni ignored their squabbling. "Forensics thinks they're targeting base metals, anything that can be sold for scrap. So, don't forget to visit junk yards and scrap dealers."

"Boss, I reckon it's a teen gang with an older experienced leader."

"I think so too, Cleatus. Takes someone who's been around to sell these items. Another reason we think it's a local gang is that they have also been stealing soap detergents, allergy medicines, and pregnancy tests."

Piggy laughed. "Gotta be a gang of women! They'll steal anything."

Loni opened her mouth to jump Piggy and then controlled herself. "I see your desk's a mess. Are you ready to go work on the robbery?"

"Don't have time, Lieut. Still working on the Carboni case."

"Doing what?"

"Jeez, Lieut. Ya ain't done piddle about who did in that poor dead child at the hospital."

The room became deadly silent, everybody waiting to see what would happen.

Piggy leaned back in his chair and declared, "Tying down loose ends."

"Exactly what loose ends?"

"Still looking for them."

"Piggy! You will get your ass out of that chair and go with the others!"

Loni looked around. "Hey, anybody seen Bobbi? She had the addresses for you to check on."

Still comfortably leaning back in his chair, Piggy wiggled a finger toward the front of the room.

Ginger stared at Piggy. "That's it?"

Piggy stared back at Ginger.

"Jeeez, Piggy. The lieutenant is right. You get any lazier we'll have to shovel you outta here like a sack of shit." Piggy just sat and stared at Ginger until she huffed back at him. "Tell you what, Piggy. You show me a way you can get any lazier, and I'll pay you fifty dollars."

Piggy sat without even a tic and barely moved his lips. "See that pocket sitting on my manly chest? Why don't you just stick that fifty dollars in there?"

"Why don't you just stick this up your ass!" Ginger flipped Piggy the bird and sat back down in a huff.

"Talk about lazy," Harry added to the conversation. "I got a gun nut neighbor who lost over a hundred collector guns in a flue fire just last week. He could spend thousands on guns, but he was too damn lazy or stupid to pay for cleaning his flue."

"Hey, you're badmouthing a good friend of mine. He lost ever'thing in that fire."

Harry barked a laugh. "Just saying."

Loni walked toward Bobbi's desk. "When Bobbi gets back . . . good, there she is." Loni watched Bobbi come out of the restroom. "Bobbi. Could you get those robbery addresses to everybody?" Loni turned to her crew. "Go to lunch and canvas this afternoon before we all go home to a nice weekend." Loni shouted over the scraping chairs and rustling papers as her detectives packed up to leave. "Hey, everybody! If I don't see you at quitting time, don't forget to show up at the gun buyback tomorrow!" Loni heard a jumbled babble of groans and voices coming at her all at once.

"Can't, Lieut. Going to a funeral."

"I got a sick kid at home."

"You don't have any kids."

"I do so! I got goats."

"I got a sick chicken."

"I don't give a flying fuck," Loni raised her voice over the hubbub. "I will see ALL of you bright and early tomorrow at eight. Got it!"

Everyone looked up at Loni's uncharacteristic swearing, but only Piggy spoke. "What'cha up to the rest of the day, Lieut?"

"I got a funeral to attend."

"Whose?" asked Bobbi.

"Carlotta Carboni's."

"Jeez, Lieut. You know that woman that well?"

"Not that it's any of your business, Piggy, I go to murder victim's funerals, especially unsolved ones, to see what I can see."

"See what? Another dead body?" Piggy grinned. "Bet they had a hell of a job cleaning her up."

"Piggy!" Loni warned.

"Further, it's only unsolved cuz you won't admit who done it."

"Come on, Piggy." Don grabbed his arm and pulled him toward the stairs. "We better get out of here before she decides to bury you."

The afternoon was actually warm as Loni parked her car next to an old beat-up pickup with several holes that looked like bullet holes. She couldn't identify the original color, and she glanced around before she poked a finger into one of the holes. The pickup was so battered and covered in mud that she couldn't detect any recent collision damage.

Already running late, Loni hurried into the funeral home and looked for the viewing area. A sign pointed her to a room lined with a few rows of chairs. She spied Chief sitting in the back and joined him, hoping he could give her names for the people she didn't know. "Afternoon, Chief."

Chief grunted and sat still and pale as a corpse, seeming unaware of his surroundings. Loni was beginning to believe that he could be seriously ill and briefly wondered if she should ask him what his doctor had said. Rejecting that idea, she leaned back and watched people arrive and carefully sit in the portable metal chairs. Wispy white clouds were painted on a light blue color of the walls and ceiling, and "Heaven Bound" was splashed across the front of the room in darker blue. A skinny podium stood on a small platform, and a silver casket sat on a wooden box painted black. The casket was closed.

"Hey, Chief. Know who owns that beat-up pickup out there?" Loni whispered.

"No idea."

The murmuring quieted when a tall gaunt man stepped behind the podium and stared out at his audience with a frown on his lined face. His dark orange skin-tone under the florescent lights indicated too many hours in a tanning bed. Loni ignored what he said as she studied the few people around her and noted that she had questioned most of them in the hospital. The row of chairs in the front where relatives usually sat were empty. Both of the cleaning women, a night security guard, and the head of the hospital CEO were all there. But no Mike Kenyon. No one sat close to each other in the other chairs. None of them seemed to be grieving or fidgeting. Loni didn't recognize the three women wearing business suits. Or the two men dressed casually in blue trousers and white dress shirts. She wanted to ask Chief who they were, but Loni felt a wall of illness between them.

Grateful that the talk was short, Loni left first and moved quickly outside, surreptitiously taking photos of the people with her cell phone. There were no pall-bearers. Instead two men who evidently worked for the funeral home brought the casket out on a cart and wheeled it down the disabled ramp to a waiting hearse. Loni slowly walked to her car with the other mourners.

The people from the hospital were almost cheerful as they quietly talked while they got in their cars. The cars trailed the hearse that wound its way up a hill to the graveyard on top. Loni waited for someone to claim the pickup but no one did. When everyone had left, she hurried after the procession and parked a distance from the grave. The breaking surf of the ocean slammed into rocks, and white foam flew high and hanging before it floated back down. Spendy real estate for the dead to enjoy, Loni mused. She left her car to join the people at the gravesite as they watched the two men settle the casket onto the belts above the hole.

Of the eleven people who had gone to the cemetery, no one sat in the front chairs assigned to family. Looking around, Loni noticed that the chief wasn't there. Again, neither was Mike Kenyon. The tall man from the funeral home concluded the graveside service by opening his bible and reciting the Lord's Prayer in monotone before he closed the service and walked back to the hearse. He climbed into the driver's seat and drove away. Loni stood in amazement. Did no one love this woman? Did no one care?

On her way home, Loni drove by the funeral home, The pickup was gone. Damn! She realized she should have stayed with the pickup. She didn't even get the license plate!

Turning on her phone, Loni found a text message from Jenna and laughed as she read, "Do I own a T-Bird now?"

Loni texted back, "Hell no!" She waded through her chores, supper, and bed but Jenna didn't return her text.

Chapter Sixteen

"Good morning, Molly."

Molly's voice matched her welcoming grin. "Hey, thanks for coming."

They walked together to set up the parking lot for the gun buyback. "Oh, God." Molly groaned. "Burt's here already."

"Who's Burt?"

"A gun nut and a nasty little man."

Burt looked like a puffed up banty rooster ready for the attack as he bustled over to them and pushed into Molly's space. "I'm fed up with you lesbians trying to take our guns away from us!" he loudly announced.

"Really?" Loni stepped between Molly and Burt and motioned her hand toward five men standing on the sidewalk. A couple joined them, and two men stood in the parking lot talking to the driver of a car that had just pulled in. "Looks like I'm the only lesbian here."

"I ain't talking to you."

"You are now."

Burt's disgust washed over Loni before he turned back to Molly. "Listen, little girl." His voice accelerated in both speed as the volume rose. "You got us old white men awake now, and you're gonna be really sorry. We got a real president now who supports us. All we wanted was to be left alone. Just you wait, little girl."

"Are you threatening Molly?"

Burt tried to stare her down, but he was so short that he had to look up at her. "Who the hell are you?"

Don jumped into the fray. "Hey, hey, slow down. She's the boss, Burt."

Burt ignored Don and turned to Piggy. "Damn, Piggy. Don't tell me you put up with a skirt?"

"Everyday. She don't know no better," Piggy cajoled Burt.

"Do something about it, Piggy. She's only a woman!"

"I been trying, but she thinks Obama was our greatest president," Piggy complained.

Loni tried to calm down both the men. "I said he was a good and caring man."

Burt snorted. "I and millions more patriotic Americans disagree with you. He's a threat to our American way."

Loni got pissed. "I've heard all that before from Piggy. I ask you. Eight years with Obama, and you still kept your damn guns. You don't have death panels, you don't live in Federal Emergency Management Agency camps, and you don't live under Sharia Law. He cut the inflation rate in half, decreased the federal deficit by seventy percent, and reduced interest rates by almost two percent. The economy for the middle and lower class is always better under Democratic presidents. And gay marriage hasn't damaged your precious way of life. So, what the hell is your problem?"

Burt never heard a word Loni said when he turned back to Molly and spat out words, spittle coming out of his mouth. "This ain't right and you know it." He continued to glare at her from his bearded Santa Claus façade before he spit toward her foot and turned toward the entrance to the police station. Loni hurried around him and blocked his way as he started to go inside after a young woman with a Colt six-shot pistol in her hand. "Anything you want to buy, you have to do it outside." He snorted again and stomped back to Piggy, shouting and waving his arms in the air.

Loni ignored him and watched the HPD volunteers direct cars and pedestrians as catcalls from the highway trashed the gun buyback. She turned back to Burt when she heard him call out to an elderly, white-haired man walking up with a gun in his hand. "I'd like to buy that."

Molly dashed up. "Burt?"

Burt puffed up again and said, "I'm looking to buy this gun."

Molly frowned. "We need a background check on the owner first."

"Fine. You take care of that. I'm buying this gun."

Molly turned to gun owner. "That okay with you?"

The man nodded. "He's offering more than you are."

"That's okay. We just need to get someone out here with the authority to help you make the deal."

"I can do that." Loni called the police office on her radio. "A buyer out here wants one of the guns from a seller." Listening a minute, Loni said, "State police will be right here."

Burt huffed in exasperation. "Stupid bureaucrat! Only good at wasting everybody's time. Takes five idiots to get nothing done." His anger built with every step as he paced up and down. The gun owner watching Burt looked ready to rabbit but before Burt exploded again, a state police officer arrived. Molly greeted him and turned to Burt. "Local police aren't authorized to do background checks on sellers. Only the state police can do that. Captain Hargrove here will be glad to help you."

The captain calmly asked the gun owner, "May I please see your carry permit?"

Loni kept a close eye on the smirking pseudo Santa as Officer Hargrove called in the permit number. He nodded toward Burt who grumped and handed a wad of crumpled money to the seller who scuttled back to his car. Burt turned on Molly again and waved the gun in her face. "Jesus, lady! Took me an hour to buy this gun. You're just another freaking government waste!"

Loni started to stop Burt's haranguing, but Ginger wandered up and wriggled between Molly and Burt. Ginger pointed at Burt's gun and batted her eyelashes as she purred in her sweetest voice, "I'm looking for a protect gun. Can I axe y'all 'bout identifying the parts?"

Burt pointed at Molly. "Your girlfriend there can help you."

"But I hear you be the expert on guns. Ya'll know ever'thang. Help me here, please. I only wants to know, is that a Walther?"

"Yes." Some of the fire went out of Burt's expression as he preened at Ginger's southern flirting and Texas drawl.

"I hear it's a special gun with extraordinary parts. That true?"

"I'm not sure what you're asking." Burt looked confused.

"May I?" Ginger reached for the gun. Burt handed it to her and sneered when she clumsily ejected the magazine. She checked to make sure it wasn't loaded and then put it back. "I was told parts of this gun were special but I think they were spoofin' me. Could you tell me if I learned this right?" Ginger pointed at the handle. "I was told this was the bollocks. That true?"

"Sure," Burt responded with a derisive smile.

"And this is called the foreskin?" Ginger pointed to the side of the gun barrel.

Burt grinned with a shrug.

"And this," Ginger pointed to the cock. "This thingy under the cock? Is this the pubic bone?"

Burt's grin turned into a smile.

"I really thought they was just teasing me." Ginger smiled. "I guess that's why y'all love your guns so much and spend so much time pettin' like they was an extension of your penis. Feels really good, huh?"

The smile slid off Burt's face, and he turned beet red. He snatched his gun from Ginger's hand and clomped off.

Turning to Loni with a shit-eating grin on her face, Ginger said. "Can I go home now?

The gun buyback was brisk although occasionally threatened by fast-rolling clouds that could hold rain. Loni watched for a squall while she focused on supervising volunteers and keeping Burt at bay. The ring on her cell phone broke her concentration. Recognizing it, she swiped at her phone and said, "Hey."

"What are you doing right now?" Loni heard Jenna's melodious voice.

"Waiting for your call."

"Why?"

Loni decided to go for it. "Every time I hear your voice, I sort of fall apart."

A barely audible sound buzzed quietly before Loni heard Jenna take a deep breath and murmur, "Would you say that again?"

"I said I miss you," Loni whispered as she searched for a private place.

"You could come to see me."

"When."

"I'm hoping tomorrow afternoon and stay for supper? Meet my daughter?"

"What time?"

"Around five?"

"Okay." Loni waited for the usual hang-up but nothing happened. "Hang up."

"You first."

"When did we become ten years old? Hang up." Loni heard Jenna's laugh just before she hung up.

Chapter Seventeen

The rising moon over the coastal range filtered through the great fir trees on the eve of Winter Solstice as Loni's long day ended. On the lonely road to Jenna's home, she slowed at the spot where she and Jenna were run off the road, but she didn't stop.

As Loni walked onto the porch, Jenna opened the door and pulled her into the hallway. She led Loni into the library lined with books from floor to ceiling on three walls. Windows on the fourth wall surrounded French doors that opened out onto a view of the lake. Locking the door behind her, Jenna pulled Loni onto the couch facing a burning fire. She kissed Loni's dimples and then her mouth while Loni pulled her closer.

"Anybody else here?"

"Last I saw they were all in the family room watching the telly. And as you noticed, I locked the door," Jenna purred.

"Who are 'they'?"

"My sister, her husband and three children. And my daughter."

"No grandmother?"

"No. She's in Portland."

"Causing more trouble?"

"Probably."

Loni leaned back pulling Jenna with her, and they quietly sat, soaking in the feeling of being together alone. Jenna ran her finger over Loni's forehead and down her nose to her lips, and Loni's eyes closed. All her thirsty nerve endings reached out and circled around Jenna, melding them together until Loni finally felt complete. "Times like this makes me feel like we've never been apart."

Jenna kissed her again, deeper and longer. She whispered against Loni's mouth. "This never changed."

"Hey." Loni nuzzled her ear. "Don't stop now, but you said you needed to talk."

Jenna reluctantly released Loni and sat back. "Do you really think someone is trying to kill me?"

"At the very least, set you up for murder. I thought it was Guy until he ended up dead." Loni shook her head. "I feel like I'm going in a circle. Now I've got three deaths and no sure suspects."

"Maybe you should straighten the line out."

Loni was confused. "What do you mean?"

"Start looking at who had what to gain by getting rid of me. My ex-husband, for example. Right now he's furious with me. He called today, threatening to take my daughter away from me."

Loni sat up straight. "Can he do that?"

"No. He's just mad because he lost access to my grandmother's money. He's using Loni Lyn to get some of it." Jenna sat forward and took a deep breath. "My grandmother recognized you at the hospital, and she told Barelli about our years together."

Loni was lost in thought for a few moments before she spoke. "No, that doesn't compute for me. He lost the money with the divorce, and I don't see how your imprisonment or death would change that." Loni didn't want to scare Jenna when she had so many other problems.

Jenna leaned back into Loni and refused to let go. "Please. I don't want to think about it anymore. I want to think about our good times. Do you remember?"

"Like what?"

"Like how we had everything planned. Our own law firm. What our house was going to look like. How many children."

Loni giggled. "We just couldn't agree on which one of us would get pregnant."

"First," Jenna reminded her. "Who would get pregnant first?" Tipping back Loni's head with a finger under her chin, Jenna kissed Loni deep and hard. "I once believed you were my soul mate. Do you believe we can go back there?"

Loni was ready to answer Jenna when she saw a red laser beam panning across to Jenna's cheek. Twisting her body, Loni threw Jenna to the floor just as the glass shattered behind them spraying shards everywhere. A bullet pierced the opposite wall. "Stay down!" Loni ordered as she crawled to the French door leading out to the side patio. She carefully opened it and slipped out. Working her way around the house, she stayed in the deep shadows and reached the front just in time to hear the diminishing sound of a boat motor.

Back in the house, Loni found Jenna's living room filled with her sister's family all asking questions at the same time. She held up her hand for quiet and called the police station. "There's been a shooting at the Davenport house. No one hurt, but I need a couple of officers to walk the perimeters tonight." Loni interrupted the desk sergeant. "No. I don't need Adanna. I can dig out the bullet. Not much else to investigate. The shot came from a distance, out of a boat, and the shooter escaped. I don't think they'll be back tonight, but you never know." Loni hung up just as Jenna walked in with bedding and a pillow.

"I think," Jenna's brother-in-law got up into Loni's face, "maybe no one's really after Jenna. Maybe it's you they're after."

Jenna sputtered, attempting to interrupt. "But—"

"Think about it, Jenna. You only get attacked when you're with her." The brother-in-law turned to Loni. "I'm sure we're well-protected now. Having you around is too dangerous. You should go!"

Jenna's voice matched his. "You can't tell me who can visit me!"

"This isn't up for debate, Jenna. She's leaving."

"It's okay, Jenna. It's probably for the best." Loni decided she wanted to drive around the lake looking for where the attacker came from. Maybe someone had a missing boat."

Jenna walked Loni to the door with a soft goodnight.

Loni drove around the lake but found nothing. The few houses on the other side were still and dark. Circling back to Jenna's house, Loni waited in her car until two burly cops knocked on her window. She explained what had happened and stayed long enough to watch them board up the broken window.

Chapter Eighteen

Loni arrived at work still mulling over how to protect Jenna. The elevator grunted and ground its way to the top, and Bobbi bounced out. Loni watched her stuff the tail of her light blue blouse into her dark blue skirt as she noticed her makeup was smeared and her hair needed combing.

Ginger hooted. "Top of the morning, Bobbi. You're missing a button on your blouse. I like that color, by the way. Is that a russet?"

Piggy laughed. "I'll button it for you."

Bobbi blushed and grabbed at the top button hole on her blouse. "Compliments of my youngest. He didn't want to go to the sitter's this morning and wouldn't let go of me." She tossed her purse in her desk's top drawer in disgust. "His older brother told him he was flunking kindergarten and might as well not go back. Wait 'til I catch up with him tonight."

Harry came out of the bathroom and stared at Bobbi. "Which kid threw up on you this morning?"

"Wasn't a kid. It was my husband. And he didn't throw up on me. He had a hangover and wouldn't get out of bed to take our son to kindergarten. So I had to." Bobbi wryly laughed. "But not before I threw a glass of water on him and ran."

Loni ignored Bobbi's tardiness and quieted her crew. "Somebody shot at me last night from a boat at a good one hundred yards away. That tells me he must be a good shot."

"Don't see any holes in you." Piggy snickered. "Can't be that good a shot."

At the same time, Ginger gasped. "How do you know it wasn't for you?"

"My first clue was the red laser beam in the middle of someone else's forehead." Loni turned to Harry and Don. "Can you guys check with the shooting range for the names of any experts? And after that, check around the lake for who owns speed boats. Make sure none of the boathouses have been broken into."

"First thing, Lieutenant," they said in unison. Harry added, "Just as soon as you're finished here."

"It won't be long. Moving on to the good news. Molly reported on the gun buyback, and I would like to comment on the fine job that both you guys and the HPD Volunteers did. They behaved like professionals, especially in diverting folks away unless they brought a firearm for the buyback. We're lucky to be partnered with them."

"Here, here," Ginger agreed. "The whole event was kind of fun. I even saw a cousin I hadn't seen in a hundred years."

"That's just a lie, Ginger. You ain't that old."

"For Christ sake, Piggy! I'm just saying that it's been way too long since I saw him."

Loni continued, "Molly was very pleased with Saturday's event. She told me that a hundred and thirty-two guns were turned in. They found one stolen gun and already located the owner. He'll pick it up today." Loni stopped and paused a minute. "We also received a gun used in two different murders. Ginger, I want you and Cleatus to talk to the person who turned it in. He said he bought it from a neighbor really cheap. We need to find the neighbor."

Piggy excitedly jumped in, "Twice, Lieut? Maybe a serial killer. I always wanted to catch one of those. Can I go too?"

Don answered him. "Good thinking, Piggy. Other serial killers were caught by doing something stupid. Westley Allan Dodd, for example, was considered the worst killer ever. Liked his little boys. He grabbed a kid in a theater who fought him screaming and kicking. He dropped the kid, jumped in his car, and it broke down a short distance away. Did he walk away into the night? No. He hung around and got caught."

"Yeah." Piggy cackled. "You know what's also cool? He axed to be hanged. Can you beat it? Hanged."

"I remember him," Harry ruminated. "We lived in Oregon during most of my school years. He was always in the news. I couldn't go out of my yard to play. My mom was so afraid that she'd put a leash on me when we went to the grocery store."

"Stranger Danger." Piggy reminded everyone. "Bet that's where it got started."

"Oh, God!" Loni exclaimed. "Not another discussion. Come on, guys. We've got work to do."

"Jest a minute, Lieut. This is important. Psychopaths are fascinating," Piggy pronounced. "Specially the child ones like Raymond Martin DeFord."

"Another one of your broad answers, Piggy." Don corrected him. "They're not all psychopaths. Sometimes there's a reason. DeFord, for example, had a father who hit him in the head because he wouldn't stop crying and caused life-long problems from brain damage."

"Poor fool."

"Yeah, it's parent abuse that causes it anyhow."

"Cleatus? Is that true?"

"It don't help but not always."

"True. I went to school with Randall Brent Woodfield. His parents were really nice and they worshipped him."

"The I-5 Killer?"

Don nodded. "Everybody called him Randy," Don reminisced. "I was two years behind him. He was someone I really admired. Big shot athlete, smart, good looking. He had it all." Don shook his head. "The longer I live the more I believe in genetics. He had to be a throwback to some sick sonofabitch."

"He was a prolific sonofabitch. He was suspected of killing over forty-five people before he was stopped."

Cleatus agreed. "Truly a psychopath. Never had a remorse gene."

"Yeah," Ginger said. "Then there were the real sickos like Christian Michael Longo and Robert Bryant who murdered their own families. I cannot imagine how horrible it must be to be murdered by your own father. Longo ran out of suitcases to bury his family in so he tied rocks to his two youngest children and threw them in the water alive. Robert killed his family with a shotgun."

"They say Longo's problem was anger and his failure to provide for his family increased his anger beyond his ability to control it."

"Bullshit. His church failed him here as it did in Robert's case. Both were from the same very religious background. The church made them what they were."

"That true, Cleatus?"

"People! Focus!" Loni warned.

"Just a minute, Lieut. This is important."

Don nodded. "Then there were the ones who almost got away with it. Like Homer Lee Jackson who wasn't caught for twenty years. He killed four women we know of. Can you imagine what it would be like to wait twenty years to get arrested?"

Harry smiled. "Bet for a long time he thought he did get away with it."

"Don't forget the ones that did get away with it like the 1994 triple murder of three women at the Leathers Oil Company gas station in Gresham."

"Yes, but they figured it was another worker but they couldn't prove it."

"Are we through yet?" Loni demanded.

"Hang on, Lieut. I got another. They all got a sickness. It's that name I can never pronounce. This one had a shoe fetish. You know, Cleatus?"

"Retifism, Piggy. You talking Jerry Brudos."

"Right, Jerry Brudos. He stalked, raped, tortured, killed. He did it all. Ain't that something?"

"Stop!" Loni demanded. "Are you through listing every serial killer known in Oregon?"

"Lord no, Lieut. We're jest started."

"No, Piggy. You *jest* finished. Let's move on people. NOW!"

"But this is important!"

"And no, Piggy, you can't go!"

Piggy sat at his desk sulking as Loni watched Harry and Don leave for the shooting range. She was lost in her thoughts about Jenna when Bobbi threw a pencil at her to get her attention. "Call for you, Lieutenant. Adanna. Line One."

Loni groaned, "Thanks, Bobbi. I'll take it in my office." She closed the door and said, "Hey, Adanna. What's up?"

"We found your bullets, Loni."

"I'm not following—"

"Out of your gun. At least, the one registered to you. They were embedded in a pickup found burned out this morning under an old railway trestle up the river. The cops on site dug a couple out and brought them to me."

"You tell them to locate the owner?"

"Yeah. He didn't know anything."

"Did the owner report it missing?"

"Not until this morning."

"Really? Who'd it belong to?"

"That's the odd thing. The truck's registered to our DA. We called. He said he thought somebody had borrowed it, but he didn't know who and never did know who and didn't know how long it had been gone."

"Where'd he keep the truck?"

"Behind his garage."

"Really? And he never noticed it missing?"

"Said he just thought a friend borrowed it. He decided maybe someone stole it from whoever borrowed it."

"Really. Did he tell you which friend might borrow his truck without his knowledge?"

"Said he wasn't sure so he'd ask around."

Loni snorted in disbelief. "Time I had another talk with good old Jimmy."

"Good luck with that. I called him again just before I called you and asked him for a list of his friends that borrowed his pickup. His clerk said he just left on vacation. She didn't know where or how long."

"Neither, apparently, does anyone else." Loni sighed in resignation. "Thanks, Adanna."

"What's your interest in this truck?"

"Whoever was driving it tried to kill me?"

"Yeah. That would get my attention, too. I'll let you know."

"Thanks. I mean that."

The phone rang again. This time it was Chief's office calling off his meeting with Loni because he was sick. Worried, Loni glanced at the call slip Bobbi handed to her. "Piggy!" Loni raised her voice over Piggy's argument with Cleatus. "You're the next in the rotation." She waved the paper at him. "Somebody robbed the convenience store out on Hawford this morning."

"In a minute!" Piggy answered. "I'm trying to teach Cleatus something." He turned back to Cleatus. "I don't believe in that global warming crap. Weather changes all a time. Ain'tcha ever heard of El Nino? Some years hotter. Some years colder. This heat wave don't mean nothin'." Piggy was on a rant. "I say just live your life ignoring all that other crap and be happy. Ya'll need to read the first book in the Bible."

"Piggy, there's climate change and there's weather. Two different things. Too late to stop the damage no-how."

"What'd he say?"

"He said weather is what we get all the time. Climate change is a study of weather over time and the polluters need to be stopped."

"I don't care. People still got rights."

"For themselves. Not for anyone else!"

"Maybe they knows what's best better'n you."

"I don't care what they think they know, Piggy. They should not decide for me."

"Sure they do."

"Listen, Piggy." Loni attempted to end the discussion. "Don is trying to say that your freedom ends where his nose begins. But if you don't get moving, I might be tempted to change the shape of your nose."

"What does my nose have to do with anything?" Piggy looked confused.

"It means if my behavior doesn't interfere with your space, you can't tell me what to do. You don't get to be my moral judge."

"You're wrong. One thing, you queers mess up my space good."

"How?"

"I have to worry about saying politically correct bullshit for one."

"Damn. You're so right. Being a caring, decent, kind man is just wrong."

"Don't mind him, Lieutenant. He seriously hates being a nice person," Don interjected.

Piggy couldn't let it go. "You kid, Lieut. But it's true, especially with what I deal with all day. Scums. The lot of them."

"So," Don asked, "Becoming a worse scum is your goal in life?"

"Jeez, ever'body believes in something."

"I agree, Piggy." Don said. "But fanatical believers deal in spirits I can't see, voices I can't hear, a life hereafter I can't touch. And my biggest problem is when the so-called true believers hide behind religion in their judgmental robes preaching hate while protected by the church from any criticism for their absurd and dangerous behaviors."

"Not my fault what crazies do."

"It is when your church members participate in protecting them."

"True, Don." Cleatus drawled. "Ya'll want something, ya just say 'It's God's will,' and ever'one expect you to willingly fall on your petard."

Ginger snorted. "He said go fuck yourself."

"He did not, Ginger. What the hell's a petard?"

"A bomb, Piggy."

"Why didn't you say so, Cleatus? I didn't understand a word you said," Piggy complained.

Don scowled at Piggy. "He said when some people get a little power, then they force us to do things their way by saying God said it and we can't prove no different."

"Yeah," Cleatus continued, "they get away wid it even though they lie as we is indoctrinated to accept any proffering of faith as gospel."

Ginger grinned. "There you go, Piggy."

"That's just crap, Ginger. Just last Sunday my preacher prayed for homos like to you to give up your sinful ways." Piggy was waving his arms to emphasize his point. "See, Ginger? He cares about you."

Ginger laughed her loud honking blast. "Know what, Piggy? I'm so grateful God answered my prayer instead of your sick-ass preacher's."

"Out! Out!" Loni watched her detectives gather at the stairs and start down before she called, "Bobbi! A minute?"

Bobbi followed Loni back into her office.

"The cleaners? Find anything?"

"Nothing useful." Pulling on her raincoat, Bobbi continued through plastic crackles, "No unusual spending, no red flags in their social media. Nothing in their history to indicate they had the training in any kind of medicine. Sorry."

Bobbi waved goodbye, and Loni impatiently waited for her crew's return while she cleaned her desk from the sandwich she had brought for lunch. The detectives had been busy with unfinished cases including the spate of neighborhood robberies. Harry and Don came back with information about a local gang who may be doing the robbing. Ginger and Cleatus called about meeting two fellow cops who wanted them to check out an abuse report from Child Services. They had picked up an almost naked seven-year-old kid off the street who had said he was helping his mother's boyfriend make "special medicine." Ginger had wanted to know what to do with the meth lab they found.

Frustrated by her inability to solve Carlotta Carboni and Guy Murphy's murders, Loni said, "Jesus, Ginger. How hard can it be? After you arrest the assholes just take a match to the damn thing and walk away."

"Come on, Lieutenant!"

"I know. I know. Did you get a warrant to enter?"

"Didn't have to. We saw the lab equipment through the window so Cleatus called it exigent circumstances and we went in. The chemical stench was so bad it left us with headaches so we got out."

"Any close neighbors?"

"Yeah. It's one of those little salt-box houses in that settlement on the edge of town."

"Good. Now you need a warrant before anyone can go back in. Call in a hazardous materials team, and ask around to see if you can find the owner. If you do, tell the owner we're confiscating his house because it's so dangerously polluted."

"Wow." Ginger whistled through the phone. "Can we do that?"

"Only if the owner doesn't properly clean up the mess. Tell him that."

"Guess this'll teach him to keep a better eye out for his property."

"It tends to work that way. Get your mask on and gather what evidence you need for an arrest. Soon as the hazmat team arrives go home and clean up."

After she talked to Ginger, Loni searched the DA's credit cards for any regular travel places. One stood out. Wier River. Bank records showed regular payments to the bank on a piece of property there.

"Hey, Lieutenant," Bobbi interrupted Loni's research. "I found a bank transfer from Giovanni's labs to Mike Kenyon. Looks like the lot of them were in it together."

"Now if we can only prove it. I'm beginning to wonder if the DA isn't part of it. He's disappeared again."

"Still can't find him?"

"In the wind along with Mike Kenyon."

"Too bad Piggy's not here. He'd know."

"Guess I sent him off too soon. I could have asked him questions about the DA, though he always says he doesn't know where the DA goes."

"Is Piggy working on something?"

"Damned if I know." Loni was pissed, and her agitation had her walking the floor like a new father. "I think I need to call in sick and go home. I really don't feel good." Loni stumbled through the words as she planned ahead and struggled to drag on her heavy leather coat. "Tell the boys I'll be back in the morning.

"Do I need to know where you're really going?"

Loni headed for the stairs. "You already know. Keep it to yourself, okay?"

Despite her irritation, Loni enjoyed the trip to the small town of Wier River. She knew it was a business trip and that she should not be driving old Highway 30, but she had read about the road and Sam Hill. He had convinced the state of Oregon to build the road so that he could get to a castle he had built up the gorge on the Washington side. He named it Maryhill, after his wife who never lived there.

The famous winding road was patterned after the great scenic roads of Europe, edged with building blocks. She crossed old English style bridges and admired the spectacular deep drops to the river far below that reminded her of the Grand Canyon. The vast view filled with occasional red and yellow smears among the variegated greens tumbled down the cliffs into the blue of the Columbia River. She wanted to stop at the falls and the Bonneville Dam just to stand and stare, but she was running out of time before Jenna was arraigned.

They could come back together and visit everything she missed on this trip. Next time, she could see the full-scale replica of the English Stonehenge that Sam Hill built as a tribute to World War One soldiers lost in the war. Loni read that he was buried near his Stonehenge.

The weather had turned dense and dark by the time Loni got to Wier River. The heavy rain made her grateful for the slow drive through town. Her address led her to a building with the sign reading "Taoist Acupuncture." She cautiously stepped inside the red door and saw cane chairs lining a wall papered with cherry trees in pink blooms. Opposite a staircase at one end was a short counter. Behind it sat Mister DA himself.

"Afternoon, Jimmy."

The DA jerked up, surprise on his face. "What the hell are you doing here, Loni?"

"Looking for you."

"And you're looking for me why?"

"Got some questions and I've had a hard time tracking you down to ask them."

"Okaaaay." The DA seemed unsure of himself. "About what?"

Loni sat across from him in one of the cane chairs and looked around. "Too many things aren't adding up. And I really need them to add up."

"Okaaay. About what?"

"About the Carboni case. And before you say anything, I won't stop until I get some answers. You can try to fire me if you want."

"You don't think I can fire you?"

"I believe I work for the city, and the mayor is my boss. True?"

"Go on."

"I need to know where you were on the morning of December fifth, and the night of December thirteenth?"

"I was here."

"Can you prove that?"

The DA picked up the phone and said, "Would you please come down here and bring your calendar?" Hanging up, he turned to Loni. "I'm going to tell you something I would rather not have spread around town."

A tall, distinguished Indonesia man came around the corner from the stairs. He was carrying a curly-headed boy around seven years old still in his pajamas. The man tried to wipe away the snot hanging down from boy's nose but only succeeded in smearing it down the chin. Mystified, Loni looked from them to the DA

"This is Loni Wagner, dear heart, the lieutenant in charge of our major crimes division." The DA turned to Loni. "This is Hasan, my husband, and our son. When he got sick, I came home."

Loni felt her mouth drop open. She closed it with a snap and grinned. "Glad to meet you, Hasan."

A smirk crossed the DA face as he said to his husband, "Check the fifth and the thirteenth on your calendar and tell me where I was."

"I don't need to check. The fifth you were sick as a dog with food poisoning. I took you to the hospital." He turned to Loni. "It's just down the street if you want to check. The thirteenth was when Eddie came down with the flu." Hasan turned to Loni. "Jimmy drove into work that morning. He was back home by noon." Hasan turned back to Jimmy. "You remember. You left at seven to get to Harborville to get some cases to the grand jury." Hasan turned to Loni. "That's when Jimmy took some vacation days to be here. He would never stay away from home when his son is sick."

"Tell me who took your pickup last."

"Why?"

"We found it burned out under an old railroad trellis. Bullets from my gun were embedded in it."

"Damn!" The DA was quiet a few seconds. "I already told the chief. The last time I saw it Piggy and I went fishing. Wait a minute!" The DA turned on Loni, his limbs jerked in his anger as his smooth Asian face turned red. "Are you accusing me of murder? Because of what I ordered you to do?"

"I think you should get back to your job before the judge has you arrested for dereliction of duty. She really is worried about you. At least give her a call?" Loni said, inching to the door as she nodded goodbye to Hasan. "I'll see you back home, soon, right?" Loni jumped out the door before the DA could say anything else.

Chapter Nineteen

"So? How'd it go with the DA?" Bobbi asked Loni the first thing before she got her coat off.

"Like everything else on this case." Loni quietly hung up her coat and sat across from Bobbi. "He had an alibi. I still think he's involved. But I don't know how."

"Sorry." Bobbi commiserated with Loni as she handed Loni a phone message slip. "Your friend from Portland called yesterday. She wants you to call her back."

Loni picked up the phone. "Hey, Leslie. Sorry I couldn't get back to you yesterday. I was out of town." Loni listened and took notes for a few minutes before she hung up. She sat quietly for several minutes before she turned to talk to Bobbi. "She said Carboni was always alone when she came in. Apparently, she was on shopping sprees except for one stop at the Western Lab. That's what one of her snitches said. He was the hotel bell boy who called her a cab for the lab. Nobody recognized the other photos." Loni rubbed her face in frustration until she suddenly flashed onto the gray hair she found at the scene. "Bobbi! Have you heard back about that gray hair I gave Adanna?"

"Not yet."

"Look into it, okay?"

"You really think that just one hair could lead us to the killer? It could have been there for months before Carboni fell on it."

"Only other place we haven't looked, Bobbi. And the place was really clean. Call Adanna and see if she's processed it yet."

The creaking elevator door opened and expelled Adanna. "Hi everybody! Hey, Lieutenant, how's it going?"

Bobbi grinned. "That fast enough for you, Lieutenant?"

"You're magic, Bobbi." Loni beamed as she welcomed Adanna. "I'd love it if you have good news for me."

"Don't know how good it is. Your shooting victim? He'd been weighted and dumped not far off shore. A shrimp fisherman caught the body in his net and brought him in. They said he jumped off just as soon as he tied up at the dock and won't go near his boat again. Want a boat cheap?"

"Nope. Ask your boyfriend."

Adanna shook her head. "That's not funny!"

"I thought it was." Loni grinned at Adanna's frustration. "How do you know it was him?"

Adanna smiled knowingly. "Your bullet was in him?"

"Okay, I get it."

"Only it wasn't your bullet that killed him. I wanted you to know. He had a bullet in his head from an unregistered gun."

Loni gave Adanna a quick hug in thanks. "You have no idea what a relief that is. So far in this crazy job I've never killed anyone and I really hope I never do."

"I understand. I've known people who have had to kill. No matter what, it changes you."

"And not for the better. Who was he?"

"Henry Lewis Alito. Couldn't find anything else about him."

Loni tilted her head in thought. "Where did he live?"

"His address is a box number in Cherry Junction. I called. Said he lived up the Soda Fork Road in the Cascades. No exact address."

"Isn't the chief's lodge up there somewhere?"

Adanna shrugged.

"Time I talked to the chief. Bobbi? Would you send me his address?"

"Thought you already talked to him." Adanna said to Loni.

Loni pulled to the side of Chief's house and started to get out when her phone rang. She swiped it on. "Hey, Adanna." Loni listened a minute. "Oh, god, I forgot all about your report." A few seconds passed before Loni spouted out in shock, "You're fucking kidding me!" She listened a few more seconds before she said, "Damn, Adanna. I should have caught that. That's why you were so careful about getting that report to me. I'm really sorry." Another few seconds ticked by. "I know, I know. It's my job to catch the bad guys. It's your job to prove they're the bad guys. Next time I promise to read your reports."

Damn! Loni dropped her phone back into her pocket just as Chief walked out his back door carrying fishing gear. *I really messed up.*

"Hey, Loni. You come to go fishing with me?"

"Glad to see you're feeling better, Chief." Loni studied him. "Maybe another time. Just needed some advice from you."

"Fine. Why don't we talk about it while we're enjoying ourselves." Chief kept walking down a boat ramp to a floating building with Loni following him. At the foot of the ramp, he propped open a door leading into the building and walked on in with Loni following. She watched him climb onto the back of a small white fishing boat parked inside. The back was open to the lake.

"You coming?" he said over his shoulder.

"Not this time. I'm hoping you can help me figure something out."

"We can talk about it on the water. Get in."

Loni shook her head. "Not today. I've got to get back." She tried to keep her voice even. "Hey, Chief, I didn't know you lived on Brown Bear Lake," she said while she casually ran her index finger along the red stripes on the side of the boat and watched Chief stow his rods and ice box on board. "Did you know Doctor Giovanni and her family lives just across on the other side?"

"Might have. Anything else?"

"Yes. Piggy said you were a good friend of the DA's. That you helped him after he lost his family and got him the job in Harborville."

"Sure," Chief's voice was ragged. "So what?"

"Adanna said she saw a plant called Doll's Eye in your greenhouse. I thought maybe the DA got the poison for Guy Murphy from your greenhouse.

"You blaming the DA for the murders?"

"Right now he's our best bet."

The chief ducked his head. "No. He hasn't been here for a while. You got proof it was the Doll's Eye plant that poisoned Guy Murphy?"

"Not yet. But all the symptoms are there."

Chief studied Loni a minute. "Maybe it's not only the Dolls Eye that sees too much. You're not really here about the DA, are you?

"Not really. I had a good visit with him in Wier River." Loni sighed. "Chief. You have the right to remain silent. Anything you say can and will be used against you in a court of law—"

Chief broke into the Miranda warning. "Stop it, Loni!" he warned in a stern voice.

"You have the right to have an attorney present during questioning—"

"Stop!" The chief dropped into a deck chair on the boat, his face in a stiff frown. "Loni, it would be best if you got the hell out of here and kept your mouth shut. Right now!"

"If you cannot afford an attorney, one will be appointed for you. Do you understand these rights?"

"How the hell did you figure out it was me?" Chief demanded.

"Adanna found your hair at the scene under the body. After that it was just a matter of connecting the dots."

Chief stared at her in disbelief. "Jesus," Chief shook his head in self-disgust. "I couldn't stand to turn her over. He sat silent for a few minutes. "Might not have found it anyway."

Loni finally had to ask, "What happened, Chief? Why'd you do it?"

They stared at each other for a minute before the fire died out of the chief, and he slumped further into his chair. "What the hell," he muttered. When he looked up in despair, his eyes were wet. "I just wanted to be in love one last time. But I got obsessed and couldn't let go."

"Go on."

"Carlotta was supposed to meet me at my lodge like usual, but she didn't show. She behaved all funny and cold the last time we were together, and she left almost as soon as she got there. I was worried so I drove to her house early the next morning. Guy's car was in her driveway, and she was on the porch. She kissed him when he left, and I just lost it. I went back the next day and made her admit she was only using me."

"So you killed her."

Chief's sigh was filled with pain. "She laughed at me. She said if I wanted to know who she was really in love with, hang around another hour and I could meet her. I really lost it when she said 'her.' She wanted another woman instead of me? I asked her about the man she spent the night with. She said she was just keeping him happy. He was the dealmaker with a lab in Portland." Chief rubbed his face hard. "A scalpel was on her desk where she'd been cutting stuff out of the newspaper. I grabbed it. She ran, but I caught her at the front door."

"What about Jenna Giovanni? Why are you trying to kill her?"

"Because she's the one that stole my woman."

"You really did have it bad."

"I did. I just couldn't help myself. Carlotta was all I could think about. She was everything to me, and Jenna took her. I wanted Jenna to suffer as much as I did." The chief was quiet a few moments before he added, "And I wanted her grandmother to suffer."

"Why?"

"She killed my son." Chief sat, quietly looking at his hands. With a heavy sigh, he said, "He was ten when he fell and cut an artery. I knew Mrs. Davenport had the same rare blood type. I'd checked just in case he ever needed a transfusion. We found her shopping at the outlet mall in Carver, but she wouldn't come back to help. We couldn't find blood from anywhere else in time." Chief rubbed at his face. "After that my marriage fell apart. My wife just stopped caring about me."

"A man was caught in a fisherman's net. Name was Henry Alito. Know him?"

"Sounds familiar."

"He had two bullet holes in him. Only one of them was mine, and it wasn't the bullet that killed him."

"He was a dead man anyway."

"You can't know that! You could have tried to save him!"

The chief seemed to shake himself out of his despair. Standing, he beckoned Loni onto the boat. "Why don't we go for a ride? Maybe fish a little? We can talk some more."

"Don't think so, Chief. What do you know about Mike Kenyon?"

"I don't know who that is." He pulled a hand out of his pocket and pointed a gun at her. "Loni, get in the boat."

"Best shoot me here, Chief. I'm not getting in that boat."

A look of shock crossed Chief's face. He exclaimed, "Wifey, what are *you* doing here?"

Loni turned and saw Chief's wife standing near her, holding a Beretta handgun. Her hand shook as she stared at the chief. Tears ran down her face as she blurted out, "I heard everything! You really butchered that woman out of jealousy? And you murdered your best friend?" She shook her head in denial. "I always knew you catted around, but to murder for it? Really?"

"Shut up, Wifey. Nothing to do with you." Chief seemed to be putting himself back together.

Loni had met Chief's wife only once before at the Pride Parade, but she remembered her long flowing white hair that cast a silvery effect around her crown. A slender woman, her sweet pixy face added to a beauty that never seemed to age. Loni felt sorry for her.

"I told you to shut up!" Chief warned her.

"Nothing to do with me?" She screeched. "Nothing? That's what I always been to you isn't it? Nothing!" She slowly lifted the gun as though it weighed a thousand pounds. "No more. No more." With tears streaming down her face, she pulled the trigger before Loni could stop her.

Turning to Loni, she dropped the gun from her hand. "You can take out the trash now. I'm done."

Chapter Twenty

"Did the chief's wife really kill him?" Bobbi asked Loni as soon as she walked into the squad room.

"I turned it in as self-defense. He had a gun on me, and she saved my life."

"Good." Bobbi shook her head is dismay. "But the chief? How is that even possible?"

The elevator did its usual squawking before the door opened, revealing Harry and Don. They led a middle-aged man in need of a shave, haircut, and bath into the interrogation room and shut the door on him. Approaching Loni, Harry finally got control of his anger. "Gotta hear this one."

"Yeah," Don said, shaking his head. "It's not good, Lieutenant." Canting his head toward the interrogation room. "We arrested that guy for drunk driving."

"Anybody hurt?"

"Not really," Harry said. "According to witnesses this guy stumbled out of the driver's seat after he rear-ended a car. He tried to run, but he slipped and slid into a pole. The ice left from last night's freeze tripped him up. Here's the kicker. He wants immunity. Said Chief was his best costumer for his fenced jewelry and that's why he was in town. Now don't that beat all?"

"Says he can prove it." Don continued Harry's story. "Said Chief usually met him at his fishing lodge, but Chief didn't show up this time so he came to town to find him and got drunk."

"Can you believe this," Harry added. "He said that Chief had a girlfriend with him and that she was really something."

"Listen guys. His story's is true. The chief admitted it to me. All of it."

Both Harry and Don stared at Loni in stunned disbelief."

"Tell me you're joking!"

Loni shook her head waiting for reluctant acceptance from the two. "Do me a favor?"

Harry nodded.

Loni said, "Go back into the room with him and tell him to write everything down."

After they left Loni turned to Bobbi, "Take Harry and Don the photos of Carlotta Carboni and Jenna Giovanni along with ones of two other women about their age. Tell them to ask the guy if he can identify any of them as Chief's girlfriend."

Bobbi looked at Loni quizzically when she came back out of the room. Loni just grinned while they waited.

"Guess what?" Harry said when the two detectives bounded out of the room.

Loni beat him to it. "He identified Carlotta Carboni."

Chapter Twenty-One

Loni's brain was a foggy mess as she dodged through the milling crowd of police officers, reporters, hospital personnel, and hangers-on filing into the courtroom. She avoided looking at Jenna's grandmother and family mixed in with the crowd. She found a bench to wait until she was called as a witness.

It seemed like hours before she was finally called into the courtroom and sworn in. She waited for Sally Harper, Jenna's lawyer, to ask her questions. Out of the corner of her eye Loni watched Sally stand and move around her table toward her as Loni glanced around the courtroom, trying to ignore the DA's scowling face. She eased up when she saw Jenna wink at her.

"My client is accused of two murders and one negligent homicide. Describe what evidence you found at the first murder." Sally opened her questioning.

Loni and took a deep breath before she started her testimony. "In tracking the activities of Doctor Giovanni on the morning of Carlotta Carboni's death, I found that she did not leave work until eight-fourteen, an hour after the approximate time of the murder. This was verified by the pathologist who said that she viewed an autopsy on a child. Doctor Giovanni's footprints near Ms. Carboni's body were on top of dried blood, and Doctor Giovanni's clothes had no blood spatter when she was arrested at the murder scene. No murder weapon was found there. We also found a receipt in her purse for a bottle of wine at a local store time stamped approximately twenty minutes before the victim's death. The clerk at the store verified this."

The judge banged her gavel to stop the murmur in the courtroom. Sally followed up with another question. "Moving on to the negligent homicide. Tell us what the hospital security files revealed on the night the child died."

"Objection." The DA jumped up out of his chair. "That was not part of the exculpatory evidence, and it was obtained illegally without a warrant."

Returning to her table, Sally flipped through papers until she found the affidavit. She handed it to the judge. "We had permission from the hospital personnel. These tapes did not invade anyone's privacy. Even the hospital will agree to that."

Looking over the affidavit, the judge agreed. "Overruled. Continue."

"We used the camera images from the door entering the pediatric floor to note the times of arrival and departure for all adults. The only time Doctor Giovanni entered the pediatric floor on the nights in question was on the emergency code blue call. It appeared that Ms. Carboni was doing CPR on a child in respiratory distress when Doctor Giovanni took over and directed the resuscitation attempt. She was unable to revive the child. The pathologist believed the anesthetic combined with the child's illness was the probable cause of death. Because Doctor Giovanni was no longer a suspect, our most likely suspects became Mike Kenyon as Carlotta Carboni's accomplice in aspirating the bone marrow. He had training in an oncology department where he assisted doctors, but we know he didn't kill her. His alibi for the time of Ms. Carboni's murder is solid."

"Did he confess to the aspiration?"

"No, he seems to have disappeared. He didn't show up for work the next night and his apartment appears to have been cleaned out."

The DA was silent, and Sally continued. "Moving on to the next murder. Guy Murphy. Tell us what you found there."

"We found Guy Murphy in his garage in his car where he died. At first, his death appeared to be a suicide from carbon monoxide, but the autopsy revealed that he was poisoned."

"Do you find the source of the poison?"

"Yes."

"Please explain."

"A plant called Doll's Eye, found in the greenhouse of our police chief Alden Hazen, was the poison."

Loni's testimony caused another buzz in the courtroom, and the DA stared daggers at Loni. She stared back, daring him to object. The judge banged her gavel again.

"And?" Sally resumed.

"Police chief Alden Hazen confessed to the murders."

The courtroom exploded into bedlam as the DA jumped up screaming "I object, I object. I object."

The judge's mouth dropped open. "You're kidding!"

Loni turned to the judge over the courtroom noise. "I wish. He confessed before his wife shot him."

The judge regained her calm and pounded her gavel. In the silence, she said, "Maybe you better start explaining how your investigation led to Chief."

Loni closed her eyes to help her organize her thoughts while she waited for the courtroom to settle. After a deep breath, she listed her evidence in an almost monotone voice. "I saw a Fiesta ware coffee cup in Chief's office that could have been the missing cup from Ms. Carboni's house. He said it was from his wife's set, but it couldn't have been because hers was from a recent production. Ms. Carboni owned antique Fiesta ware."

"That's not the strongest argument I ever heard." The judge had taken over the questioning.

"There's more. Adanna tested a hair I found beneath the body. The DNA belonged to Chief."

"Anything else?"

"An eye witness said he met a few times with Chief and Ms. Carboni at Chief's hunting lodge. Our witness sold Chief expensive jewelry which he gave to her."

"That it?"

Loni paused a few seconds, reluctant to continue. She looked up with tearing eyes. "Chief told me that he was in love with Ms. Carboni, and he killed her because he found out that she was in love with Doctor Jenna Giovanni. He said he tried to kill Doctor Giovanni twice because he was crazy with grief. His wife heard the confession. He had a gun pointed at me and said he was going to kill me. She shot him defending me."

"Okay, I've heard enough." The judge picked up her gavel. "Court's dismissed." She turned to Jenna. With a sharp smack of the gavel, she said, "You are free to go."

Loni leapt to her feet, circled around, and grabbed Jenna's hand, pulling her out of the courtroom back into the adjoining conference room. Locking the door behind them, they just sat and stared at each other for a long time.

Jenna looked numb. "It's really over?"

"It's really over."

Jenna sat back, and a smile started to form on her face. "Despite everything, I'm still glad I moved home." Jenna canted her head, staring at Loni. "Can I ask you a question?"

"Maybe."

"Why did you move back here?"

"The truth?"

"Yes."

"I had great memories of our times here. I liked the town and thought it would be good a place to settle down after I left Arizona."

Jenna sighed. "And I came back to heal. And maybe hoped a little bit that our time together here would help that."

Loni shook her head with a short laugh. "And here we are."

"Where do we go from here?"

"We could go out to dinner tonight."

"You asking me out on a date?"

"Maybe. Depends."

"Depends on what?"

"Depends on where you want to go?"

"Where do you want to go?"

"Would McDonald's qualify as a date?"

"Not even close."

"They have a playground for Loni Lyn."

"How about dinner at my house?"

Loni laughed. "I remember your cooking. Including the heartburn."

Jenna jostled Loni in protest. "Matter of fact, I've become a very good cook."

"Maybe I could. Your grandmother joining us?"

"Maybe. Why don't you come and find out?"

"Only if I can stay for breakfast."

Jenna's dimples were deep as she slowly stood and closed in on Loni. "Maybe."

About the Author

Sue Hardesty was born and raised on the Arizona desert where she was either following her prospecting mom around, watching her pick-axe rocks, or riding horses with her dad helping him trail cattle. After college she moved to the Phoenix area and taught English and Communications for many years. Retirement took her out of the desert heat as she moved to the beautiful Oregon Coast where she and her partner now run their dog on the beach every morning. And where she even takes time to write a little. You can find her website here: www.SueHardestyBooks.com.

Launch Point Press
Portland, Oregon